all that we never were

ALICE KELLEN

sourcebooks
casablanca

Published by Sourcebooks Casablanca, an imprint of Sourcebooks
P.O. Box 4410, Naperville, Illinois 60567–4410
(630) 961-3900
sourcebooks.com

Originally published as *Todo lo que nunca fuimos* in 2019 in Spain by Editorial Planeta,
an imprint of Grupo Planeta. This edition issued is based on the paperback edition
published in 2019 in Spain by Editorial Planeta, an imprint of Grupo Planeta.

Cataloging-in-Publication Data is on file with the Library of Congress.

Printed and bound in the United States of America.
VP 10 9 8 7 6 5 4 3 2 1

For Neïra, Abril, and Saray.
Thanks for being there…and for everything else.

Every revolution starts and ends with his lips.

—Rupi Kaur, *Other Ways to Use Your Mouth*

AUTHOR'S NOTE

In all my novels, there are songs that accompany many scenes on paper. Music is inspiration. On this occasion, it's something more. A wrapper around certain moments, a thread that pulls a bit at the characters. You can find the complete Spotify playlist of songs I listened to while I was writing this story, but if you like, I encourage you to listen to some of the more important ones in the exact moment when they appear in the novel. In Chapter 24, "Yellow Submarine," in 48, "Let It Be," and in 76, "The Night We Met."

PROLOGUE

"EVERYTHING CAN CHANGE IN AN instant." I had heard that phrase many times throughout my life, but I had never stopped to really chew it over, to savor the meaning those words can leave behind on your tongue when you break them down and feel them as your own. That bitter feeling that comes with every "what if…" that awakens when something bad happens and you ask yourself if you could have somehow prevented it, because the difference between having it all and having nothing is only a second. One second. Like back then, when that car swerved into the wrong lane. Or like now, when he decided he had nothing to fight for and the black and gray swallowed up all the color that was floating around me just a few months ago…

Because, at that second, he turned right.

I wanted to follow him, but I hit a barrier.

And I realized I could only keep going to the left.

January

—

(SUMMER)

1

Axel

I WAS LYING ON THE surfboard while the sea swayed around me. That day, the crystalline water seemed held by a giant swimming pool; there were no waves, no wind, and no noise. I heard my own tranquil breath and the splashing whenever I let my arms drop, and then I quit and just stayed there motionless, staring at the horizon.

I could say I was waiting for conditions to change so I could catch a good wave, but I knew perfectly well that there wouldn't be one that day. Or that I was killing time, as I often did. But I remember what I was really doing was thinking. Yes, thinking about my life, with the sensation that I'd reached all my goals and lived one dream after another. "I'm happy," I told myself. And I think it was the tone that echoed in my head, that faint question mark, that made me furrow my brows, still gazing at the undulating surface. "Am I happy?" I asked myself. I didn't like that quivering doubt, vivid, demanding my attention.

I closed my eyes before taking off into the sea.

Later, with my surfboard under my arm, I went back home,

walking barefoot over the sand of the beach and the trail lined with weeds. I pushed the door open—because of the humidity, it was always stuck—left the board on the back porch, and continued inside. I placed a folded towel on the chair and didn't get dressed, sitting instead at my desk, which was the embodiment of chaos and took up an entire side of the living room. Chaos, at least, for any sane person. Papers full of notes, others with discarded proofs, the rest of it just meaningless scribbles. On the right, there was a clearing with pens, pencils, pictures; above it, a calendar with days marked out before the deadline, and on the other side, my computer.

I looked through the accumulated work and answered a few emails before continuing with the project I was working on just then, a tourist brochure for the Gold Coast. It was basic, an illustration of a beach with the curved lines of waves and the blurry shadows of surfers. The kind of job I enjoyed most: simple, quick, clear, and well paid. No nonsense about "improvising," about "keeping your suggestions in mind," just a simple "draw a fucking beach."

After a while, I made a sandwich with the few ingredients left in the fridge and served myself my second coffee of the day, cold, without sugar. I was about to bring the cup to my lips when someone knocked at the door. I didn't usually get unannounced visitors, so I left the coffee on the counter with a frown.

If I'd known in that moment what those few short raps would bring, maybe I wouldn't have opened up. Who am I trying to fool? I could never have turned my back on him. And it would have happened either way. Sooner. Later. What does it matter? From the beginning, it feels like I was playing Russian roulette with a bullet in every chamber, and one of them was fated to go through my heart.

I was still leaning my hand on the door frame when I realized this was no courtesy call. I stepped aside to let Oliver come in. He was taciturn and serious. I followed him to the kitchen, asking what had happened. He ignored the coffee and opened the liquor cabinet, taking out a bottle of brandy.

"Nice choice for a Tuesday morning," I said.

"I got a fucking problem."

I waited without saying anything, still dressed in the bathing suit I'd donned when I got up. Oliver was wearing long pants and a tucked-in white T-shirt, the kind of thing I'd have sworn he'd never wear.

"I don't know what I'm going to do; I keep thinking of alternatives, but I've tried them all, and I think...I'm going to need you."

He got my attention. Mainly because Oliver never asked for favors, not even from me, his best friend since before he'd learned to ride a bike. He didn't when he was going through the worst moment in his life and he rejected almost all the help I offered him, because he was proud or because he thought he was bothering me or because he wanted to show himself he could handle the situation, however difficult it was.

Maybe for that very reason, I didn't hesitate.

"You know I'll do whatever you need."

Oliver downed his drink in one sip, left the glass in the sink, and stood there, leaning on his hands.

"They're sending me to Sydney. It's temporary."

"What the fuck…" I opened my eyes wide.

"Three weeks a month for a year. They want me to oversee the new branch they're opening and then come back once everything's stable. I'd like to reject the offer, but they're doubling my goddamn salary, Axel. And now I need it. For her. For everything."

I watched him run a hand through his hair, nervous.

"A year's a long time," I said.

"I can't take her. I can't."

"What does that mean?"

Let's be honest: I knew perfectly well what that "I can't take her" implied, and my mouth went dry just then, because I knew I couldn't say no, not to the two people I care most about in the world. My family. Not the one you're born into—I had enough as far as that goes—but the family you choose.

"I know what I'm asking you for is a sacrifice." It was. "But it's the only solution. I can't take her to Sydney now that she's already started school, especially with her missing last year. I can't pull her away from everything she knows right now; it would be too many changes. You're all we have left. Leaving her alone isn't an option. She's got anxiety, nightmares; she's not…she's not right. I need Leah to be herself again before she goes off to college next year."

I rubbed the back of my neck, following Oliver's lead from a few minutes before and taking out the bottle of brandy. The shot warmed my throat.

"When are you leaving?" I asked.

"In a couple of weeks."

"Jesus, Oliver."

2

Axel

I HAD JUST TURNED SEVEN when my father got the pink slip and we moved to a bohemian town called Byron Bay. Before then, we'd always lived in Melbourne, on the third floor of an apartment block. When we got to our new home, it felt like a permanent vacation. In Byron Bay, you often saw people walking barefoot down the street or through the supermarket. The air was relaxed, without any real schedule, and I think I fell in love with each and every corner of it even before I'd opened the car door and struck the gruff-looking boy who would be my neighbor from then on.

Oliver had unkempt hair and baggy clothes and looked like a savage. Georgia, my mother, liked to tell that story over and over at family gatherings when she'd had one glass of wine too many. She'd say she nearly dragged him into our house to give him a bubble bath. Fortunately, the Joneses came out just when she was grabbing him by the sleeve. She let him go when she realized the root of the problem was right there in front of her. Mr. Jones, smiling in a poncho daubed with paint, stretched out his hand.

And Mrs. Jones hugged her, leaving her frozen to the spot. My father, my brother, and I laughed when we saw the stupefied look on her face.

"I suppose you're the new neighbors," Oliver's mother said.

"Yeah, we just got here," my father replied.

Their talk stretched on a few minutes, but Oliver didn't seem especially interested in welcoming us. His face was bored, and I watched him take a slingshot and a stone out of his pocket and aim at my brother, Justin. He hit him on the first try. I smiled because I knew we'd get along.

3

Leah

THE MELODY OF "HERE COMES the Sun" kept repeating in my mind, but there was no trace of sun in the black scratches across the paper. Just darkness and hard, straight lines. I noticed my heart pounding faster, stifling me, chaotic. Tachycardia. I balled up the paper, threw it aside, and lay on the bed, bringing a hand to my chest and trying to breathe...breathe...

4

Axel

I GOT OUT OF THE car and climbed the stairs to my parents' door. Punctuality wasn't my thing, so I was the last to appear, same as every Sunday when our family met for lunch. My mother greeted me by running her hands through my hair and asking if I had that mole on my shoulder last week or if it was new. My father rolled his eyes when he heard her and hugged me before welcoming me into the living room. Once I was there, my nephews clung to my legs until Justin got them to leave me in peace with a promise of chocolate.

"Still bribing them?" I asked.

"It's the only thing that works," he responded, resigned.

The twins laughed softly and I had to struggle not to join them. They were devils. Two charming devils who spent the whole day shouting, "Uncle Axel, pick me up," "Uncle Axel, put me down," "Uncle Axel, buy me this," "Uncle Axel, shoot," and that kind of thing. They were the reason my older brother was going bald (though he would never admit to using hair-growth products) and Emily, the girl he started going out with in high school and ended up taking as his wife, had given up pants and skirts for leggings, and smiled whenever one of her little bundles of joy threw up on her or drew on her clothes with a marker.

I waved to Oliver and walked over to Leah, who was at the table, which was already set, staring at the pattern of vines around the edges of the dishes. She looked up at me when I sat down beside her. I gave her a friendly nudge with my elbow. She didn't respond. Not the way she would have some time back, with a smile that took up her whole face and could light up a room. Before I could say anything, my father came over with a tray of stuffed chicken he left in the middle of the table. I looked around disconcerted until my mother handed me a bowl of sauteed vegetables. I smiled in gratitude.

We talked all through the meal: about the family's café, the surf season, the most recent contagious illness my mother had heard about. The one thing we didn't touch on remained hovering in the air, however much we tried not to pay attention. When it was time for dessert, my father cleared his throat, and I realized he was tired of pretending nothing was going on.

"Oliver, have you really thought about this?"

We all looked at him. All of us but his sister.

Leah didn't take her eyes off her cheesecake.

"The decision's made. It'll pass quickly."

My mother got up theatrically and brought her napkin to her mouth, but she couldn't help sobbing, and she walked off to the kitchen. I shook my head when my father went to follow her and offered to calm the situation myself. I took a deep breath and leaned on the counter next to her.

"Mama, don't do this. This isn't what they need right now."

"I can't help it, son. This situation is unbearable. What else can happen? It's been a terrible, terrible year…"

I could have bullshitted her, could have said, "It's no big deal" or "Everything will be okay," but I couldn't manage it, because I knew it wasn't true. Nothing would ever be the same. Our lives didn't just change when the Joneses died in a car accident; they became different lives, with two absences that were always profoundly present, like a suppurating wound that never closes.

From the day we set foot in Byron Bay, we were family. All of us. Despite the differences: The Joneses may have gotten up every day thinking only in the now. My mother might have spent her every waking second worrying about the future. They might have been bohemians, artists used to living in nature, while we only knew life in Melbourne. Maybe when they said yes, we said no; maybe we contradicted each other in arguments that lasted till dawn on the nights when we had dinner together in the garden, but still.…

We had been inseparable.

And now it was all broken.

My mother wiped away her tears.

"How can he even think of leaving you in charge of Leah? We could have worked something out. We could have done a quick renovation in the living room, splitting it so she could have a bedroom, or we could have bought a sofa bed. I know it's not the most comfortable thing and she needs her space, but no matter how good your heart is, you can't even take care of a pet."

I raised an indignant eyebrow.

"I'll have you know I've got a pet."

"Yeah, what's it called?"

"It doesn't have a name. Yet."

Actually, it wasn't my *pet*. I wasn't really one for *owning* living creatures, but now and again, a scrawny tricolor cat with a hateful face would show up on my back porch for food and I would give it the leftovers. There were weeks when it came by two or three times, and others when it didn't bother.

"This is going to be a disaster."

"Mom, I'm almost thirty; I can take care of her. It's the most reasonable thing. You all spend every day at the café, and when you don't, you've got to take care of the twins. And she's not going to spend a year sleeping in the living room."

"What will you eat?" she asked.

"Food, damn it."

"Watch your mouth."

I turned around and left the kitchen. I went back to the car, grabbed the wrinkled pack of smokes from the glove box, and walked a few streets down. Sitting on the curb, I lit a cigarette and stared at the branches of the trees quivering in the wind. This wasn't the neighborhood we had grown up in, the one where our families had grown together until becoming one. The two properties had been put up for sale; my parents had moved to a small one-bedroom house in the center of Byron Bay, close to the café they opened more than twenty years ago, when we settled here. They didn't have any reason to go on living in the suburbs when Justin and I were gone; they had lost their neighbors, and Oliver and Leah had moved to the house he rented when he wanted his independence after the two of us finished college.

"Thought you quit smoking."

I squinted my eyes toward the sun and looked up at Oliver. I exhaled a drag while he sat down next to me.

"I did. A couple of cigarettes a day isn't smoking. Not the way a smoker smokes, anyway."

He smiled, grabbed the pack, and lit one for himself.

"You've stepped into some shit, haven't you?"

I guess that was as good a term as any for being suddenly in charge of a nineteen-year-old girl who was nothing like the child she used to be. But I remembered right away all that Oliver had done for me. He taught me how to ride a bike. He got his nose busted in a fight when we were studying in Brisbane, a fight I got him into. I sighed and snuffed out my cigarette on the ground.

"We'll work it out fine," I said.

"Leah can take her bike to school. She usually spends her free time shut up in her room. I can't get her out of there, you know… Hopefully everything will go back to normal. She's got some rules; I'll tell you about those later. I'll be here every month, and…"

"Relax, it doesn't sound that complicated."

It wouldn't be for me, not the same way it had been for him. All I'd have to do is get used to living with someone, which I hadn't done for years, and keep control. Control over myself. The rest we would work out on the fly. After the accident, Oliver had felt obligated to give up the carefree lifestyle he and I had known when we were growing up to become his sister's guardian, and work in a field he didn't care for but that gave him a good salary and stability.

My friend sucked in a breath and looked at me.

"You'll take care of her, right?"

"Shit, of course I will."

"Good, because Leah...is the only thing I have left."

I nodded, and with one look, we understood each other: he was calm and knew I would do everything in my power to make sure Leah was happy, and I realized I was probably the person Oliver trusted most.

5

Axel

OLIVER SMILED AND RAISED HIS glass.

"To good friends!" he shouted.

I toasted with him and took a sip of the cocktail they had just served us. It was the last Saturday before Oliver left for Sydney, and I had insisted we go out for a bit. We had ended up in the same place as always, at Cavvanbah, an open-air bar on the edge of town near the seashore. It was named after the aborigines' term for the area, and it meant "meeting place," which summed up the spirit and identity of Byron Bay. The building where they served the drinks and the few tables were painted an island blue that matched the thatched roof, the palm trees, and the swings hanging from the ceiling around the bar.

"I can't believe I'm going."

I nudged him and he laughed humorlessly.

"It'll just be a year, and you'll come back every month."

"And Leah, fuck, Leah…"

"I'll take care of her," I repeated. I'd been saying the same words all day since that morning when I opened the door for him and we worked out our plan. "We've always done this, right? Stay above water, get ahead, that's what it's all about."

He rubbed his face and sighed. "If only it was that simple."

"It is. Come on, let's have some fun." I got up after one last sip. "I'm going for two more; you want the same?"

Oliver nodded, and I walked away from the table, stopping a few times to greet acquaintances. It was a small town, and almost all of us knew each other, even if just by sight. I leaned on the bar and smiled when Madison grimaced after serving drinks to the two people next to me.

"Back for more? You trying to get drunk?"

"I don't know. Depends. If I do, will you take advantage of me?"

Madison suppressed a smile while she grabbed a bottle. "Would you like me to?"

"Always, you know that."

She looked me dead in the eye as she pushed the glasses forward. "You want me to wait for you, or you have plans?"

"I'll be here when you wrap up."

Oliver and I spent the rest of the night drinking and reminiscing. About that time we called his father because we were drunk on the beach, and instead of picking us up and taking us home, he decided to draw us in his sketchbook while we were laid out, then copied the picture and hung it all over my house and the Joneses' to remind us of what idiots we'd been. Or another time when we got into trouble in Brisbane buying pot: We smoked until I was completely gone, and then, giggling, I threw the keys to the apartment we were sharing into the sea. Oliver went to look for them fully dressed, high as a kite, while I was on the shore cracking up.

In those days, we promised each other we would always live this way, the way we did in the place where we'd grown up, which was so simple, relaxed, anchored in surfing and counterculture.

I looked at Oliver and held back a sigh before finishing my drink.

"I'm going to go; I don't want to leave her alone any longer," he said.

"Okay." I laughed when I watched him stumble getting up, and he flipped me the bird and tossed a few bills on the table. "We'll talk tomorrow."

"We'll talk," he responded.

I spent a while there with a group of friends. Gavin talked to us about his new girlfriend, a tourist who had arrived two months back and wound up staying indefinitely. Jake told us three or four times about the design of his new surfboard. Tom just drank and listened to the others. I stopped thinking while the place cleared out in the early morning hours. When the last customer left, I walked around the building, opened the back door, and snuck in.

"Remind me again why I'm so patient."

Madison smiled, closed the blinds, and came over with a sensual smile on her lips. Her fingers wove through the loops on my jeans, and she pulled me close until our half-open mouths collided.

"Because I make it worth your while," she purred.

"Refresh my memory."

I took off her skimpy top. She wasn't wearing a bra. Madison rubbed against me before unbuttoning my fly and kneeling slowly. When her open mouth took me in, I closed my eyes, leaning my hands on the wall in front of me. I sank my fingers in her hair, trying to get her to go faster, deeper. I was about to come when she stepped back. I put on a rubber. Then I sank inside her against the wall, ramming her, shivering every time I heard her say my name, feeling the moment: the pleasure, the sex, the need. That was everything. And it was perfect.

February

—

(SUMMER)

6

Leah

I KEPT LOOKING AT MY joined hands while the car drove over the dirt road and the afternoon sun tinted the sky orange. I didn't want to see it, didn't want to see the color, or anything else that would bring back the memories and dreams I had left behind.

"Don't make it hard on Axel; he's doing us a big favor, you realize that, right, Leah? And eat. Try to be good, okay? Tell me what you're up to."

"I'm trying," I answered.

He went on talking until he braked in front of a property surrounded by palm trees and wild brush growing untamed. I'd only been to Axel's place a few times, and everything struck me as different. I was different. In the past year, he had been the one who dropped in at our apartment now and again to hang out. I closed my eyes when a thought lashed me, the thought that said to me, if this had happened before, the mere thought of sharing the same roof as him would give me butterflies in my stomach and a knot in my throat. Now, however, I felt nothing. That was how it was since the accident, that was the mark it had left in me, the immense, desolate emptiness that made it impossible to build anything because there was nothing to base it on. I just no longer *felt* anything. And I didn't want to either. It was better to live like this, lethargic, than with the pain. Sometimes there were highs, some unexpected lightness, as if something were trying to open up inside me, but I managed to control it eventually. It was like being in front of a pile of pizza dough full of lumps and bubbles just before passing the roller over it and flattening it out.

"You ready?" My brother looked at me.

"I guess so." I shrugged.

7

Axel

I WANTED TO GO BACK in time just to tell my past self that I was a dumbass for saying this wouldn't be complicated. It was fucking complicated right from the get-go, when Leah set foot in my house and looked around without much interest. Not that there was much to see. The walls were bare, without a picture in sight, the floors were wood, just like the furniture with its different colors and styles, the living room was separated from the kitchen by a counter-top, and, according to my mother, the décor resembled a tiki bar.

As soon as Oliver left, with just enough time to reach the airport, I started feeling uncomfortable. She didn't seem to notice; she just remained silent, following me while I showed her the guest bedroom.

"Here it is. You can redecorate or..." I closed my mouth before adding, "Or whatever it is girls your age do." She wasn't one of those beaming youngsters that run all over Byron Bay with their surfboards on their backs in summer dresses. Leah had left all that behind, as if somehow it connected her to her past. "You need anything?"

She looked at me with immense blue eyes and shook her head before putting her suitcase on the bed and opening the zipper to take out and arrange her things.

"Whatever you need, I'll be on the porch."

I left her alone and took a deep breath.

No, it wasn't going to be easy. Within my chaos, I had a set routine. I got up before dawn, had a cup of coffee, and went surfing, or swimming if there weren't any waves; then I made myself lunch and sat down at my desk to organize my work. I usually made some progress, doing a little of this and a little of that, never in an especially organized way unless I was on a tight deadline. Later, I had my second and last cup of coffee for the day, normally while I looked at the landscape through the window. I wasn't a bad cook, but I rarely turned on the stove, more because I was lazy than anything else. In the afternoon, same story: more work, more surfing, more hours of silence sitting by myself on the porch, more peace. After teatime came my nightly cigarette, a little reading or music, then bed.

So that first day Leah showed up at my home, I decided to stick to my routine. I spent the afternoon working on one of my latest commissions, concentrating on putting together a linear image, adding details until I thought it was perfect.

When I put down my pen and got up, I realized she still hadn't emerged from her room. The door was half-closed, just as I'd left it. I went over, knocked, and opened slowly.

Leah was lying in bed listening to music with her hair spread over the pillow. She looked away from the ceiling and took off her headphones as she sat up.

"Sorry, I didn't hear you."

"What were you listening to?"

"The Beatles."

There was a tense silence.

I would venture that everyone who knew the Joneses knew the Beatles was their favorite group. I remembered long nights at their house dancing to their songs and singing aloud. When I started accompanying Douglas Jones, Leah's father, years later while he was painting in his studio off the backyard, I asked him why he always worked to music, and he replied that it was his inspiration, that nothing is born inside you, not even the basic idea— what you bring to it is the way you portray it. He explained that the notes marked the way for him, and the voices shouted every brushstroke. Back then, I used to imitate everything Douglas did, admiring his paintings and the easy way he smiled at all hours, and so I followed in his footsteps and tried to find my own inspiration, something that would get inside me, but I never did, and that's probably why, halfway down the road, I wound up taking an unexpected detour and becoming an illustrator.

"You want to catch some waves?" I asked.

"Surf?" Leah was tense as she looked at me. "No."

"Okay. I'll be back soon."

I was nervous as I crossed the few feet between my home and the ocean, looking at the orange bike leaned against the wooden railing of the porch. Oliver had left it there after taking it out of the car. It was just an object, but one that represented changes I still hadn't absorbed.

I waited, waited, and waited until the perfect wave came. Then

I arched my back, positioned my feet, and rose, coming down along the wall of the wave and, once I was really going, surfing away from the break and finally jumping down into the water.

When I got back, the door to the guest room was closed. I didn't knock. I showered and went to the kitchen to make some dinner. I had gone—unusually—to the store the day before. I rarely bought much, but I had tried to bring some variety into the fridge. All I knew that Leah liked were strawberry lollipops; she always had one in her mouth when she was little, and she'd spend hours chewing on the plastic straw. That and the cheesecake my mother made, but that was no surprise, everyone knew it was the best in the world.

While I cut a selection of vegetables into strips, I realized I didn't know Leah as well as I thought I did. Maybe I never really had. Not deep down. She was born when Oliver and I were ten, and no one expected another addition to the family. I still remember the first day I saw her: she had chubby pink cheeks, little fingers that grabbed on to anything in arm's reach, and hair so blond it was almost transparent. Rose, Leah's mom, spent a long time telling us how from now on we would have to take care of her and act right when we were around her. But Leah spent the day crying or sleeping, and we were more interested in hunting bugs on the beach or playing.

When we went off to college in Brisbane, she had just turned eight. When we returned after staying there awhile to work and go through our internships, Leah was almost fifteen, and even if we came back a lot, we had the feeling she had grown up all of a sudden, as if one night she had gone to sleep a girl and had woken up the next day a woman. She was tall and thin, with few curves, like a beanstalk. She had started to paint while I was away, following in her father's footsteps, and one day, when I crossed the yard and stopped in front of the painting on the easel, I couldn't help but wonder at the delicate lines, the dashes of almost quivering color. My hair stood on end. I knew it couldn't be Douglas who had painted it, because there was something different about it, something...I couldn't explain.

She walked out the back door of her home.

"Did you do this?" I pointed at the painting.

"Yeah." She looked at me warily. "It sucks."

"It's perfect. It's...so different."

I turned my head to look at it from another angle, absorbing the details, the life throbbing in it, the confusion. She had painted the landscape there out front—the curved branches of the trees, the oval leaves, the thick trunks—but it wasn't a real image; it was a distortion, as though she had grabbed all the elements and mixed them in the blender of her mind and then thrown them out all jumbled, with her own special interpretation.

Leah blushed and stood in front of the picture with crossed arms. Her sweet angel face frowned and she looked at me reproachfully.

"You're kissing up to me."

"I'm not either, damn it. Why would you think that?"

"Because my father asked me to paint them," she said, pointing at the trees, "and I did this, and they don't look anything like them. It started out right, but then...then..."

"Then you did your own thing."

"You think?"

I nodded and smiled at her. "Keep doing that."

In the months to come, every time I went to see my parents or the Joneses, I would spend a while with her looking at her latest work. Leah was… She was her. There was nothing else like her. She didn't have influences; her lines were so distinctive I could have picked them out anywhere. She was light, and there was something that drew me to her, as if her pictures compelled me to keep looking, keep discovering…

8

Leah

I GOT OUT OF BED with a sigh when Axel shouted that dinner was ready. He had made some vegetable tacos that were steaming on his so-called coffee table, a surfboard with four wooden legs in front of the sofa. Apart from his desk covered in junk, it was the only table in his house, unless you counted the old trunk where he kept his record player. Everything there was very him, with that furniture that matched despite being so different, the order in the disorder, the reflection of inner peace in the small things.

I envied him. That way of living, so unworried, so relaxed, always looking ahead without stopping to look back, always focused on the now.

I sat on one end of the sofa and ate in silence.

"So you're taking your bike to school tomorrow."

I nodded.

"Would you rather I drive you?"

I shook my head.

"Sure, your call." Axel sighed. "You want some tea?"

I looked up at him slowly.

"Tea? Now?"

"I always have some at night."

"It's got caffeine," I whispered.

"Doesn't bother me."

Axel took the plates to the kitchen. I looked at him over my shoulder as he did. His hair was dirty blond, like ripe wheat or the sand on the beach at dusk. I looked away from him quickly, confused, pushing aside the colors, burying them.

Axel called me a few minutes later, cup of tea in one hand and a pack of cigarettes in another.

"Come out on the porch?" he proposed.

"Nah, I'm going to bed. Good night."

"Good night, Leah. Get some rest."

I got under the sheets even though I wasn't cold, and hid my head beneath the pillow. Darkness. Just darkness. In Axel's house, you didn't hear a single car pass down the street, no distant voices; there was just silence and my thoughts, which seemed to shake and shout and try to break out. When I felt anxiety bearing down on my chest and my breathing turning irregular, I closed my eyes tight and grabbed the sheets, wanting everything to be gone. Everything.

The next morning, I found him in the kitchen.

All he had on was a wet red swimsuit. He was making toast. He smiled at me. And I hated him a little for that, for smiling at me like that with those perfect lips and that gleam in his eyes. I tried not to look at him and opened the fridge to take out the milk.

"Sleep well?" he asked.

"Yeah," I lied. I'd had nightmares again.

"You sure you don't want me to take you?"

"Sure. Thanks though."

I left there, him, not long afterwards, and didn't stop pedaling till I'd reached school and left the bicycle chained to a fence painted blue. The wooden building was small with a patio surrounding it. I looked down when I walked through the door and didn't talk to anyone. Before, this had been my favorite moment of the day: getting to class, finding my friends, telling each other the latest gossip, and walking together to class. But I couldn't do that anymore. I had tried it, I really had, but there was a barrier between them and me, something that wasn't there before.

When I walked past Blair with my head low, hair partly covering my face, I wished she hadn't gotten a job there. Probably that's why I kept my hair so long, to avoid attention, to hide the feelings I knew everyone could see in my eyes. If I could have had a superpower, I would have chosen invisibility. That way I could have escaped those looks of pity, the ones at first and the ones that came later, the ones that seemed to scream that I was weird, that no one understood me, that I wasn't trying hard enough to come back to the surface and breathe...

I spent the whole morning sitting at my desk, tracing spirals in the corner of my math notebook, concentrating on the ways the lines curved and on the soft movement of the black pen. When class was over, I realized I'd barely heard anything the teacher said. I was putting my books into my bag when Blair entered the room timidly and came over. Almost all my classmates were already gone. I looked at her restrained, wanting to escape.

"Could we talk a sec?"

"I...uh, I gotta go."

"Just for a few minutes."

"Okay."

Blair took a breath.

"I heard your brother's got to go to Sydney for a while and I wanted you to know if you need anything, anything at all, I'm still here for you. I always was, honestly."

My heart started thumping.

I wanted that, I wanted everything to go back to the way it was, but it couldn't. Every time I closed my eyes, I saw the car turning over and over, a blurry green furrow that meant we were no longer on the road, a song that cut off suddenly, a frozen scream. And then...and then they were dead. My parents. I couldn't forget it, I couldn't get away from the scene for more than a few hours, as if it had happened last night and not almost a year before. I couldn't walk next to Blair and smile every time we crossed paths with a group of surfer tourists or talk about what we were going to do in the future, because all I wanted to do was...nothing, all I could think about was...them, and no one could understand me. At least, that was the conclusion I came to after several sessions with the psychologist Oliver sent me to.

"It doesn't have to be the same, Leah."

"It can't be," I managed.

"But it can be different, new. Wasn't that what you used to do when you painted? Take something that existed and interpret it differently?" She swallowed nervously. "Couldn't you do that with our friendship? We wouldn't have to talk about anything if you didn't want to."

I nodded before it was over, leaving a little crack open between us. Blair smiled and then we left school together. She waved goodbye as I got on my orange bike and pedaled away.

9

Axel

HER BEDROOM DOOR WAS STILL closed.

She had been in my house for three weeks, and every day when she got back from school, she would eat whatever I prepared for her in silence, without protests or objections, then shut herself up between those four walls. The few times I entered, she was listening to music on her headphones or drawing with a fine-point pen, nothing interesting, just geometric figures, repetitions, pointless sketches.

Probably the longest sentence she spoke to me was on the first night, when she told me tea had caffeine. After that, nothing. If there hadn't been an extra toothbrush in my bathroom and I hadn't started to go grocery shopping now and then, I would hardly have noticed her presence. Leah only came out to eat lunch and dinner and go to school.

Naturally, my mother came by a few times with food, even though I had dropped by the café several times to tell her everything was fine, eat a free piece of cake, and spend some time with Justin, who was supposed to take over the business if my parents ever gave up their addiction to work.

"How are things?" he asked me.

"I guess fine. Or not. What the fuck do I know?"

"It's a tough situation. Be patient. Don't do your usual thing."

"My usual thing?"

"You know the kind of dumb shit that crosses your mind."

I laughed and downed my coffee in one sip. I had never been close to Justin; we weren't the type of brothers who go out together and hang or get drunk. We didn't have anything in common, and probably, if we weren't bound by blood, we would have been two strangers and would never have spoken more than a few words to each other. When I was little, it often struck me that he was stuck in the life we left behind in Melbourne, as if they'd jerked him away from there and dropped him in the middle of a place he didn't really understand. For me, it was the opposite. This stretch of coast was mine, almost made to measure for me: the freedom, being able to go around barefoot whenever I wanted, the relaxed life, the bohemian atmosphere, everything.

I walked around Byron Bay after saying goodbye to my brother and bought some organic fruit. Then I called Oliver on my way home. We'd talked the day before, but he had to hang up right away after just a few words because someone told him he had a meeting.

"How's it going?" he asked me.

"I've got some more questions."

"I'm all ears," he replied.

"Leah spends the whole day shut up in her room."

"I told you, she needs her space."

"Can I take that space away from her?"

There was silence on the other end of the line.

"What are you trying to tell me, Axel?"

"You never asked her to just stop locking herself away?"

"No, that's not how it works, the psychologist told us…"

"Do I have to go along with all that?" I asked.

"Yes. It's a matter of time. She's had a hard time."

I held back the impulse to contradict him and bit my tongue. Then he talked to me about his work out there, the organizational stuff he'd been doing for those three weeks. If he was lucky, maybe he'd be able to cut his stay in Sydney a few months short. I didn't want to let myself feel relieved before I knew for sure.

It was Saturday. She'd spent the whole morning shut away, and it was starting to try my patience, even though Oliver would arrive on Monday and I would have my normality back for seven days. It's not that I didn't understand her—of course I understood her pain—but that didn't change things, didn't change the present. According to the psychologist Oliver had taken her for numerous sessions with, she wasn't working her way through the phases of grief properly. In theory, she was stuck in the first, denial but I didn't agree with all that. Maybe that's why I knocked on her door.

Leah looked up and took off her headphones.

"The waves are nice; grab your board."

She blinked, confused. That was when I realized that every time I proposed something to her, it came across as a question. A question Leah felt justified in saying no to. But this wasn't a question.

"I'm not in the mood. Thanks though."

"Don't give me that. Move your ass."

She looked at me with alarm. I saw her chest rising and falling in time to her accelerated breathing, as if she hadn't seen the attack coming after all those days of calm. I hadn't planned it either, and I had promised my best friend I wouldn't do something like this, but I trusted my instincts. And I had an instinctive need to get her out of that room, a desire to drag her away from that place. Leah sat up stiffly, tense.

"I don't want to go, Axel."

"I'll wait for you outside."

I lay in the hammock stretched between two beams on the porch, where I normally read at night or closed my eyes while I listened to music. I waited. Ten minutes. Fifteen. Twenty. Twenty-five. After half an hour, she appeared, nose wrinkled with distaste, hair in a ponytail, face uncomprehending.

"Why do you want me to go?"

"Why do you want to stay?"

"I don't know," she answered softly.

"Me neither. Let's go."

Leah followed me in silence and we crossed the short distance separating us from the beach. The white sand received us warmly under the midday sun, and she took off her dress and stood there in her bikini. I don't know why, but I looked away and stared at the surfboard before passing it to her.

"It's short," she complained.

"Like it should be. Makes it more agile."

"Slower," she replied.

I smiled, not at her answer, but because it was the first time in those three endless weeks that we were having what you might call a conversation. I went toward the water, and she followed me without complaining.

The city was a mecca for surfers, but the waves weren't usually big. Still, that day the phenomenon known as "the Byron Bay wave" was on display. It happened when the three points came together at high tide, creating one long wave that advanced to the right, starting at the edge of the cape and entering the bay in regular, synchronized tubes.

I never missed an opportunity like that.

We headed out toward the depths. Once there, we didn't say a word, just sat on our surfboards and waited, waited for the perfect moment... Leah reacted and followed me when I made a sign and took off, smelling a good wave on its way, sensing a growing energy in the calm water.

"It's coming," I whispered.

Then I swam out to sea, hurrying, and stood up on my board before sliding into the wave, skirting it, gathering speed to make my move. I knew Leah was following me. I could feel her behind me, opening her way on the wall of the wave.

Happy, I looked over my shoulder.

A second later, she was gone.

10

Leah

THE WATER STRUCK ME, AND I closed my eyes.

Then the color was gone, and I felt safe again from those memories that try sometimes to creep in, the life that was no longer there, the things I used to want and no longer cared about. Because it wasn't fair that everything remained the same now that nothing was the same. I was so far away from my former life, myself, that sometimes I felt like I had died that day, too.

I opened my eyes.

The water was whirling around me. I was sinking. But there was no pain. There was nothing. Just the salty taste of the sea in my mouth. Just calm.

And then I felt him. His hands pulling me into his body, his strength, his momentum tugging us upward. Then the sun hit us as we broke the surface of the water. I felt nauseated. I coughed. Axel ran his fingers down my cheeks, and his eyes, their blue so dark it looked black, stared me straight in the face.

"Fuck, Leah, babe, are you okay?" he asked, calling me *babe*, the way he had before. Ever since I was a child.

I looked at him, shaken. Feeling...feeling something...

No, I wasn't okay. Not if I was feeling him again.

11

Axel

PANIC. LOSING SIGHT OF HER—THAT was panic. My heart was still in my throat when we got back home, and I couldn't stop thinking about her sinking in the choppy waters, how fragile she looked. I wanted to ask her why she hadn't tried to come up, but I was scared to break the silence. Or maybe what I was really afraid of was her answer.

I stayed in the kitchen while she showered, looking out the window, tossing around the idea of picking up the phone and calling Oliver. When Leah came out and looked at me, nervous and ashamed, I had to hold back to keep from letting loose on her.

"How are you?"

"Fine, I just got lightheaded."

"When you fell in the water?"

She looked away and nodded.

"I'll be in my room," she said.

"Fine. But I want to talk to you tonight."

Leah opened her mouth to protest, but then she went into her room and closed the door. I took a deep breath, trying to calm down. I walked barefoot onto the back porch, sat on the cracked wooden steps, and lit a cigarette.

Damn right we needed to talk.

I took a last drag before going in again. I walked over to my desk and rummaged through the papers until I found a blank sheet. I grabbed a pen and wrote down all the questions that had occurred to me in those three weeks. I put the paper down close by and went on writing while I made dinner. I got the salad ready and knocked at her door. She didn't object when I said we should have dinner outside.

The sky was covered in stars and I could smell the sea.

We ate in silence, almost without looking at each other. When we were done, I asked if she wanted tea, but she shook her head, so I went to the kitchen to put the plates in the sink. When I came back, Leah had her back turned, leaning on the railing and staring into the darkness.

"Sit down," I told her.

She sighed loudly before turning around. "Is this necessary? I'm leaving the day after tomorrow."

"And coming back a week later," I replied.

"I won't bother you." She looked at me, pleading. She reminded me of a frightened animal. "I didn't want to go; you're the one who made me get in the water…"

"That's beside the point. We're going to spend a lot of time together this year, and I need to know things." I took a sip of tea and glanced down at the sheet of paper in my hand covered in questions. "To start with, don't you have any friends? You know what I mean, people to hang out with, like other girls your age."

"Are you kidding?"

"No, absolutely not."

Leah paused. I wasn't in a hurry, so I got in the hammock and left my tea on the wooden railing while I lit a cigarette.

"I used to. I do. I think."

"How come you never go out then?"

"Because I don't want to, not anymore."

"How long is it going to be that way?" I asked.

"I don't know!" She was breathing fast.

"Fine…" I noticed the wrinkles in her forehead, the way her throat moved as she gulped. "That answers three of my questions." I looked at the paper. "How's school going?"

"Normal, I guess."

"You guess or you know?"

"I know. Why do you care?"

"I never see you studying."

"It's not really any of your business."

I tapped my chin a few times. Then I looked at her. As an equal. Not as if she were someone who needed my help and I was ready to give it to her. I saw fear in her eyes. Fear because she knew what I was going to say to her.

"I don't want to have to remind you of this, but for a year, your brother's been killing himself working for you, so you can go to college, so you can get ahead…"

I closed my mouth when she started sobbing.

I got up, feeling like an asshole, and hugged her. Her body shook against mine and I closed my eyes, holding on, holding on even though it hurt, because I wasn't about to say sorry for what I'd said, because I knew this was how it had to be.

Leah pulled away and wiped off her cheeks.

I stayed there beside her, my arms on the wooden railing around the porch, the damp night breeze blowing around me. I grabbed my notes.

"Next up." I had her right where I wanted her: open right down the middle, shaking. Stripped of the armor she wore at all hours. "Why aren't you painting?"

If I hadn't seen so many different things in her eyes, I could have sifted through the parts I was dissecting to try and understand her—but I wasn't there yet. "I can't stand colors."

"Why?" I whispered.

"Because they remind me of before, and of him."

Douglas Jones. Always covered in paint, colors, life. I had a lot of questions left on the page. *Why can't you accept what happened? Why are you doing this to yourself? How long do you think you'll be like this?* I balled it up in my hand and slipped it into my pants pocket.

"Are you done?" she asked, uncertain.

"Yeah." I lit another cigarette.

"I thought you quit."

"I did. I don't smoke. Not the way smokers do."

She smiled. It was a timid, fleeting smile, but for a millisecond, it was there, illuminating her face, tensing her lips, just for me.

12

Leah

I DON'T REMEMBER WHEN I fell in love with Axel. I don't know if it was one day in particular or if the feeling was always there, asleep, until I grew up and became aware that it was love, wanting someone, yearning for a glance from him more than anything else in the world. Or at least, that's what I thought when I was thirteen, when he was living in Brisbane with my brother. If he came to visit, I would spend the night before sleepless with butterflies in my stomach. I used to write his name in my day planner, talk to my friends about him, memorize his every gesture, as though they hid some important message. Later, when Axel came back and settled in Byron Bay, I started to love him down to my bones. All I needed was to have him close and let that feeling grow even as I kept silent, as though it were in a locked box where I protected it and nurtured it with my daydreams.

The first time he set eyes on one of my pictures, it was as if the world stopped, every blade of grass, every flap of a bird's wings. I was breathless, looking out the window while he turned his head, keeping his eyes on the canvas. I had left it there after spending the morning painting that stretch of woods that grew behind our house, trying to follow my father's instructions.

When my legs would obey me, I went outside.

"Did you do this?" he asked me.

"Yeah." I looked at him warily. "It sucks."

"It's perfect. It's...so different."

I could feel myself blushing as I crossed my arms. "You're kissing up to me."

"I'm not either, damn it. Why would you think that?"

I hesitated, not taking my eyes off him.

"Because my father asked me to paint them," I said, pointing at the trees, "and I did this, and they don't look anything like them. It started out right, but then...then..."

"Then you did your own thing."

"You think?"

He nodded before smiling at me. "Keep doing that."

Axel praised that canvas full of lines that even I had struggled to understand, though, in some way I couldn't explain, they fit, molded to each other, worked. His dirty blond hair shook in the breeze, and I felt the need to come up with the perfect mixture that would give me that tone: a base of ochre with a little brown, shadows at the roots, the sunlight sprinkled on the lightest tips as they curled softly. Later I would focus on his skin, its tan concealing the few freckles on his nose, his eyes almost closed, his smile mischievous, astute, but at the same time unworried, there in his disorder, in himself...

13

Axel

I THOUGHT I WOULD FEEL fucking relieved the day Oliver came back to spend the last week of the month with his sister, but I hardly noticed the difference. That was how faint, almost airy, Leah's passage through my home had been.

Over the following days, I kept up the habit of cooking. I don't know why, but I was finding it relaxing. My life returned to what it always had been: waking up at dawn, coffee, beach, lunch, work, coffee number two, and a chill afternoon. I started walking around the house naked again, leaving the bathroom door open when I showered, playing loud music at nighttime, jerking off in the living room. The difference was I had my privacy, I could do all the things I couldn't do in her presence, and I did, less because I wanted to than to mark my territory.

Friday I had managed to wrap up two commissions, so I decided to hit the waves for the afternoon, searching for them, gliding over them until I felt my muscles swell with the effort. It was still daytime when I returned home and found my brother sitting on the sofa and my six-year-old nephews careening through the living room. I raised an eyebrow, leaving behind a trail of water (why bother mopping when the water dries on its own? You just have to be patient). Justin walked over toward the kitchen.

"What made you think you could burst in without asking?"

"You gave me a key," he reminded me.

"Yeah, for emergencies."

"This is one. Besides, if you'd ever answer the damned phone instead of leaving it off for days at a time, I wouldn't have had to come. I need your help."

I grabbed a beer out of the fridge and passed him one too, but he refused it.

"Talk," I said after the first sip.

"Today's our anniversary."

"And I should care because…?"

"I forgot about it. I don't know where my head was. Emily's been pissed off all day—you know how it is—slamming doors, giving me weird looks I don't understand, that kind of thing. Finally I remembered what day it was, and fudge, man, now…"

"Don't ever say *fudge* under this roof again."

"It's for the kids. They're sponges, I swear."

"Get to the point, Justin."

"Can you watch them? Just for tonight."

I closed my eyes and sighed. When did my house turn into a family inn? It's not like I didn't want to. I loved my nephews, I adored Leah, but not the responsibilities they brought with them. I had always done my own thing, and I liked being alone. It suited me. I wasn't one of those people who felt the need to relate to people; I could go for weeks without seeing anyone and I wouldn't miss it. But apparently, I was now doomed to experience the effects of life in common. I had only ever taken care of the twins once, and that led me to my next point:

"Why don't you leave them with Mom and Dad?"

"Today's the cake contest."

I imagined my mother at the flea market, all the food, music, and hubbub out there practically in the suburbs, criticizing everyone's desserts, probably making the other competitors cry with her nasty looks just so she could come in first. Byron Bay was famous for its many cafés, and all of them had their own house-made cakes. But no doubt about it, my family's were the best.

"Fine, I'll do it," I agreed, looking at him with amusement. "But I hope your makeup sex is worth it."

Justin punched me in the shoulder. "There won't be any makeup."

"Oh, so it's going to be a savage hate fuck. You never cease to amaze me."

"Can it. Emily doesn't know I forgot and she never will. I booked a room in Ballina. I'm going to tell her it was a surprise and that's why I haven't said anything to her all day."

I laughed, and he gave me a look that could kill.

"As far as the kids go, I put everything they could possibly need in a backpack along with a change of clothes. We'll come pick them up tomorrow morning. Try and act like a normal person. Don't let them stay up till dawn. Remember to keep your phone on."

"You're giving me a headache."

"Thanks for this, Axel. I owe you one."

My brother left after hugging and kissing his kids goodbye

extravagantly, as if they were going off to war and he'd never see them again. When he closed the door, I frowned and they burst out laughing.

"Okay, boys, what do you feel like doing?"

Connor and Max smiled, revealing their gap teeth.

"Eat candy!"

"Paint with you!"

"Get into the hammock!"

"Best if we make a list." I went to my desk, grabbed a piece of paper, and started to write down every stupid thing my nephews uttered. Nonsense, and of course most of it sounded like a blast. That was the best part of being an uncle: every time I saw them, all I had to do was have fun.

When night fell, we'd had our dinner of spaghetti and ketchup (Connor's plate was more ketchup and spaghetti), I'd taken out the old video game console I kept in the closet to play with them, and they'd gotten my permission to swing around in the hammock for a while. I let them use some of my paints, and when I came back to the living room after washing the dishes, I found Max painting a tree on the wall next to the television. I shrugged, thinking I had more than enough paint and that I'd repair the disaster tomorrow. I got behind him and grabbed the hand with the brush in it.

"Softer lines, see?"

"I want to paint too," Connor said.

Before I realized it, it was past midnight and I had a stretch of wall covered in children's paintings and I hadn't turned on my phone. Justin was going to kill me. It was bedtime. Both of them complained at once.

"What about the candy?"

"It's on the list," Max reminded me.

"I don't have any. Well, now that you mention it…"

That week, when I went to the store, I had grabbed a handful of those strawberry suckers shaped like hearts that Leah liked when she was little. I took a few out of the cupboard and handed them out. I found my cell in my underwear drawer. I had six calls from Justin. I wrote him to tell him all was well. I also had a message from Madison saying we should see each other Saturday night. I responded with a simple yes and went back to the living room.

"Okay, boys, now it really is bedtime."

They didn't put up a fight. I accompanied them to the guest room and they both curled up in the same bed. Just before turning out the lamp on the nightstand, I saw the papers Leah had left on the table. I grabbed them and took them out onto the porch. I lit a cigarette and looked at them. One by one. Slowly. Looking closely at the spirals that filled the first page, a mechanical, numb drawing, like the kind I did. I looked through a few more until I found something that truly caught my eye. I blew out a lungful of smoke all at once and turned the page as I realized that, viewed horizontally, those quivering lines made a face in profile. It was drawn in charcoal. Black tears were sliding down a girl's face, frozen forever now on that paper, and something in her expression struck me as tender within her sorrow. I ran the tip of my fingers over the tears, smearing them until they became grayish streaks. Then I pulled my hand away as though they'd burned me, because I never drew that way, trying to express something intimate; it just didn't work that way for me.

14

Leah

FOR MONTHS, I'D FELT SELFISH and useless, unable to get ahead, but I didn't know what to do about it. One day, with my eyes red and swollen from so much crying, I found myself throwing on a raincoat so the pain wouldn't get me wet, and somehow I realized then that happiness, laughter, love, and all the good things I'd known couldn't touch me either.

I read once that feelings are somehow mutable, that sorrow can transform into apathy, for example, and manifest itself through other sensations. I had provoked this. I had made my emotions remain ravaged, frozen in a way that made it possible for me to cope with them. And yet...Axel had poked holes in that raincoat in fewer than three weeks. I had been afraid of that from the beginning. So much so that I didn't want to return to his hope, that place that was so his that it made me feel hemmed in.

I guess I was still thinking about that when, on the last night before he left, Oliver said we should have pizza for dinner and watch a movie. My first impulse was to say no. My second one was to take off running and shut myself up in my room. And the third...the third would have been something similar if Axel's words about the effort my brother was making for me hadn't kept repeating in my head. My voice shook when I uttered that soft yes. Oliver smiled, leaned over toward me, and gave me a kiss on the forehead.

March

—

(AUTUMN)

15

—

Axel

LEAH RETURNED. AND WITH HER, the closed door, the silence in the house, the furtive glances. But something was different. Something was new. She didn't take off running when dinner was over; instead she stayed sitting there awhile, distractedly balling her napkin in her hand or offering to do the dishes. Sometimes, in the afternoons, while eating a piece of fruit and leaning on the counter, she would look at the sea through the window, distant, lost.

That first week, I asked her three times if she wanted to come surfing with me, but she rejected the offer, and after what happened last time, I didn't force it. I didn't say anything when the tricolor cat came to visit me and Leah went to give it leftovers from dinner. I didn't say anything that first Saturday night when I was lying in the hammock and I heard her steps behind me. I had put on a record, and I don't know why, but I had this thought that the chords in the song that was playing had grabbed her by the hair and pushed her out on the porch, note by note.

"Can I stay here?"

"Of course. Want some tea?"

She shook her head and sat on one of the cushions on the wooden floor.

"How was the week?"

"Same as always. Normal."

I had lots of questions to ask, but none that she would respond to, so I didn't bother to bring them up. I sighed, relaxed, contemplating the starry sky, listening to the music, living that instant, that moment.

"Axel, are you happy?"

"Happy…? Of course."

"Is it easy?" she whispered.

"It should be, right?"

"I used to think it was."

I sat up in the hammock. Leah was sitting up, hugging her knees against her chest. She looked small under the darkness of the night.

"There's something wrong with what you just said. Before you were happy because you didn't think about it, and who does when they have the world at their feet? In those moments, you just live, just feel."

There was fear in her eyes. But also longing. "Will I never be that way again?"

"I don't know, Leah. Do you want to be?"

She swallowed and licked her lips nervously before taking a deep breath. I knelt beside her, took her hand, and tried to get her to look me in the eyes.

"I can't…breathe…"

"I know. Slow. Easy…" I whispered. "I'm here, babe. I'm right beside you. Close your eyes. Just think… Think about the sea, Leah, about a choppy sea that's starting to calm down. Are you seeing it in your mind? There's almost no waves left…"

I wasn't even sure what I was saying to her, but I got Leah to breathe slower, more relaxed. I accompanied her to her room, and something quivered in me when she said good night at the door. Compassion. Impotence. What do I know?

That night, I broke my routine. Instead of reading a little and going to bed, I turned on my computer and pushed aside the things I had on the keyboard before searching for *anxiety*. I spent hours reading and taking notes.

Post-traumatic stress disorder: a psychiatric affliction that appears in people who have experienced some traumatic moment in their lives. I took more notes: *Sufferers have frequent nightmares and recall the experience. Other typical signs are anxiety, palpitations, and increased sweating.* I went on, incapable of sleeping: *A sense of distance, paralysis in the face of normal emotional experiences. Loss of interest in hobbies and pastimes.*

I found out there were four types of post-traumatic stress.

In the first, patients constantly relive the triggering event. In the second, they are hyper-excited, constantly perceiving danger or surprise. In the third, they focus on negative thoughts and their sense of guilt. And in the fourth…shit, the fourth was Leah, one hundred percent. *They adopt evasion as a tactic. Patients show and transmit emotional insensitivity or indifference about daily activities, and avoid places or things that make them remember what happened.*

On Sunday I got up at dawn, as always, though I'd only slept a few hours. It was a sunny day, but the temperature had dropped. I made coffee, let Leah sleep, grabbed my surfboard, and walked down to the beach. But when I saw the dolphins so close to the shore, I retraced my steps, because I couldn't let her miss that, and I needed her to be there by my side in the waves now that I was starting to understand her, like a riddle I wanted to crack or a puzzle I was still missing a piece to.

I knocked on her door, but she didn't answer, so I opened it softly. That was my first mistake. I took a breath when I saw her in the bed on her back, wearing nothing but a T-shirt and white panties. Her naked legs were wrapped in the sheets. She moved a little and I closed the door and left.

"Fuck," I said while I was putting on my leash.

I spent several hours in the water.

I guess that's why she came looking for me.

Still out in the water, I saw her sitting close to the shore, legs crossed, eyes pinned to the horizon. I came out a little later, exhausted, my board under my arm. I flopped down beside her, stretching out on the sand without uttering a word.

"Sorry about last night. I didn't want to scare you."

"It's anxiety, Leah; it's not your fault. The harder you try to avoid it, the more you think you can, the worse it will be. Things aren't always easy, but little by little, you'll make it."

"No one believes me, but I am trying."

I believed her. I was convinced that she was struggling every single day to get ahead without realizing that she was the one holding herself back. She wanted it. But her instincts were stronger, and her instincts were shouting at her that the path to her goal was too arduous, that the best thing would be to stay where she was, huddled down, protected, anchored in a place she herself had built.

———————

The next day, after seeing her disappear up the drive on her orange bike, I got in my pickup and headed to the café to call in the favor my brother owed me and get a free breakfast. I ordered coffee and a piece of cake.

"How did the night go? A fuck to remember?"

"My wife isn't just some fuck, Axel. Watch your mouth."

"Okay, you're right. She's a grade A fuck. Sorry."

My brother scowled at me and I laughed because I meant it. Emily was such a catch, I still had a hard time figuring out what she was doing with Justin.

"Oh, is there a grade A fuck around?" My father showed up with his customary smile. He liked to toy with slang and sound like the surfers and hippies in the area, but it never came out right, and Mom always gave him a friendly slap on the neck whenever she heard him.

"Forget it, Dad. Axel. He's an idiot."

"Your kids think I'm the coolest uncle ever."

"My kids are six," he replied, rolling his eyes. "And I'm still mad at you for letting them paint your walls. What were you thinking? The other day they trashed the living room and couldn't understand why we were yelling at them."

"I told them they could do it one time. If they did it again, that's not my problem. I've got to go; we'll talk tomorrow."

"Take it easy, dude!" my father shouted with a grin.

I tried not to laugh as I said goodbye, got into the truck, and drove awhile to the next town over. It's not that I couldn't buy what I wanted in Byron Bay, but there was less variety and the prices were usually higher. I took my time choosing. I wanted everything to be new, unused, without marks or memories. I used the occasion to get some work materials I needed. When I got back home, I went out to the porch and got everything ready. Then I put the sushi I'd bought in the fridge and waited, smoking a cigarette, until I saw her pedaling in the distance.

16

Leah

"SO THINGS ARE BETTER..." BLAIR looked at me.

I nodded without taking my eyes off the purple ribbon hanging at the end of her braids. The color was intense, alive, like the skin of an eggplant. I took a deep breath and then did the thing I'd been avoiding for so long, taking an interest in another person, breaking the layer of indifference.

"You good too?" I asked.

Blair smiled before telling me what her job had been like those first weeks. Since her mother was a teacher there, she'd recommended her as a kindergarten assistant while she was studying early childhood education. She had never wanted to leave Byron Bay. I had always dreamed of going to college, studying fine arts, and coming back with a head full of ideas to make real. And when I imagined myself doing it, I saw him looking at my pictures, analyzing them with that way he had of softly tilting his head.

How far away all that was...

"We could meet for a coffee one day. Or a Coke, I don't know, whatever you want. You know, we don't even have to really talk."

"Okay," I agreed quickly because I couldn't stand to see Blair like that, almost begging for some time with me when she ought to be running away from me and not even bothering to ever speak a word to me again.

With the palms of my hands sweaty despite the cool breeze, I got on my bike and pedaled as fast as I could to Axel's house, as if with every turn of the wheels I was trying to leave my nerves behind. And I did; at some point on the ride, I was empty, and when I arrived, I felt a shiver as I saw him leaning on the wooden railing with a cigarette between his fingers. I buried that shiver. I buried it deep. In my mind, I scratched the dirt with my fingertips, dug a hole, put in that hole any glimmer of emotion I felt, and covered it up.

With a knot in my throat, I parked my bicycle and climbed the stairs. I had been concentrating so hard that I didn't even notice there was something else there, something that hadn't been on the porch when I left that morning. I shook when I saw it. A spotless easel of bright wood with an empty canvas resting on it.

"What's this?" my voice broke.

"This is for you. What do you say?"

"No." I was almost begging. "I can't... There's no way..."

Axel swallowed as if he hadn't expected this reaction. I tried to escape to my room, but before I could get into the house, he grabbed my wrist and pulled firmly. Shit. I felt his fingers surrounding my skin...his skin...

"I've seen your drawings. If you can do it on paper, why not here? It's the same thing, Leah. And I need you to do it. I need you to start moving forward."

I closed my eyes. I hated him for saying that.

I need... He needed it? I swallowed my frustration, still trembling.

"I'm supposed to meet up with a friend."

Axel let me go. His eyes drilled into me in the midday silence, and I shrank before him, realizing he could see right through my raincoat...

"So you're meeting a friend. Who? When?"

"Blair. We haven't set a date."

"Isn't that a requirement to meet up with someone?"

"Yeah, but we'll talk about it later."

"Sure. Next year. Or the one after," he joked.

"Fuck you, Axel."

17

Axel

I HEARD THE DOOR SLAM when Leah disappeared, but I didn't move. I stayed there in front of the white canvas I'd bought her that morning, my heart frantic. How fucking long had it been since my heart had beat like that, so chaotic, so fast? My life was usually like a sea without waves, calm, serene, easy. I'd only had to face the truth one time, and that was when the Joneses died.

I remember that day as if it just happened.

A few hours before, Oliver and I had gone out and gotten drunk with a group of English tourists who invited us to finish the party in their hotel. When the phone rang, we were already taking the gravel path out, laughing about things that had happened the night before. The sun shone high in the clear sky, and Oliver picked up the phone, still smiling.

I knew it was something bad when I saw his face, as if something inside him had shattered. Oliver blinked and grabbed the post in front of him, crumpling to his knees. He murmured, "An accident," and I took the phone from his hands. My father's voice was on the other line, hard, like a smack across the face: "The Joneses had an accident." I could only think of her.

"Leah? Dad…" I gulped. "Is Leah…?"

"She's hurt, but not badly."

I hung up and held Oliver's shoulders while he vomited in the garden of that hotel. My brother picked us up on a nearby street ten minutes later. Ten minutes that were eternal, while Oliver lost control and I gathered what strength I had to keep him on his feet.

18

——

Leah

I DIDN'T LEAVE THE ROOM the whole afternoon. But I did open my backpack, take out my books, and do my homework. When I finished, I put on my headphones and let the music fill me. It was the one link with the past I allowed myself, because I couldn't...I couldn't do without it. Impossible.

"Hey Jude" played, then "Yesterday."

When "Here Comes the Sun" came, I skipped it.

I went back to "Yesterday," to "Let It Be," to "Come Together."

For the first time in ages, the hours in those four walls where I had felt so safe became eternal. I walked out to go to the bathroom around nightfall and Axel was gone, so I went to the kitchen to grab a bite, not looking toward the back porch, because I was still painfully conscious of what was out there. I opened a few cabinets until I found a box of Tim Tam cookies, but my hand drew back when I saw what was next to them: a bag full of strawberry lollipops shaped like hearts. I was about to grab one when Axel came in. Still wet, he left his surfboard in the doorway and looked at me cautiously.

"I'm sorry about earlier. Really sorry," I said.

"Forget about it. What do you want for dinner?"

"I don't want to forget about it, Axel. I can't. I feel like I'm drowning every time I do something normal, something I used to do, because that's like saying life will just keep going on its merry way, and I don't understand how that's possible when a part of me is still inside that car with them and can't get out."

Axel ran a hand through his damp hair and sighed. And then... he said something that broke me. *Crack*.

"I miss you, Leah."

"What?" I whispered.

He leaned on the bar in the kitchen between us.

"I miss the girl you were before. You know, watching you paint, joking with you, that smile you used to have... And I don't know how, but I'm going to get you out of there, out of wherever you are, and bring you back."

He didn't say anything else before getting in the shower, but those words were enough to give me a bout of tachycardia. I stood still, my eyes focused on the window and one hand on my chest, afraid that any movement might provoke an earthquake and the ground would slip away beneath my feet. But it didn't. The calm was almost worse. The absence of noise or chaos. Calm and nothing else. Like the hint that a storm is coming, or you're in the eye of the hurricane.

19

Axel

WHEN I SPOKE TO OLIVER that night, I didn't tell him anything that had happened in the afternoon. When I hung up, I realized that I was hardly telling him any of the things that were taking place under this roof, where we lived, in which things only had the importance that we wanted to give them. And despite everything, Leah and I got along well with each other; we could get angry and then have dinner like two civilized people. Or spend days without saying more than a few words to each other, and it wasn't weird. Somehow, we fit together, even with the sadness that was eating away at her and the desperation I was starting to feel, because if there was one flaw I had, it was impatience.

I'd never been the type to wait.

I remember when I was little, I wanted to buy a remote control car, and I pressed my parents about it for days. My brother had been begging them for months to take him to get a board game so boring I rolled my eyes as soon as I heard its name. And so, according to my childhood logic, one afternoon I took my brother's piggy bank, stole all the money out of it, and put it back without anyone noticing. My parents took me to get the car, thinking I was spending my own savings, and Oliver and I played with the toy on all the roads and trails behind our home, setting obstacles with stones, tree trunks, and leaves to see if it could climb them. For weeks, I saved the money I made for good behavior or doing chores, and little by little, I put it back in Justin's piggy bank. When he decided to buy what he wanted, I had sold the car, now half-destroyed, to a kid from school, and he wasn't missing even a cent.

The moral of the story is, why wait till tomorrow to get something you can have today?

At that moment, my impatience was killing me.

For Leah. Because I needed to see her smile.

The next day, when she got up, I noticed the bags under her eyes.

"Rough night?"

"Kind of."

"Stay home. Rest."

"Are you giving me permission to skip school?"

"No. You're old enough to know if you need to go to class. But if you want my opinion, I think you'll be wasting your time, staring at the chalkboard without grasping anything, because you look like you're about to fall over. Sometimes it's better to gather your strength before diving back in."

Leah went back to bed. I spent a while in the waves before returning home and making a sandwich. I sat down at my desk to try and make some headway on work I had left aside the day before to go get that easel that was now gathering dust on my back porch. I wrote down on a piece of paper my upcoming deadlines and pinned it up beside the calendar. Then I got to work on some commissions until Leah came back out of her room at midmorning.

"Did you get some rest?"

"A little. Is there any milk left?"

"I don't know. I need to go to the store."

"Maybe...maybe I could go with you."

"Sure. I could use the help."

That, and I was happy to get her out of there, so she'd at least have a bit of fresh air. I concentrated on my most important job while she sat at the bar eating breakfast. When I was done, to my surprise, she came around the desk and bent over my shoulder to see what I was doing.

"What is it?" she asked, squeezing her eyebrows.

"I'm offended you asked. It's a kangaroo's ears."

"Kangaroos don't have ears that long."

I realized our first trivial conversation was going to revolve around the length of kangaroo ears. I asked her to grab a stool from the kitchen and sit down next to me. Elbow to elbow, I laid out the drawings in front of her.

"The deal is this: Mr. Kangaroo has to tell the kids why it's bad to throw trash on the ground, leave the water running, or eat burgers until you pop."

Leah blinked, her brows still knit.

"What's that got to do with its ears?"

"It's a cartoon, Leah. Doing it that way makes it funny. You know, exaggeration, like giving it big feet or little rat arms. Kangaroos don't laugh like this in the real world either."

I pointed to the glimmering white teeth I had drawn in one of the panels and saw how a smile trembled on Leah's lips before suddenly disappearing, as if she had realized it and taken a step back. I wanted to keep her a little longer by my side, because the alternative was watching her shut herself up in her room.

"What do you think of my artistic gifts?"

She tilted her head. Thought. Sighed. "I think you're wasting your talent."

"This from the girl who stopped painting..."

She gave me a harsh look, and I felt relieved to see her react, giving an immediate response. Cause and effect. Maybe that was the deal: grab onto the string and start pulling, pulling it tighter and tighter....

"So what's your excuse?" she replied.

I raised an eyebrow. I didn't see that coming. "I don't know what you're talking about. You want a coffee?"

She shook her head as I got up to go to the kitchen. I served myself a cup, cold, and sat down beside her at the desk again. I showed her a few other jobs, the most recent ones I'd done, and she listened attentively without asking more questions or taking any particular interest in anything. Being with her was easy, comfortable, like all the things I loved in life.

I went on working, and she grabbed her headphones and walked out to the back porch. While I drew the background of trees behind Mr. Kangaroo, I couldn't stop looking at her. Because there, with her back turned, with her elbows leaning on the wooden railing listening to music, she looked so fragile, so diffuse, so vague...

That was the first time I felt the quiver.

But at the time, I didn't know that tingling sensation in my finger-tips meant I wanted to draw her, capture her in lines, and keep her for myself, grab hold of her in fingers covered in paint. I wouldn't manage to capture her as she was, live, whole, until much later.

I left after a half hour, pulled off her headphones, and put them on. She was listening to "Something." With the first chords, that bass like a carpet under the notes, I realized it had been ages since I'd heard the Beatles. I swallowed and thought of Douglas in his studio telling me how to feel, how to live, how to be the person I was in that moment, and I asked myself if there was a part of me that had turned my back on that. I took off the headphones and handed them back.

"Are we still on for going to the store together?"

We drove into the city, crossing it to the opposite end. I parked almost at the door, we entered the supermarket, and we walked together up the aisles. Leah grabbed some cookies for breakfast and white bread without crust.

"What are you doing? That's almost offensive."

"Everyone hates the crust," she responded.

"I love the crust. What's the point of bread that's white all over, with nothing to break the monotony? Fuck that. You eat the edges first, then you go for the center."

I watched a timid smile cross her face before the curtain of blond hair came between us when she bent over to grab a package of spaghetti. Twenty minutes later at the register, I realized Leah was relaxed, as if the clouds always circling around her head had cleared up a little, and I told myself I had to figure out a way to get her out of the house more, pull her away from the apathy that covered her every day. Next month things would change, even if I didn't yet have a plan.

When we walked outside, we almost tripped over a girl with round brown eyes who had her dark hair in a ponytail on top of her head. She smiled at Leah with a caring look and waved her hands as she spoke.

"What a coincidence! I just called to see if you were okay since you weren't at school, but then I remembered you don't have a, uh…"

Leah didn't react, so I butted in. "A cell phone."

"Right. My name's Blair. We already know each other though."

I didn't remember her. I'd met several of Leah's friends when I used to see her out and about surrounded by other girls, going from town to the beach and from the beach to town without a care in the world, laughing like a kid.

"Pleasure. Axel Nguyen."

"I didn't sleep well," Leah managed to say.

"I hear you. Still though, if you're up for that coffee…"

"She's up for it," I said.

Leah tried to kill me with her eyes.

"I came here to pick up some shampoo, but I'm not busy."

"She isn't either." I gave Leah a bit of cash. "Go get a bite to eat together. I've got stuff to do. We'll meet back here in an hour?"

I saw panic swirling in her eyes. A part of me wanted to make it disappear, but the other part…the other part was happy, god damn it. I swallowed my compassion and turned my back on that silent plea her lips didn't manage to utter.

20

Leah

I WAS STUCK THERE STANDING in the middle of the sidewalk while Axel disappeared down the street. I felt my pulse quicken and looked at the ground. There was a leaf just next to Blair's foot. It was reddish, with little membranes inside it like a skeleton growing under its colorful skin. I looked away as I thought of the tone, of the mix that would produce that color.

"Come in with me for the shampoo, and then we'll eat something?"

I agreed—how could I not? Axel had made me do it, but it was also impossible not to see the hope in Blair's eyes. She was always so transparent, even when she tried not to be. So I walked back inside with her to the toiletries section, and then we went to a nearby place that served all kinds of salad and fresh fish.

"So it looks like living with Axel is going well."

I walked around the table and sat down in front of Blair. "It's fine. This hasn't been his best day."

She looked at me with interest after the waiter took our order and left. I glimpsed the rhythmic shifting of her legs beneath the table and knew she was nervous, unsure how to break the ice, and that only made me feel worse.

"Do you still have...feelings?"

I knew what she meant without her saying another word.

"No." *Because I don't feel anything anymore*, I wanted to add, but I swallowed the words. How far away that time seemed when I spent every day with Blair, pretending to be grown-ups when we were just little girls, talking to her constantly about him, about Axel, about how I loved him, about how special he was, about how when I blew out the candles on my cake on my seventeenth birthday, the thing I wished for was to kiss him someday and know what it would feel like to do it. I took a deep breath, uncomfortable, my throat dry. Then I decided to try and act normal for the next forty-five minutes, or as normal as I could be.

"How's work?"

She smiled, excited, happy to have something to talk about. "Good, good, but it's a lot bigger sacrifice than I expected. The kids won't stay still for a moment. I swear, I had sore muscles the first week. And the parents... Well, basically some of them should have to take a class before they're allowed to procreate."

I grinned, and it almost hurt. "It's what you always wanted to do."

"It is. And you? Are you going to go to college?"

"Seems like it." I shrugged.

That had been my dream a long time ago, but it seemed vague just then, and a burden. I didn't want to leave. I didn't want to be alone in Brisbane. I didn't want to have to meet new people when I wasn't even capable of relating to the people I grew up around. I didn't want to paint or study or anything like that. I didn't, but Oliver...

My brother had gone from living glued to his surfboard and walking barefoot at all hours to being the administrative director for a major travel agency, because he'd always been an ace with numbers, and one of the partners at the company knew my father and offered him the job two weeks after the accident. I remember Oliver told him, *You won't regret it*, and my brother was a man of his word, the kind who always does what he says. The same way he saved his last dollar so I could go to college.

However much I hated the idea, I didn't want to disappoint him, hurt him more, cause him more problems, but still, I didn't know how to stop feeling this way, so sad, so empty...

"Axel seems like a straight shooter," Blair said.

"He is." And I was pissed at him.

"He also seems like he cares about you."

I looked down at my plate and concentrated on the intense green of the lettuce, so vibrant, the red of the tomato, the amber of the pumpkin seeds, the yellow of the corn, and the dark brown, almost black, of the raisins. I took a breath. It was pretty. Everything was pretty: the world, color, life, like I used to see it before. If I looked around, all I saw were things I wanted to transform—make my own version of the salad, of the dawn in front of the sea, of the woods behind my old house that made me want to spend the rest of my life with a brush in my hand when I saw Axel's expression as he looked at them.

21

Axel

LEAH WAS ALREADY AT THE door of the supermarket when I got there. She was mad. I ignored her furrowed brow, we got in my car, and we spent the whole drive in silence. I carried the grocery bags into the kitchen, and I hadn't started to put the things in the cabinet when she appeared, gorgeous and incensed, surrounded by new outlines showing curves that had been vague the month before. Her eyes were gleaming.

"How could you do that to me?"

"That? Be more specific, Leah."

"Betray me like that! Trick me!"

"You are thin-skinned."

"And you're an idiot."

"Maybe, but did you have fun? What's it like hanging out with another human being? Nice? Now's the moment when you say, 'Gee Axel, thanks for helping me take this step and being so patient with me.'"

But none of that happened. Leah blinked, trying to hold back tears of frustration, turned around, and went to her room. I closed my eyes, tired, and rested my head on the wall, trying to focus. Maybe it had been a bit rushed, but I knew...no, I felt that it was what I had to do. Despite her, even despite what I would have liked. Because seeing her like that, so pissed, so hurt, was a thousand fucking times better than seeing her empty. I remembered what I had thought that morning, about holding a string in my hand and pulling till it tightened...and that was what made me go to her room and open the door without knocking.

"Can I come in?"

"You already are in."

"True. I was trying to be nice."

She tried to strike me dead with her stare.

"Let's get to the point. Did I trick you? Sure, a little. Was it for a good cause? Yeah. So I want to let you know I'll be doing it again. And I know you think I'm an insensitive fucking asshole who enjoys pouring salt in your wounds, but one day, Leah, one day you'll thank me. Remember this conversation."

She brought a trembling hand to her lips and whispered to me to go before she got up, opened the window, and grabbed the headphones from her table.

The next few days, we barely talked.

I didn't care. I couldn't stop thinking about all I'd read about PTSD. And at least I had found a way to break the paralysis and apathy for a few seconds, and that was better than nothing. When Leah got mad, there was no indifference in her eyes, and her feelings took over and she couldn't do anything about it. So I had her there, I was pulling the cord slowly, I just had to find the right way to do it.

———————

Oliver came to pick her up on the Monday of the last week in March. She was still at school, and I hugged him harder than usual because I missed him and I couldn't imagine what it must be like to be in his shoes. I took two beers out of the fridge and we walked out to the back porch. I lit up a cigarette and passed him one.

"Quitting smoking is great," he said with a laugh.

"Fantastic. Liberating." I blew out my drag. "How are things in Sydney?"

"Better than last month. How about here?"

"More or less the same. Leah's making slow progress."

He looked at the tip of his cigarette and sighed. "I can hardly remember what she was like before. You know, when she used to laugh at everything and was so...so intense that I always used to be afraid of when she'd get older and wouldn't be able to manage her emotions on her own. And now look at her. Fucking ironic."

I swallowed the words that were burning on my lips. If I hadn't, I would have told him that for me she was still the same, still every bit as intense, even when she locked herself away and forced herself not to feel anything because if she did, it would be sorrow at what had happened and guilt at the idea of continuing to enjoy life when her parents no longer could, as if she thought that were unjust. Oliver had assimilated the tragedy from a different perspective, emotional, sure, but with that practical orientation he had little choice over. He had cried at the funeral, said his goodbyes to them, and gotten drunk with me the night afterward. Then he had gotten to work, organizing the family's bills and taking care of Leah, who was stuffed to the gills with tranquilizers.

I had been thinking about death a lot lately.

Not about what happens when it comes, not about the goodbye we all have to say one day, but about how to confront it when it when it takes the people you love most. I asked myself if sorrow and pain were instinctive feelings, or if we had been taught these ways of dealing with the horror.

I finished my cigarette.

"You in the mood?" I jutted my chin out toward the sea.

"Are you serious? I came here straight from the airport."

"Come on, it'll be like in the old days."

Five minutes later, I had lent him a bathing suit and a surfboard, and we were walking over the sand. It was windy that day and the water was cold, but Oliver didn't hesitate when we walked out into the water. A few rays of sun filtered through the spiderweb of clouds that covered the sky, and we tried to catch a few waves, but they were low and weak. We managed to ride a few, with short quick movements, then we lay on our boards facing the horizon.

"I met someone," Oliver said.

I looked at him with surprise. Oliver didn't *meet* women, he just slept with them. "I didn't see that coming."

"Doesn't matter, because it can't happen."

"Why? Is she married? Does she not like you?"

Oliver laughed and tried to push me off my board. "It's not the right time to start a relationship. I'll be back here in a few months, and then there's Leah, my responsibilities, money issues, lots of stuff…" We fell silent, each thinking about his own affairs. "You still seeing Madison?"

"We hang out sometimes when I get bored, but I hardly ever do now that I'm a full-time babysitter."

"You know I'll always owe you for this, right?"

"Give me a fucking break."

We emerged from the water and I saw Leah's bicycle leaning against the wooden posts of the porch. When Oliver found her in the kitchen, he hugged her hard, even if his swimsuit was wet, and she complained. He pulled away, grabbed her by the shoulders, and looked at her closely.

"You look good."

Leah grinned. "You don't. You need a shave."

"I've missed you, pixie."

He embraced her again, and when our eyes crossed as he pulled her into his chest, I saw gratitude reflected in his eyes. Because he knew…we both knew she was better, a little more awake.

22

Leah

CHAOS BROKE OUT WHEN I stepped into the Nguyen house. The twins leapt at me, grabbing my legs the same way they did with everyone, while their father tried to pull them away and Emily gave me a kiss on the cheek. I managed to make it to the kitchen following Oliver, and Georgia hugged us both as if she hadn't seen us in years. She mussed Oliver's hair and pinched his cheek, saying he was so handsome it was a crime to let him roam the streets. Me she swayed softly with, as if she thought she might break me if she squeezed me too tight. I don't know why, but I felt more excited than I had in weeks. Maybe because it smelled like flour, and I remembered the afternoons she and Mom spent in our kitchen talking and laughing with a glass of white wine in their hands and ingredients all over the counter. Or because my defenses were down.

The idea terrified me. Feeling so much again....

I went to the living room and sat down on the edge of the sofa wishing I could melt into the wall. I spent a while staring at the little threads sticking out of one side of the carpet, listening to

Oliver's serene, strong voice while he talked with Daniel about a game of Australian football. I liked seeing him with Axel's father because things returned to how they had always been, animated but also relaxed, as if nothing had changed.

Axel arrived half an hour later. Last, naturally.

He nudged me with his elbow when we sat down to dinner. "You ready for more fun tomorrow?"

"What kind of nonsense is that?" his mother said. "I hope you're not bothering her with your madcap ideas. Leah needs calm, isn't that right, dear?"

I nodded and dug around in my food.

"I was kidding, Mom. Pass the potatoes."

Georgia passed him a bowl from the other side of the table, and the rest of the meal went on as always: Conversations about any and all topics, the twins throwing peas, Axel laughing at them while his brother and Emily reproached them with sour looks. Oliver talking to Daniel about his job in Sydney, me counting the minutes until we could go home so I wouldn't have to die inside little by little, seeing around me all the things I didn't know how to appreciate anymore.

It was as if I didn't remember how to be happy.

Is that something you can learn? Like riding a bike? Keeping your balance, putting your hands on the right place on the handlebars, back straight, eyes looking ahead, feet on the pedals...

More importantly, was that what I wanted?

April

—

(AUTUMN)

23

Axel

LEAH CAME BACK HOME WITH her headphones hanging over her shoulders, her eyes shifty and more timid than normal, as if she were afraid I would do something rash, like throw a pajama party or play the tambourine at three in the morning. I could tell she was avoiding me. If I went into the kitchen, she left; if I walked out onto the porch, she went inside. Maybe it shouldn't have gotten to me, but it did. It damn well did.

"Do I have some kind of contagious disease no one in my family's told me about because I'm going to die and they want me to spend my last days in peace or something?"

She forced herself not to laugh. "No. Not that I know of."

There was that little something that was different from the first month. Back then she would have just said no and taken off running. Now, even though that was what she wanted to do, she stayed there before me, defiant.

"Then maybe it would be nice if you stopped avoiding me."

"I'm not. It's hard to hang out with you."

"Hard? We live together," I reminded her.

"Yeah, but you're always on the beach or working."

"I'm here now. So it's perfect. What do you want us to do?"

"Nothing. I was…I was just going to listen to some music."

"Good plan. Then you can help me make dinner."

"But Axel! We don't…"

"We don't what?"

"That's not how we work."

"Actually, we don't work period. Or better said, you don't work, but we're going to change that. I'm tired of walking into the room and seeing you walk out, and if you're wondering, yes, this is a temporary dictatorship. I'll see you on the porch in five minutes."

I dug through the records gathering dust next to the wooden trunk where the record player stood. Finally I found it, the Beatles on vinyl. I wiped off the cover with the sleeve of the sweatshirt I had put on because the nights were getting cooler, and I played it.

"I'm So Tired" started to play softly while I was walking onto the porch. I sat down on the cushions, and Leah settled down beside me, as though drawn out by the music. My elbow rubbed her arm, she trembled, and then our bodies pulled further apart.

When the first chords of "I Will" sounded, she gave a long sigh, as if releasing a held breath. I asked myself what the music must be making her feel, so close to me there. Her lips were open slightly and her eyes lost in the sea where night was falling.

"I like this one," I said.

"*I will*," she whispered the lyrics in reply.

"One day in the studio, your father made me listen to it from beginning to end with my eyes closed."

She started to get up, but I quickly grabbed her arm and held her beside me.

"He told me they said Paul McCartney had to find inspiration in the person next to him to write. He had a couple of muses, among them his dog when there were no women around. Then Linda appeared. And this was one of the songs he played for her. You know what Douglas told me? That the first day he saw your mother, he heard the notes of this song in his head. That's why he always put it on whenever he painted anything related to love."

Leah batted her eyes and I felt my heart sink when I saw the tears in her eyelashes, and I asked myself how I would draw them if someone asked me to that exact moment when they were moving like a pair of wings trying to ward off sorrow.

"Why are you doing this to me, Axel?"

The pleading tone in her voice... Fuck. I wiped away one of her tears with my thumb.

"Because it's good for you. Crying."

"But it hurts."

"Pain is the collateral damage of living."

She closed her eyes, I felt her shiver, and I hugged her.

"Then I don't want to live..."

"Don't say that. Don't ever fucking say that."

I pulled away from her, afraid that she would fall to pieces, but what I saw was the opposite. She seemed stronger, more whole, as if some piece inside her had slipped into place. I wanted to understand her. I wanted...I needed to know what was happening inside her. To enter, to dig around, to open her heart and see everything.

And impatience was overwhelming me, curiosity consuming me. I tried to give her space, but I wound up taking it away.

"I knew that about my father," Leah said so softly that the night breeze swallowed her words and I had to bend down to hear them. "He told me that if you hear a song in your head when you find your soul mate, that's a gift. Something special."

I nodded, quiet, leaning back against the wood.

"Did that ever happen to you?"

I was trying to be light, to lift the mood a little, but Leah looked at me very sternly, lips clenched tight and eyes shining after crying.

"Yes."

24

Leah

DAD WAS ALWAYS LISTENING TO music and I adored every note, every chorus, every chord; when I walked back from school with Blair and saw our roof in the distance, I always imagined our house like four magic walls with melodies and colors, emotions and life inside. My favorite song when I was little was "Yellow Submarine." I could sing it with my parents for hours, covered in paint in my father's studio or hugging Mom on the couch, which was so old it swallowed you up when you sat on it. It stuck with me as I grew up. The childish rhythm, the disordered notes, the unpredictable lyrics that talked about the town where I was born, a man who traveled through the sea and talked about what life was like in the land of the submarines.

A week after my sixteenth birthday, Axel came to our house, talked with Dad in the living room for a while, and knocked on the door to my room. I was mad at him because I was childish and he hadn't come to my birthday, choosing to go to a concert with friends in Melbourne and spend the weekend there. At that age, things like that got to me. So I scowled at him when he came in and set my paintbrush down on the open watercolors case on the table.

"Why the long face?"

"I don't know what you're talking about."

Axel grinned, that grin that made my knees quiver. And I hated him for provoking that feeling and not even knowing it, for still treating me like a girl when I felt like an adult around him, for breaking my heart several times...

"What's that?" I pointed at the bag in his hand.

"This?" He gave me an amused look. "It's the present you're not going to get unless that wrinkle you have here disappears..." He bent over and I held my breath while he smoothed out my forehead with his thumb. Then he handed it over. "Happy birthday, Leah."

I was so excited that I forgot my anger in a split second. I tore the wrapping paper and opened the little box impatiently. It was a thin supple nib from a well-known company, and it had cost a fortune. He knew I had started using them to perfect my other techniques.

"You bought this for me?" My voice shook.

"So you can keep creating magic."

"Axel..." I had a knot in my throat.

"I hope one day you'll dedicate a painting to me. You know, when you're famous and you're all over the art galleries and you can barely remember the idiot who didn't come to your birthday."

My eyes were foggy and I couldn't really see his expression, but with my heart pounding in my chest, I heard that childish melody, the notes swirling in my mind, the sound of the sea accompanying the first notes...

He couldn't imagine the words getting caught in my throat, yearning to come out. The words that burned. That slipped back inside. *I love you, Axel.*

When I opened my mouth, all I said was: "We all live in a yellow submarine."

Axel knitted his brows. "Are you talking about the song?"

I shook my head, confusing him. "Thanks for this. Thanks for everything."

25

Axel

STARTING APRIL 9, THE BEGINNING of the first vacation period, we started spending entire days together. Leah refused to get in the water in the morning, but when she did get up early, she would walk along the beach and sit in the sand with a cup of coffee in her hands. I would see her from afar while I waited impatiently for the next wave in the silence that accompanied the dawn.

We would have lunch together without talking much.

Then we'd work. I managed to make a space for her on my desk, and while I dealt with my commissions, she would do her homework and study in silence, an elbow leaned on the edge of the surface and her chin in her hand. Sometimes I was distracted by her even breathing or the movement of her legs beneath the table, but in general it surprised me how easy it was to have her beside me.

"Can I put on some music?" she asked one day.

"Sure. Choose the record."

She put on one of my favorites, Nirvana.

After the first week of vacation, we had a routine marked out. At dusk, I would work a little longer while she would go to her room alone, lie down on the bed or draw with a little nub of charcoal. She'd come out to help me with dinner, and when she was done, we'd hang out on the porch.

One night, the cat came around.

"Look who's here." I got out of the hammock and stroked her spine. She responded with a purr. "That's how I like her, sweet and grateful," I said with a hint of sarcasm.

"I'll go find her some food."

Leah showed back up with a can of tuna and a bowl of water. She sat on the ground, legs crossed, in a red pilled sweater and shorts. Watching her while she fed the cat, I thought…I thought that someone should paint that scene. Someone who was capable of it. The moment of peace, the bare feet, the blond hair unkempt and wild, the freshly washed face, and the sea whispering in the background.

I looked away from her and took a sip of tea.

"Bluesfest is coming in two days. We're going."

Leah looked up at me and frowned. "I'm not. Blair invited me and I told her I couldn't."

"Oh. Busy schedule? Doctor's appointment? Social engagement? If not, I'd advise you to turn on the phone that's in there gathering dust and tell Blair you made a mistake. Go with her. That way I can be on my own a little."

"You say that like I'm a burden."

"Nobody said that," I replied.

But maybe she was right. I liked her making progress, but I

also missed spending a night on my own without responsibilities, without worrying about anyone else.

And so, on Friday at dusk, I took Leah out to Tyagarah Tea Tree Farm north of Byron Bay, where Bluesfest is held, one of the most important music festivals in all of Australia. The area was also a koala habitat, the organization worked to take care of them, and tourists could go there and watch them. The year before, they had planted 120 mahogany trees, and they were financing protection programs overseen by the University of Queensland.

We saw dozens of white tents in the distance as we approached one of the entrances, spread out over the acres of meadow. We waited at the gate because Leah was supposed to meet Blair there. She agreed to after I threatened to accompany them.

"Are you serious? Like you'll be our chaperone?" she had asked, unable to believe it.

"Yeah, unless you start acting normal, hanging out with your friends and letting me do the same with mine. Otherwise you'll have me there watching you braid each other's hair and trade multicolored friendship bracelets. Your choice. There's two options. Both are fine with me; I'm getting drunk either way."

"Do I have permission to do the same?"

"Nope. Not a drop of alcohol."

"Fine, relax. I'll call Blair."

I didn't give a sigh of relief until I saw her friend appear, walking toward us with a smile. I greeted her distractedly, thinking of how badly I wanted a beer, to hear some music, to relax, and to talk about whatever, anything that didn't include tension or walking around on eggshells.

"Remember to keep your eye on your phone," I told her.

"Fine but don't…don't take too long." She gave me a pleading look, and I was about to change tack and drag her home, away from there, to the security of those four walls where she seemed to feel comfortable.

But then I remembered that shine in her eyes when I broke that shell she protected herself with, and I realized I had to keep pushing.

"I'll call you later. Have fun, Leah."

I walked inside and didn't look back. Same as every year, the festival was packed and it took me a while to find my friends near the stalls where they were serving food and beer. I greeted Jake and Gavin with a clap on the back and ordered a beer. By that time, there were already several groups playing. Tom showed up a few minutes later, already a bit tipsy.

"It's been weeks since I've seen you around."

"You know, man, I live with a teenager full-time now."

"Where'd you leave her?" Tom looked around.

"She's with her friends. Tell me what's what."

We'd known each other since high school, but we'd never had a deep friendship. If they asked me for a favor, I'd do it, and Oliver and I had gone out with them for years, before and after we left Byron Bay, at night or to catch a few waves. All my friends, except for Oliver, had been more or less like that: simple, superficial, with that feeling that they would never go further than where they started. But that was enough for me.

"Didn't think you'd be here." Madison showed up later, when we'd already been there a few hours and I was worried enough about Leah to consider sending her a text to make sure she was okay.

I shook my head. I wasn't the type to get tensed up or worried.

"How are things?"

"Good. Tom's already soused."

I bent down and she stood on tiptoe to kiss me on the cheek, and when she decided to get closer to one of the stages, I didn't hesitate to follow her. The music filled the night, and people were swaying along to the melody. I danced with her and felt like that was all that I needed. This was the life I knew: easy, unworried, with nothing to get under my skin. I took her hand and smiled before turning her around. Madison tripped over her feet and almost fell, but I grabbed her in midair and we both cracked up laughing under the dark sky of deep night. Then I felt my cell phone vibrate.

I let her go and walked away from the music.

"Axel? Can you hear me, Axel?"

"I hear you. Is this you, Blair?"

"Yeah. I need your help..." I couldn't understand the words that followed. "I can't find her... We're close to the second stage, by one of the food stalls, and I...I didn't know what to do..."

"Don't move. I'm on my way."

I ran to the other end of the field with my heart in my throat. The mere thought that something might have happened...

I found Blair where she said she would be.

"Where's Leah?"

"I don't know. We were fine all night. She seemed like she was having fun... She was like the person from before, but then she went off with a guy we know and it's been more than half an hour and I can't find her. She left her bag, I got worried, I didn't know what to do…"

"Stay here, I'm going to try to find her."

I walked around the stage trying to pick her out from the crowd drinking, laughing, and jumping to the sound of the music, but it seemed impossible that I could see her among all those people. I left behind unknown faces, tons of long-haired blonds that weren't her. I looked all over, shaken, my nerves raw. I was thinking of all my options, putting a fucking poster with her face on all the lampposts or readying my speech for Oliver about how I lost his sister the way you lose a Lego, when I saw her.

I took a quick breath of air and walked toward her. She was all I saw. Her, and the boy's hand under her T-shirt caressing her back, and her eyes closed, as if in a trance; how she didn't react when he kissed her on the lips and pressed into her body, which danced to the rhythm of a slow song, swaying under the spotlights and lampposts like a marionette under someone else's control.

"Get away from her!" I grunted.

The boy let her go and Leah looked at me with half-shut, shining eyes. She wasn't just drunk; she'd spilled a drink or two on herself, she stank of rum, and her T-shirt was soaked. I grabbed her hand and dragged her off in a hurry, ignoring her protests. Or babbling. Or whatever it was.

We got out and away from the multitudes.

I put her in the car. She didn't say a word. She hardly looked at me. And that was better, because anything would have been enough to make me fly off the handle and start screaming.

Of all the scenarios I had imagined could occur at Bluesfest, this was the one I hadn't expected. I thought she'd spend the night pissed off, on her own in some corner. Spend a little time with her friend and then call me when she got bored. I never thought I'd find her drunk and...in this state.

I parked in front of the house, still on edge.

The silence grew denser when we went inside and I threw the keys on the sideboard. I ran a hand through my hair, thinking of what to say and how, but finally I let go and shouted.

"So it's true, I really am your fucking babysitter. What were you thinking, Leah? You go out one night after a year of not doing anything, and you end up like this? Can you not control yourself and act like a normal human being? What the fuck were you doing with that dude? Are you serious? How could you even think of just vanishing without your phone, without telling anyone, and...?"

I stopped talking. I stopped because Leah wrapped her hands around my neck, leaving frozen the words I would never utter, and kissed me. *Fuck.* She stood on tiptoe and kissed me. My stomach turned when her lips grazed mine, and I had to grab her hips to push her away.

"What are you doing, Leah...?"

"I just wanted...to feel. You said..."

"Yeah, but not like that. Leah, babe..."

I stopped, uncomfortable, seeing her there so vulnerable and small and broken. I just wanted to hold her for hours and relieve whatever she was starting to feel. I had forgotten how she was, that intensity that blinded her, that impulsivity that called to her to leap into the void.

Ironically, she was everything I wasn't.

"I don't feel good," she moaned.

A second later, she vomited on the living room floor.

"I'll clean this up, you take a shower."

Leah stumbled off, and I wasn't sure if she was well enough to shower on her own, but she stank like rum and I thought the water might clear her head.

I didn't understand that last wounded look she gave me. That night, I didn't understand anything.

I cleaned the mess while I listened to the water coursing through the pipes.

She had kissed me. Me. Leah.

I shook my head, confused.

I went to the kitchen when the water turned off. I looked around in the cupboards, but I couldn't find any tea. I had used the last bag the night before. I tried to find something that would take the taste of Leah off my lips. And I wound up finding some cookies just as I heard her sweet voice behind my back.

"I need to know why you never noticed me."

I turned around, surprised. There she was. Naked. Totally naked. Her skin wet, a puddle of water at her feet, her curves outlined under the moonlight coming through the window, her breasts small, round, and firm.

I was so stunned I couldn't look away. My mouth went dry.

"Jesus. You want to give me a heart attack? Cover up, please."

No, shit, don't, because... My heart was about to jump out of my chest; if I blinked, I'd look down and see it lying there on the living room floor. *Fuck...fuck...* I don't know when it happened or why, but my brain disconnected, as though someone had flipped a switch, and I stopped thinking. With my head, at least. I got hard.

That was the only thing that made me react. The excitement.

I grabbed the blanket on the sofa and wrapped her in it. Leah grabbed the edges almost from inertia, and fortunately, she held it over her body. I took a deep breath, my pulse still beating at a thousand, feeling like I was on fire there in front of my best friend's sister. I wanted to bang my head against the wall.

"Go to bed. Now. Please."

Leah blinked, about to cry, her eyes still glassy from the alcohol, and she went to her room. I stayed there, my breathing agitated, trying to take in all that had happened in a matter of hours.

26

Leah

"LEAH, YOU NEED TO FEEL life. Always."

"But what if what we feel isn't always right?"

We were sitting on the steps of the back porch, and my mother was slowly braiding my hair, twisting the tufts between her fingers.

"You can be wrong. You can make a million mistakes. People are like that, we screw up, but that's why regret exists, knowing how to say you're sorry when you need to. But listen, you know what's the saddest thing about not doing something because you're afraid? As time passes, when you think about it, you have to ask yourself for forgiveness for not being brave enough. And reconciling with yourself is sometimes harder than doing it with others."

27

Axel

"I NEED TO KNOW WHY you never noticed me."

The words echoed in my mind for the rest of the night. Lying in bed, unable to sleep, I remembered the day I went into Leah's room to wait for her because her mother had told me she'd be there soon. I often hung out in the Joneses' house whenever my parents went there to visit. I'd talk with Douglas, laugh with Rose, or examine Leah's latest paintings.

I saw magic in her. All the things I never had.

I remembered an afternoon years back when I was waiting sitting in the chair at her desk. I was flipping through some scattered drawings among her papers. When I pushed some aside, I found a day planner open and full of notes like *Turn in Biology homework Wednesday* or *B&L, friends forever*. And next to them, a red heart with a name in the center: Axel.

I held my breath. I thought it might be a coincidence. Probably some classmate of hers had the same name, or some famous dumbass singer. Anyway, when she got home from school with a huge smile on her face, I buried the memory in some faraway part of my mind and left it there.

I didn't look for it again until the night when everything started to change.

28

Axel

THE SUN WAS ALREADY UP when I woke up.

I was disoriented when I opened my eyes. I wasn't used to being in bed with the sun shining high in the sky. But I mean, I also wasn't used to popping a boner looking at a naked Leah or staying awake till 5 a.m. unable to stop thinking about something that hadn't happened.

I sat up slowly, exhaling.

While I was heading to the bathroom, I started thinking of all I needed to say to her. It was going to be complicated to start with, because I didn't know what the hell to say. *First rule: No kissing.* I clicked my tongue, cranky. *Second: No getting drunk and throwing up in my living room.* As far as getting out of the shower like that, well, we'd need to talk that over, too.

Things were going to be different all right. And she needed to start cooperating.

I opened the door resolutely, angrily, but when I looked up, I was frozen, unable to turn my head away from the window that opened onto the back porch.

Leah was there in front of a canvas that was no longer white, and she was filling it with chaotic black and gray marks. I walked over to the window frame in silence, as if every brushstroke were pulling me toward her. I watched her run the brush across the canvas with a trembling hand.

I don't know how long I stood there on the other side of the window before deciding to go out onto the terrace. Leah looked up at me and I sank into her reddened eyes. Afraid, ashamed, wanting to run away.

"Last night never happened," I said.

"Okay. I'm sorry... I'm really sorry."

"You can't be sorry about something that never happened."

Grateful, Leah lowered her head and I stood beside her, looking closely at the canvas. I could see it well now. The gray splashes were stars in a dark sky; the lines falling downward and ending in curls made it seem as though the night were made of smoke. Really, all of it was smoke. I realized that as I saw how it twisted at the edges, as if that gloom were trying to escape the edges of the canvas.

"It's fucking sinister," I said with admiration.

"It was...it was supposed to be a present," she stuttered.

"A present."

"A present. An apology. For you. Painting, you know."

"Leah, did you start painting again for me?"

"No. I just..." The brush shook in her hand, and she tried to set it down on the railing, but I grabbed her wrist to stop her.

"I don't want you to stop. Not because you regret something that never happened, but because I need it. Even if it's black and white, I don't care. I need what was there before. To see through you the things I could never find in myself. Look at me, babe. Do you understand what I'm trying to tell you?"

"Yeah. I think so."

29

Leah

HE NEVER TOLD OLIVER WHAT happened the night we went to Bluesfest. That week with my brother was a mental rest, without pressure, without anyone nipping at my heels. Axel made it hard for me to breathe. It was as if all the feelings I struggled to keep under control overflowed when he was there, and I didn't know what to do about it. Every time I took a step back, Axel pushed me forward.

"I was thinking…" my brother told me on Saturday, one day before he left again, while he was drying his hair with a towel. "You want to go out to eat? We could take a little stroll too."

"Sure."

"I didn't expect that answer."

"So why'd you ask?"

Oliver laughed and I felt a tickle in my chest. My brother was so… He was incredible. So loyal. So self-made. When the knot in my throat started to overpower me, I forced myself to control those feelings. I could. Because he wasn't Axel. He didn't keep pulling, taking me to the limit; he left me the space I needed to keep from drowning.

We walked awhile through Byron Bay without talking and wound up at Miss Margarita, a cute little Mexican restaurant we used to go to with our parents sometimes. When I hesitated, Oliver took my hand.

"Come on, Leah. Axel's probably got you starving to death with his vegetarian bullshit. Don't tell me a taco with real meat in it doesn't make your mouth water."

We sat at an outside table. From there, at the end of a street with a few stores on it, we could see the blue of the sea.

We ordered tacos and burritos to share.

"Goddamn, this is worth every dollar," my brother said, licking his lips after a bite. "You can't imagine how bad the Mexican place by my work is. The first time, I almost asked them to give me my money back, but you know, I was new and I didn't want to make a scene in front of everyone else." He licked his fingers. "This sauce drives me wild."

"Everything's good out there?" I hadn't asked him much about his job. Not because it didn't interest me, but because I felt so guilty, so bad…knowing my brother was wasting his life, doing things he never wanted to do to take care of me…

"Yeah, of course, great."

"Oliver, I know you."

"Look, there are good days and bad days. It's not like Byron Bay; nothing is, you know that." He exhaled and passed me half his burrito. "There's a girl, too, who complicates things."

"What girl?"

"My boss. You want to hear something funny? I'll tell you if you smile like you used to."

I smiled in response because I couldn't help it when I saw his eyes shining and him looking so relaxed, leaning into his chair.

"That's what I'm talking about. You're gorgeous when you smile, you know?"

"Don't change the subject," I said, a little uncomfortable.

"Fine. But don't tell anyone."

"Of course I won't."

"Family honor."

"Family honor," I responded, though I knew he was just going on about this to stretch out the conversation and hold my attention.

"The second night I spent in Sydney, I was still in a hotel, bored, feeling kind of shitty, and I decided to take a walk by myself. I wound up in a cocktail bar drinking. I'd been there twenty minutes when she came in. She was stunning. I asked her if I could buy her a drink and she said yes. We talked awhile, and we ended up...you know, back in my room."

"You don't have to talk to me like I'm a little girl."

"Fine. I fucked her."

I tried not to laugh.

"So just take a guess who I found the next morning when they told me to go to the office and meet the boss?"

"Are you serious?"

"Fuck yes. There she was."

"So...?"

Oliver smiled and took a deep breath, as if he had just revealed something he'd had bottled up a long time. I saw the satisfaction in his eyes and realized that for a long time now I hadn't been thinking about anything, I'd just been there, in the present, listening to my brother—an ordinary, everyday situation.

"We should probably go."

He nodded and got up to pay.

I stayed there awhile sitting on the patio, trying to figure out what I was feeling. It was like floating in the middle of nowhere, in limbo, in a place at once vague but very alive, full of contrasts, fears, longings, things impossible to understand.

Oliver respected my silence while we walked back. When we reached a street I knew well, I stopped. "You mind if I walk myself home?"

"Doesn't Blair live here?"

"Yeah. I need to talk to her."

"Sure. Gimme a kiss."

He bent over to reach my cheek and then walked off at a rapid clip. I waited awhile in the same place until I got the courage to knock. Ms. Anderson opened up, surprised until compassion got the better of her and her dark eyes turned pitying. I looked down; I couldn't bear to watch that grief welling in them.

"Dear, it's so nice to see you here! It's been so long since..." She didn't finish the phrase before stepping aside. "Blair's in her room. You want anything? A juice? A coffee?"

"Thanks but no."

She pointed the way to her daughter's room. I walked down the hall a bundle of nerves.

My pulse was pounding. So many happy moments I'd lived there...

I sucked in a breath and opened the door.

When Blair saw me, she brought her hand to her heart.

"I can't believe it!" She smiled and struck her pinky finger jumping out of bed to come toward me. "Ow! God damn it! It's nothing. Pain is just mental, isn't that what they say? Come in, sit down. Everything okay? Did something happen? Because if you need anything, you know...yeah, you know."

"I don't need anything. I just wanted to tell you I'm sorry."

I felt like I was spending all my days saying sorry. But I felt so guilty, so bad, so poisonous... I knew I was hurting all the people I cared about, and even still, I couldn't help it, because the alternative was too...just too much, period.

"Why would you do that?"

"Because of what happened at the festival."

"Don't be an idiot. I was happy you decided to go."

"I shouldn't have gotten drunk and I shouldn't have put you in a bind."

Blair waved it off. "Forget about it. The important thing is you were there."

"Thanks for being the way you are," I whispered.

I sat at the foot of her bed, close to her. I looked around the room, stopping at the photos of the two of us and of other friends all over the corkboard hanging over her desk, next to a painting I had done for her for her birthday that showed her delicate outline against a shifting sea. For me, Blair had always been like that, the calm amid the chaos. The calm inside me. Once, my father told me we all need an anchor, and in a way, she was that for me.

"Next time we'll do something chill," she said.

"Yeah, that's probably better. I don't know what was up with me."

"How do you mean?"

And I don't know if it was because I didn't know what else to say before I left, if it was the nostalgia in her eyes, or if it was just that the moment we were living through was so strange, but I blurted it out, head swimming, throat dry as a bone: "I got naked in front of him."

"What?"

"In front of Axel. And I kissed him."

"Jesus Christ, Leah, are you serious?"

"I wasn't myself," I said defensively.

Blair's face softened and her eyes filled with tenderness. She stretched out a hand and laid it on mine before hugging me and warming me up inside, as if from that contact emanated memories, the feeling of familiarity, of friendship. "Don't you see, Leah? You're more yourself than ever. Don't you remember? You used to always be this way. Visceral. Unpredictable. You would do whatever strange shit popped into your head, you'd drag me along with you, and that...that made me feel so alive. I miss that."

I got up trembling. "I need to go."

30

Axel

LYING IN BED, SHE TOOK off her bra and pulled my hand toward her. I fell down on my knees next to her. I stared at her body, stretching out an arm to caress her legs, rising up slowly. Madison opened them so I could touch her, and when I did, she arched her back in reply and moaned.

Then I thought of another pair of breasts, smaller, rounder, different. *Fuck*. I shook my head to get rid of the image, the memory.

I lay down. Madison climbed onto my body, put a condom on me, and I forgot everything, the rest of the world, anything that wasn't the two of us moving at the same rhythm, her groans in my ear, the pleasure growing more intense, the need, sex, the moment. Just that.

May

—

(AUTUMN)

31

Axel

ON THAT OCCASION, I DIDN'T wait a few days or even hours. As soon as Leah got home, I grabbed her suitcase and took it to her room. She looked at me disconcerted.

"What is this?" she asked.

"We're going to put things in order. Talk. You know, normal stuff. I've been thinking all week about what you said, and I've realized I should have understood it earlier. You need to feel. That's it, isn't it, Leah?"

"No." She was scared.

"Let's go outside."

Once we were on the porch, she crossed her arms. "I promised you I'd paint."

"And you will. But that's not enough. One night, right here, you asked me if you would ever be happy again, remember? And I asked you if you wanted to be, but you couldn't answer, because you had an anxiety attack. So answer now. Come on."

She was so blocked, so lost… "I don't know," she panted.

"You do know. Look at me."

"Don't do this to me, not like this."

"I already am, Leah."

"You have no right…"

"But I do. I goddamn well do. I told you, Leah. I told you I wouldn't stop, even if you did think I was pouring salt in the wound. I told you you'd thank me. And I'm not going to stop; know why? Because I've helped you open up. I can tell. I'm not going to allow you to close back up. So answer the question: Do you want to be happy?"

Her lip trembled. Her eyes were molten lava, intense, piercing me, as though she wished to hurt me. I wanted to see her like that forever. Like that. Full of emotions, even if they were bad, even if they were directed at me. I could take that.

"I don't want to!" she shouted.

"Finally you're being honest."

"Fuck you, Axel!" She tried to go inside, but I stood between her and the door.

"Why don't you want to be happy?"

"How can you ask me that?"

"By opening my mouth. By doing it."

"I hate the way you are. I hate you right now."

I took it. I repeated to myself that hate was a feeling. One of the strongest ones, the kind that can shake a person, just as it was shaking her. "You can cry, Leah. You can cry with me."

"With you… You're the last person…"

She couldn't finish the sentence before a sob escaped her throat. And then I took a step forward and grabbed her softly, hugging her, feeling her shaking against me. I closed my eyes. I could almost feel her anger, her rage, her pain, so intense that I knew they were blinding her, anchoring her to a place where the only thing you can think is *It isn't right, it isn't right, it isn't right.* A part of me took pity on her; sometimes all I wanted to do was sit down beside her in silence and give her space, but then I'd remember that girl full of color who had to be hidden somewhere inside her, and then the idea of setting her free was all I could think about; I was obsessed.

I spoke with my lips in her tangled hair. "I'm sorry I ambushed you like this, but it's better for you. You'll see. You'll understand. You'll forgive me, won't you, Leah? That hatred, it's not all for me." She smiled through the tears. "We'll do this together, okay? I'll take care of everything; you just follow me. I'll guide you if you're willing to give me your hands."

I put my hand out to her. She hesitated.

Her eyes looked slowly at the palm of my hand, as if stopping to examine every line and mark. Then her fingers grazed it timidly and stayed there. I squeezed them in mine.

"Deal," she said.

Two days later, I crossed my arms in front of her. "First rule: my routine is your routine. From now on, when you're in my house, you'll do as I do. That means surfing every morning. No, let me finish before you start complaining. We're a team, that's the idea. If I'm out in the waves—and there's no way that's not happening— you'd better be by my side. We'll eat together. In the afternoon, while I'm working, you'll do your homework. After that, there'll be a little free time; you know I'm quite flexible. Don't laugh; I'm being serious. Why are you looking at me like that?"

Leah raised an eyebrow. "You're not remotely flexible."

"Who the hell says that?"

She rolled her eyes.

"All right, so no one says it. Next. After dinner, we'll hang out on the porch; then it's bedtime. You know most tribes work this way? There's an order, a series of activities throughout the day that have to be done, and a pyramidal structure. It's that simple."

"Why are you at the top of the pyramid?"

"Because I'm the cool one. Obvs."

"So this is gonna be like living in jail."

"Yeah, but consider the alternative. You've been here for three months and haven't done anything. This way you won't get bored."

"It's not fair!" she replied, indignant.

"Babe, eventually you'll figure out nothing is."

Leah huffed and she seemed like more of a girl than ever. I was about to go on telling her how our days would go when she walked past me, smiling. I followed her with my gaze until I was able to make out the tricolor cat sitting in front of the back door, on the porch, not going inside, as though she respected my space and wanted to mark the limits.

"She's back," Leah said. "Do we have anything for her?"

I groaned and went to the kitchen. Leah came up beside me, opened a cabinet, and froze when her fingers touched that bag full of strawberry suckers. She pulled her hand back and grabbed a can of tuna.

I sat down next to her on the porch.

"Where do you think she's from?" she asked.

"Who knows. Probably from nowhere."

"Axel…" She shook her head.

"What? If I was a cat, I'd want to be wild. Look at her; she probably lives in the woods hunting, and when she wakes up one day and feels lazy, she says, 'Fuck it, I'll stroll over to Axel's house and empty out his pantry.' So here she is."

Her laugh filled the porch, me, everything.

The cat purred after finishing, while Leah stroked her back, and then she lay down on the floor and didn't move, looking at us under the evening sun on a regular, ordinary Wednesday. I stretched my legs. Leah was sitting cross-legged.

"So, picking up where we left off: Do you understand?"

"What's there to understand. I have to do what you do."

"Exactly. You're so reasonable, babe."

"Don't call me that," she whispered with a hard, intense stare.

"What?"

"That…*babe*," she managed to say.

"I've always called you that. It's not… It doesn't mean…"

"I know." She looked down, and her blond hair hid her expression.

I needed a few seconds to take that in, to try and understand it. I had the feeling that I had spent years around a person I'd never managed to fully understand. I had remained on the surface, without scratching through or clearing the dust lying over the things people try to forget and leave locked up in the attic. And in those moments, I had her there in front of me, so different from what I remembered, the same, but different. More complex than ever, more mature but also harder to understand.

"Fine. I won't call you that again."

"It's not the word; it's the way you say it."

"You want to tell me what you mean?"

She shook her head, and I didn't push it.

I got up, went over to the record player, and chose an Elvis Presley LP. I put the needle in the groove and stood there watching the vinyl spin softly while the curved lines shifted. Then I went outside.

We spent that afternoon of music in silence.

32

Leah

I REMEMBER THE FIRST TIME my heart broke. I had imagined it would be a hard crack, blunt, something that happened all at once. But it wasn't; instead it was piece by piece, little sharp fragments. That was how I rang in the new year.

I was fifteen and my parents had gone to Brisbane to celebrate with the Nguyens, to a party with friends who had an art gallery Dad had worked with. I begged for weeks, and finally they agreed to let me stay with Oliver and Axel.

I had never put on makeup before, but that day Blair helped me: a little mascara, blush, and almost transparent lipstick. I wore a tight black dress for the first time and left my hair down. When I looked at myself in the mirror, I saw myself as mature and hot. I smiled until Blair started laughing behind my back.

"What are you thinking?" she asked me.

"That I'd like for tonight to be my first kiss."

Blair sighed aloud and grabbed the lipstick from my hands to put it on herself there in front of the mirror. She turned around and arranged my hair over my back.

"You could kiss any guy in class."

"I don't like any of them," I answered, certain.

"Kevin Jax is so into you and he's so handsome, any girl would kill to go out with him. Have you noticed his eyes? They're different colors."

I didn't care about Kevin and I didn't care that Axel was ten years older. I could only think of him, of that tingling I had felt ever since he'd come back to Byron Bay, about how it moved me when he looked at me or I saw him smile, as if everything else just froze.

Oliver raised an eyebrow when I walked out to the dining room. "What are you wearing?"

"A dress."

"A very short dress."

"This is how people wear them," I answered, and when I saw he wasn't convinced, I walked over and hugged him. "Come on, Oliver, don't be a wet blanket, it's my first New Year's Eve without our parents."

"Don't make it hard on me."

"I won't. I promise."

He smiled and kissed me on the forehead.

I said goodbye to Blair and helped my brother with the preparations for dinner, even if almost everything was premade. Oliver set the big table in the middle of the living room, and I stretched a tablecloth over it and laid out the silverware and glasses. The doorbell rang while I was setting a fork down over a yellow napkin. I remember that detail because, at that very moment, I heard Axel's voice and my stomach got tight, and so I focused on the little checked print.

"Where do I leave the drinks?" he asked.

"Probably best to put them in the fridge," Oliver said.

I turned around to see him, weak in the knees.

I don't know what I expected. I don't know if I thought he'd see me in that dress with my eyes made up and suddenly I wouldn't look like a little girl to him even if I still was. He noticed. I know he did. I know because Axel's always been transparent. But he didn't seem surprised.

He put away the bottles and gave me a kiss on the cheek.

"Babe, can you put down one more setting?"

I hated him. I hated that *babe* that he used with me like I was some kid, in that tone that must have been nothing like the way he talked when he was with a girl he liked. So tender, so older brother–sounding...so everything I wanted it not to be.

A while later, everyone else showed up. Jake, Tom, Gavin, and two brunettes.

I hardly opened my mouth during dinner. Not that I had the chance to, because Axel, Oliver, and their friends talked about their stuff the whole time, stories from their past, stuff they'd done the weekend before, what they were thinking about doing next weekend, stuff that only concerned them and that I didn't have any idea of. I was playing with my food when Axel spoke to me.

"You starting classes this month?"

"Yeah, in a few weeks."

The girl next to me said something I didn't manage to hear, and he cracked up laughing and looked away. I concentrated on my dish again, trying to ignore Axel's smile as he looked at Zoe. Next to her, I felt small and irrelevant, as if he could see right through me. And I was for the rest of the night, while they all drank and talked and saw off the new year clinking their glasses, and I sat there with nothing to drink but water.

The knot in my stomach got worse when Axel finished his third drink and started flirting with Zoe. He danced with her when a song came on the stereo, sliding his hands down her curvy body, squeezing her against him and laughing with shiny eyes, whispering words in her ear.

"Leah, are you okay?" Oliver was looking at me.

"A little tired," I lied.

"Go to bed if you want. We'll turn down the music."

"No need. Good night."

I kissed my brother on the cheek and said goodbye to the rest of them without even really looking at them, then climbed the stairs and went to my bedroom. I turned on the lamp on the nightstand and pulled my dress over my head, leaving it wrinkled at the foot of the bed. Sitting at my desk, I took off my makeup with a damp rag. I looked at the black streaks covering it when I finished, and thought how those dark marks were a perfect representation of my night. All of it was my fault, for thinking he'd notice me. All I had gotten was a glance. One. Not much better than that fraternal *babe*. Any token gesture from Axel was enough to hold in my memory, to grab on to...

I put on my pajamas and got into bed.

I couldn't sleep. I listened to music for hours, tossing and turning, thinking about him and how I'd felt like a child, regretting not going with my parents to that party in Brisbane where at least I could have avoided bothering my brother.

I don't know what time it was when I heard the first knock on the wall, followed by laughter. I gulped when I heard Axel's voice from the next room before she hushed him and there were no more sounds for a few minutes. Then her moans and the soft knocking of the bedstead against the wall filled the room.

I wanted to vomit, and I closed my eyes.

Him ramming her. More moans.

Pain. And a piece. A broken shard. Another one.

I hid my head beneath my pillow to cry.

That was how I found out there are hearts that break a little at a time on eternal nights to be forgotten, during years of invisibility, days of imagining the impossible.

33

Axel

I LOOKED AT HER, LYING on the board. I watched how she caught a wave and moved through it with her body leaning forward and her legs flexed, keeping her balance as she climbed the wall.

I smiled when she fell and swam over.

"No one would guess you haven't practiced in a year."

Leah looked at me gratefully and climbed her board. We stayed there in silence, looking at the morning breaking over the horizon. There weren't many waves.

"Why now? Why at dawn?"

"Don't you think surfing's a great way to start the day?"

"I guess. When did you start?"

"I don't know. I'm lying. I do. It was because of your father. You want to hear the story?"

She hesitated but eventually agreed.

"It was years ago. I was kind of disappointed in myself. You know what that's like, Leah? The feeling you've failed, that no matter how hard you try, you're not finding what you need.

Anyway, he came to see me one afternoon. I had just bought the house, and I don't know if you know this, but I did it because I fell in love with it, or worse, I fell in love with the idea of all the things I was going to do here. But…it didn't work out that way. Douglas brought a few beers and we sat on the porch. Then he asked me a question I didn't want to hear."

"If you had been painting…" She guessed in a whisper.

"I said no, I hadn't. Someday, Leah…someday I'll explain to you why and maybe then you'll learn to treasure who you are." I sighed. "I told him what was going on and Douglas understood; he always did. That night he helped me to put the easel up in the closet and put away all the paintings I had scattered around the living room. I cleared off my desk and decided to devote myself to something else. We went on talking for a while. About everything and nothing, about life; you know how your father was. When he left, I stayed out on the porch all night, counting the stars and drinking and thinking…"

"This is going to hurt…" Leah murmured.

"Yeah. Because that night, I understood there was no point in being unhappy. And at some point, however much it hurts you to go on living, you're going to understand that too. I realized that I had to enjoy every day. I thought the best way to start was focusing on what I liked the most: surfing, the sea, the sun. Then I would make it up as I went along. But I would choose pleasure, little things, music, calm. I would choose the things that fulfilled me."

"But nothing fulfills me, Axel."

"That's not true. Lots of things fulfill you, but they're all related to your past, your parents, and you don't want to go back there, so you avoid them, but weirdly...weirdly you're still stuck in that moment. Doesn't that strike you as ironic?"

Leah looked out at the waves while the early morning sun caressed her skin and created shadows and bright spots on the canvas of her face. I felt that tingling again in my fingertips. Again, I thought someone should draw her at that very instant: sitting on her surfboard, back straight, face sad.

"I guess you're right. But I can't..."

"With time you will, Leah. Trust me."

"How? It always hurts. Always."

"There are three ways to live life. There are people who just think about the future. You've probably known lots of them, those people who spend the whole day worried about things that haven't happened yet, the illnesses they might suffer one day and so on. They always have goals, but they almost enjoy reaching them more than whatever it was they had to do to get there. They save money, and that's a good thing, but they do it for that *big trip we're going to take someday* or *the home we're going to buy when we retire.*"

A smile pulled at the corner of her lips. "Your mother's a little like that," she said.

"My mother is completely like that. And it's not bad to look ahead, but sometimes it's frustrating because what if something happened tomorrow? For twenty years, she's been dreaming of going to Rome, and my father's tried to get her to several times, but she always finds an excuse to put it off because, from her point of view, traveling is never a priority; it's always a lark. What she should do is dip into her savings, go, and live that experience now, this very month."

"You're right," Leah said.

"Then there's the people who live in the past. People who have suffered, who've been harmed, who've been scarred by something. People stuck in a reality that no longer exists, and I think that's the saddest thing of all. Knowing that one moment, all the things that are gone because of it, all the things that only exist in their memory, will always be with them."

"That's me, right?" she asked very softly.

"Yeah, that's you. Life has taken its course and you've been left behind. I get that, Leah. I know that after what happened, it was impossible for you to gather your strength and get back up. Still more, you didn't want to. I've been thinking this over these days, trying to understand how it must have been easier for you to give up than to face your pain, and then I guess you just made the decision. How did it happen?"

"I don't know; it's not like there was a concrete moment..."

"Are you sure? Not some kind of breaking point?"

I remembered those first days after the accident. Leah was in the hospital and had cried and shouted in my mother's arms as she held her as tight as she could, trying to calm her down. All that had been...pain in its maximum expression. The kind you feel when you lose the people who matter most to you in the world. Nothing out of the ordinary. Not even during the funeral.

That's how loss is. Mourning. Grief. And then, as time passes, you lick your wounds, you assimilate what's happened, and the changes it brings in your life, what you've left behind, the implications of it.

That's the step she never took.

She got stuck in the earlier phase, in mourning. She spent so long soaking in that grief that a part of her subconscious must have thought it was easier to build a fence and isolate herself, and instead find calm that way.

"I told you. There wasn't a moment when things changed," she answered, and I realized she was being sincere. She grabbed the surfboard when a stronger wave moved us. "You're missing one, Axel. Talk to me about the third way of living."

"The present. You can go on having memories; that's not bad. It's not bad to think about the future sometimes either, but most of the time, the mind shouldn't be dealing with the past or something that might not happen, but instead on the here and now."

"That's you." She smiled at me.

"I try. Look around, look at the sun, the colors of the sky, the sea. Is it not fucking incredible when you really stop to look at it all? When you feel it? Leah, the feeling of being in the water, the scent of the beach, the warm breeze..."

She closed her eyes and her face filled with peace, because she was next to me feeling the same thing I felt, fixed in that moment and not on anything else, like a tack in the wall that doesn't move, that doesn't go forward or backward, but just remains.

"Don't open your eyes, Leah."

"Why?"

"Because now I'm going to show you something important."

She remained still. There was no sound. All we had around

us was the sea and the sun up high. And in the middle of that calm, I started laughing, and before she could figure out what was happening, I pushed her off her board.

"Why'd you do that?!" she shouted.

"Why not? I was getting bored."

"What's your problem?"

She jumped at me and my head went under before I dragged her down with me to the bottom. We emerged a few seconds later. Leah was coughing. I was laughing. At that moment, just as the sun was about to fully rise, I realized how close we were, that I had an arm around her waist and that, for some reason, this was now as comfortable to me as it used to be, years ago when Leah would come and surf with Oliver and me, whatever the occasion.

I let her go, nervous. "We should go ahead and get out, or you'll be late to school."

"This from the guy who just shoved me off my surfboard like a little boy."

"I almost forgot how much you like to talk back."

Leah blew out a breath, unable to hide her smile.

34

Axel

"GIVE ME A FUCKING BREAK."

"Watch your mouth, son. Manners."

My mother entered without warning, carrying enough bags of groceries to feed an army, followed by the twins, my brother, my sister-in-law, and my father. It was Saturday, so it took me a few minutes to grasp what was happening while they greeted me.

"What they hell are you doing here? Who's watching the café?"

"Hell!" Max shouted, and his father covered his mouth like he'd just said *son of a bitch* or something worse.

"It's a holiday, did you forget?"

"Evidently."

"Where's Leah?"

"Sleeping."

At that moment, she opened the door to her room, still yawning, and the twins ran over to hug her. Maybe they were less aware that she wasn't the same girl who used to dress them up and play with them. Leah hugged them and let my mother bother me for a while.

"Why are you here?" I asked.

"Always so happy to see us," Justin said sarcastically.

"Dude, your mother thought we could spend the day together, and we tried to call you, but you had your phone off," my father said.

My mother exhaled as she unpacked the groceries. "Don't call your son dude."

"He is one, isn't he?" Dad looked at me.

I was going to say something when my mother pointed at me.

"Why do you have a phone if you don't even use it?"

"I do use it. Sometimes. Now and again."

"Leave him. He's a hermit," Justin said.

"Oliver is tired of telling you to have it charged and nearby. You live in an isolated area with a girl you're supposed to be taking care of. What if something happens? If you trip and break a leg, or you're in the water and a shark attacks you, or…"

"Fuck, Mom," I shouted, unable to believe her.

"Fuck!" my nephew Connor shouted.

"Perfect," Justin said.

Fortunately, Emily started laughing, and my brother shot her a look of reproach. He went out on the porch with the boys, followed by my father, who was smiling as usual. I stayed there, still a little out of it, watching my mother put five or six containers of prepared food into the fridge and a dozen soup packets in the cabinet. Leah made coffee while Emily talked with her, asking how school was that year.

"I brought you vitamins." My mother shook a bottle of them in front of my nose.

"Why? I'm fine."

"You could probably be better."

"Do I look bad or something?"

"No, but you never know. Vitamin deficiency is the cause of many illnesses, not just scurvy if you don't have enough C or weak bones if you don't get enough D; it's linked to other problems like depression, indigestion, even paranoia."

"Yeah, that's the one that's killing me, Mom. Sometimes I get paranoid and I think my family is going to show up at my house one Saturday without warning, but then I feel better when I realize I'm alone and it's just my imagination running away with me."

"Don't be silly, son."

I poured myself my second coffee of the day and asked loudly if anyone else wanted one. Only Justin said yes. I made it for him and walked out onto the porch, where we all ended up gathering. My father had sat in the hammock with a bohemian air, saying things like "It smells peaceful here" and "I like the vibe in your house."

"So are you surfing again?" Emily asked Leah while one of her kids crawled all over her.

"A little. I made a deal with Axel."

Leah looked at me and I felt a connection. A tie that was starting to bind us. I realized we were the only witnesses to what we were experiencing in those months, and I liked that.

"Are you forcing her?" Justin asked.

"Of course not! Or maybe, yeah. What does it matter?" I started laughing when I saw him disconcerted.

"He's not forcing me," Leah lied.

"I hope not," my mother said.

"I want to surf too!" Max shouted.

"Let your uncle teach you, you'll be *owning* it," my father said.

His remark produced varied reactions. My mother said, "Daniel you sound ridiculous," Justin frowned, and my nephews shouted with enthusiasm, jumping on top of the surfboards on one end of the porch.

Fifteen minutes later, I was with them and my father in the water. I put them on the board, which was broad and long, and they stayed sitting there while I guided them to where the waves started. My father was excited and followed close behind me. Everyone else was back on the beach chatting and eating donuts Mom had brought from the café.

"I want to stand up!" Connor started moving.

"No, we'll do that later. Today, just stay seated."

"Promise me we will later though."

"I promise," I said, cutting him off.

Connor was holding onto the edges of the board when a wave shook it. We kept at it for a while, until Max got tired and pushed his brother off. I left them in the water, playing and laughing, and looked at my father.

"Leah's looking good," he remarked.

"She's making progress. Slowly. But she'll get there."

"You're doing a good job."

"Why do you think it's me?"

"Because I know you, and I know when something gets in your head, there's no stopping you. I still remember the day you asked me if beetles were fat because they were full of daisies. We had just moved and you had seen that in one of Douglas's paintings, the weird one full of colors that I used to make fun of, saying he must have smoked something before he painted it. I told you no, but obviously you weren't convinced. You had to see it with your own eyes. So two days later, there I found you, on the porch dissecting a poor beetle. And now you're a vegetarian."

I laughed. "Why would he paint that?" I remembered Douglas's picture perfectly. The colors milling together around a mound of flowers and purple-colored beetles on the ground, sliced open and full of daisies.

"Ah, he was like that; that was his magic. So hard to predict."

"Fuck." I took a deep breath. "I sure miss him."

"Me too. Both of them." My father looked away, sadder than I ever saw him, and over at the surfboard the twins were trying to climb up on. "You should customize it. Make it cooler."

He grinned softly.

They left around lunchtime, and Leah and I spent the time together in silence, as usual. In the evening, I worked awhile on a job I had to turn in at the beginning of the week, a logo and a couple of promo images for a restaurant that was opening soon. Leah stayed in her room listening to music, and I decided to give her space. She hadn't started painting again and I hadn't asked her to. Yet.

When night fell, we had dinner on the porch.

I went inside for a sweatshirt after putting the dishes in the sink, because winter was almost here and it was starting to get cool in the later hours.

I got comfortable next to her on the cushions. "You really don't want to try it?"

"No, you look like the weird tea lady."

"A joker... okay, fine."

Leah smiled timidly, but soon a shadow fell across her expression. "I realized today it must be really hard for you to have me in your house."

"What made you think that?"

"Seeing you with your family. How you hate the way they invade your space. You've always been particular. I get that, I really do. I'm sorry things are this way."

"Don't say that. It's not true."

I meant it. I hadn't even thought about it, but Leah's presence in my life didn't bother me. Living with her was simple, despite her problems, the changes that kept coming every week.

"Thanks anyway," she whispered.

35

Leah

KEVIN JAX WAS MY FIRST kiss.

Three weeks had passed since New Year's and it still hurt me to remember it. It was January and school had just started, but at the beginning, we never had to pay much attention, so Kevin and I started passing notes back and forth starting the first day.

How was the break?

Fine. Painted a lot. You?

On the beach with the guys. You walking home?

Yeah, why do you ask?

Can I walk with you?

I bit the tip of my pen and answered with a simple *yes*. When class was over, I said goodbye to Blair, who was going in the opposite direction. Kevin came over with a timid smile.

We barely talked at first, as if sending notes to each other in class had nothing to do with being face to face. But as the days passed, the discomfort faded, and I realized he was fun and really smart. He liked licorice, and sometimes he would eat one while we walked, because he said he was jealous of me always having a sucker in my mouth. It made me laugh. He was one of those optimistic people who are always happy and infect you with their joy.

"So you'll come to the beach party this Saturday," he repeated when we reached the door to my house.

I nodded, thumbs in the straps of my backpack. Kevin looked at me nervously and took a breath before speaking. "I was going to wait till then, but..."

I knew what he was thinking before it happened.

There, under the light brown trellis climbing the white fence among the wild grass, he bent over and kissed me. It was a slightly clumsy, timid kiss, as they all are at that age. I closed my eyes and noticed a tingle in my stomach that was still there as Kevin turned around and walked away.

I didn't move until I heard a familiar voice: "I promise I won't tell."

I turned. Axel arched an eyebrow and grinned.

"What are you doing here?" I asked.

"I was hanging out with your dad. Don't look at me like that, I wasn't spying on you. He seems like a nice kid, the kind that cuts your grass on Saturday mornings and follows his girlfriend to the door. I like him. You've got my approval."

"I don't need your damn approval."

"Well, now! Don't tell me you're mad!"

I repressed my desire to cry, went inside, and closed myself up in my room. My mother came up a while later with a carton of ice cream. She sat down beside me in bed, her legs crossed, dried paint all over her smock, and passed me a spoon before plunging hers into the chocolate. I swallowed and imitated her.

Later I realized a mother always knows more than it seems. That there are things, things to do with feelings, you just can't hide. That even if she respected my silence, she often knew things before I had even started to realize them.

36

Leah

IN THE BACKGROUND, "TICKET TO Ride" was playing, and every note produced another line, more precise, sharper, as though they were trying to pierce the rough surface of the canvas.

I painted without stopping. Almost without breathing. Without seeing anything else.

I painted until the sky was as dark as the picture.

I didn't even pay attention to Axel, who was lying on the hammock with a book. His eyes veered toward me when I took a strong breath. He got up slowly; he reminded me of a lazy cat, stretching out softly as he came over.

He looked at the painting and crossed his arms. "What am I supposed to be seeing?"

"I don't know. What do you see?"

The painting was black, absolutely black.

"I see you," he responded, then lifted his hand to point to a sharp corner that remained white. "You left this. Give me the brush."

He tried to take it from my hands, but I stepped back and shook my head. He raised a brow, curious, waiting for an explanation.

"I didn't leave it. Or I did, but on purpose."

Axel smiled when he understood why.

37

Axel

"READY FOR OUR EXCURSION?"

Leah looked at me and shrugged.

"I'll take that as a yes," I said.

It was the second-to-last Saturday of the month, which meant Oliver would be back in two days, and for some reason that made me feel we had no time to spare. We walked out of the house and continued on in silence. I was carrying a backpack and had made a few sandwiches and a thermos of coffee. We went around a mile down a muddy path toward the city. When we reached my family's café, we went inside and said hi to my brother.

"Where you going?" Justin asked.

"On a field trip, like kids," Leah responded.

He seemed surprised to hear her joking. A tense moment passed, and he served her a slice of cheesecake.

"To keep you strong," he said, amused.

"I already made lunch," I complained. "Anyway, what about me?"

Satisfaction gleamed in Justin's eyes. He leaned an elbow on the bar. "Order one from me, please. And be nice."

"Eat shit." I sat down on a stool and took Leah's fork, stabbed a piece of cheesecake, and brought it to my lips.

She was indignant, but then she laughed. My brother watched us with curiosity.

I went into the kitchen to say hello to my parents, then we left. The streets of Byron Bay, with their low brick and wood buildings, were full of kids skating and people coming back from the beach with their boards under their arms after surfing through the early morning at Fisherman's Lookout. We passed in front of an aromatherapy shop and a hippie truck painted in all colors with a phrase from John Lennon: "Everything is clearer when you're in love." And we took the trail to Cape Byron, the easternmost point of Australia.

"Don't go so fast," I told her.

Leah stayed by my side while we climbed the trail with its alternating stairs and dirt. The edge of the cape was covered with a blanket of green grass that contrasted with the blue of the sea. We walked around the cliff in silence. The air was tranquil.

"Are you here?" I asked her.

"Here?"

"Really here, in this instant. Stop thinking and just enjoy the path, the views, everything around us. You know what happened to me one time in Brisbane? I was an intern at a company twenty minutes from my apartment, and I passed every day down this pedestrian-only street. I don't know if I was just looking at my own belly button, if getting to work was all that mattered to me, or what the fuck, but I had been taking the same route for two months before I noticed the graffiti on this wall. I had seen it, I'm sure, out of the corner of my eye or something, like one of those things you don't bother paying attention to. That morning I stopped and contemplated it for no reason in particular. It was a tree with branches stretching out to all sides, and at the tip of each of them was a different object: a heart, a tear, a sphere of light, a feather... I stayed there so long I showed up late to work. Fascinated by an image I hadn't noticed, even though it had been on that wall for who knows how long, and that made me think how sometimes the problem isn't in the world around us, it's in how we see ourselves. Perspective, Leah, I think everything depends on perspective."

She said nothing, but I could almost hear her thoughts and see her trapping the words and hiding them away.

We kept going up Cape Byron, attentive to every step we took. I had been there many times, walking or watching the sunrise, but every occasion was different. This time because Leah was beside me and had a pensive expression, eyes centered on the waves murmuring to the left.

A half hour later, we reached the lighthouse, which rose more than three hundred feet above sea level. We stayed there awhile looking at the landscape, then decided to take a trail that bordered the bottom of the cliffs. We stopped when we found a herd of wild goats.

"I'm dying of thirst," she said, sitting down.

"Here. Take a sip."

I passed her the bottle of water and sat on the ground in front of the sea. When a wave broke against the rocks, the water came in, sliding forward until it almost touched our feet.

"Should we eat here?" she asked.

"Why not?" I took the sandwiches out of my backpack.

"You know? I think you're right. That sometimes we don't look at things the right way. I did when I used to paint. It was inevitable that I'd fixate on details, you know, tones, shapes, textures. I liked that. Absorbing it. Interiorizing it."

I looked at her profile, the slightly oval line of her forehead, her prominent cheeks, the curve of her lips, her button nose, how soft her skin looked beneath the sun, and the golden tone it took on.

"We can't do it all the time. Just in certain moments," I said.

"I guess." She took a bite of her sandwich.

I had finished mine, so I took off my shoes and got comfortable on the rock lying next to her. The sky was clear and a soft breeze was blowing. If this wasn't happiness, tranquility, life, I didn't know what could be. I closed my eyes and felt Leah moving, lying down too. I don't know how long we were there like that, if it was ten minutes or an hour, but it was perfect, and all I did was breathe.

"Axel, thank you for this. Thank you for everything."

I opened my eyes and analyzed her expression. We were close, and only her tousled hair came between us. "Don't thank me. We're a team, remember?"

"I thought you said *tribe*, and you were the chief."

"True." I laughed. I raised a hand, serious now, and touched her arm to get her attention. She pulled away brusquely. "Hey— you remember what we talked about at the beginning of the month?"

"Yeah, I remember."

"Well, we're almost at the end, and I want to ask you the same question as when we started. Are you ready?"

She shook her head, and I suppressed my desire to hold her and protect her from her own thoughts, the harmful ones, the fucked-up ones. I kept going despite her silent plea.

"You want to be happy again? With everything that implies. Assimilating the past, learning to leave it behind, smiling when you get up every morning without feeling guilty for doing it when they're no longer here. Look at me, Leah."

She did. Her eyes peered into mine while she nodded slowly, and my chest swelled with pride.

38

Leah

I LOOKED AWAY. I COULDN'T keep staring at him.

A soft quiver overcame me. A quiver with his name, because I knew it too well, so many years, so many moments... I took a deep breath, telling myself, *You can control this. You can.* I stood up.

Did I want to be happy? Yes, a part of me did.

I looked around. We were on a peak that seemed to be the furthest edge of the world, under a midday sun. The cape's form looked like the tail of a green dragon on the edge of the Pacific Ocean, with sugarcane and macadamias. I looked at the turquoise water, the shapes of the sparse clouds.

"Leah, watch out!" Axel shouted, but I didn't have time to react before a gigantic wave soaked me from head to toe. "Are you okay?"

"Are you laughing?" I shouted.

"Shit...yeah." He laughed harder.

"You're...you're..." The words got stuck in my throat while I squeezed out my T-shirt, walking away from the edge of the promontory.

"Incredible? Amazing? The best?" He was following me.

"Shut up," I said, smiling, and shoved him.

"Hey, don't touch me. Not all of us feel like getting all wet in the middle of the day."

I looked at his perfect smile, the one I had recreated so many times, drawing a waning moon, and the sparkle of his eyes, which were dark blue like the deep sea, like a stormy sky.

I shivered, not from the cold, but because of Axel.

Because of what he had always been for me. Because of the memories.

39

Leah

PLATONIC FRIENDSHIPS ARE LIKE THAT; they stay with you forever. The years pass, and while you forget kisses and people stroking your face, you do keep on remembering that smile from that boy who was so special to you. Sometimes I thought that was what I felt, because it was platonic, because it was never requited, was like a question left floating in the air: *What would it be like to kiss him?* Years back, before I fell asleep, I used to imagine his kisses. In my mind, Axel's kisses were warm, overwhelming, intense. Like him. Like his every gesture, his soft way of moving, his vivid expression full of unsaid words, his serene face with its clear lines…

I asked myself if the rest of the world saw him this way too, if those girls who turned around to watch when he passed had noticed all the things that made him special. How direct he could be, how hard he was beneath that easygoing appearance, how afraid he was to hold a brush in his hands if no one had told him what to paint…

Why was it so hard to forget a love that was never even real, that never existed?

Maybe because for my heart…it just was.

40

Axel

"ANOTHER ROUND? MY TREAT."

Oliver clicked his tongue. "I shouldn't drink more."

"*I shouldn't, it's not right, I chipped a nail*, what the fuck happened to my best friend? Come on, enjoy the night."

"I should call and make sure she's got keys."

"Cool, do that and get it over with for once."

My friend got up from the red wood table where we'd just had dinner. He walked off a bit to talk to Leah, who luckily, since she was friends with Blair again, usually had her phone on her. Not like me, it was as if my subconscious refused to give in to that device that forced me to be available twenty-four hours a day. That night, Leah had agreed to go with my parents, Justin, Emily, and the twins to a flea market outside the city, so I hoped Oliver would relax a little bit.

"Okay, everything's cool; she'll go home on her own."

"See? It wasn't so complicated."

"Order me something strong." Oliver smiled.

Like the good friend I took myself to be, I walked over to

the bar. The dinner service was over and there was a musical atmosphere in the place full of colorful chairs and weird prints. I greeted one of the bartenders, an old friend from school, and ordered two drinks.

"Bring me up to date before I'm hammered," Oliver said, licking his lips after taking a long sip. "How are things with Leah? Everything normal?"

She got naked, she kissed me, I remembered, but I ignored that fleeting thought and tried to make the image of her body fade into the background. But I couldn't. She was a fucking demon. I would go to hell for being unable to forget a single curve, a single fucking inch of her body.

"Yeah, everything's great, you know, routine."

"She's better though. She's different."

"Sometimes a change of scene is good for a person."

"Maybe. True. And how are you?"

"Nothing new. Lots of work."

"At least your job is bearable. I swear to you, one day I'm gonna get up, go to the office, and try and kill myself with the stapler. How can anyone keep from losing their mind in one of those cubicles? They're like little jails."

I laughed.

"I'm serious, you wouldn't last two days in there with all those rules and all the jerk-offs there…"

"Let me remind you I was an intern in an office."

"Yeah, maybe you forgot that you set off a fire extinguisher and sprayed the boss's office before taking off laughing like a fucking madman."

"Guilty as charged. But he was an idiot; he deserved it. It was a kind of poetic justice on behalf of my colleagues and all the future interns who were going to pass through there. They should have started a fan club for me or something."

"Yeah, just what you needed. Order another." He raised his empty glass.

"What am I, your fucking slave? I invite you to dinner, I babysit for you for free, I put up with your whining…"

The waiter passed by our table and Oliver ordered another round, giggling.

"You know what? Really the job's not so bad. I mean, it's shit, it's not my thing, but you get used to it, and actually my coworkers are nice. We go out for a drink on Fridays when we're done."

"Are you trying to replace me?"

"Have another friend like you? Not if they paid me."

I took a sip, savored it, and stretched out my legs. "Hey, weren't you hooking up with someone? What was her name?"

"Bega."

"What happened with her?" I asked.

"Nothing. I bang her. Sometimes. In the office."

"You're hooking up with a coworker?"

"I'm hooking up with my boss."

It took me a moment to realize that for him, this little slipup was a breath of fresh air, something wild that he could hold on to in the midst of a life that he had never wanted. That need to rebel somehow to feel he wasn't getting lost in his responsibilities, his schedule, order.

"Is it worth it?"

"I don't know."

"Sure." I took a sip.

"I like her, but it's complicated, she just lives to work. But what we have—that's it. I have important things to worry about, I can't risk all that. And I don't know if I want to. We're not like that, are we, Axel?"

"Like what?"

"Commitment. Getting tied down."

"I don't know."

After thinking it over a lot, I had come to the conclusion that I didn't know many things, especially about stuff that hadn't happened yet. I had realized that because I'd spent so many years clinging to what I thought I knew, that I would become a painter or that nothing would ever happen to the people close to me, my family. I was wrong. So now I never assumed anything.

"I guess I don't either," he admitted.

"So the idea is Leah's going to go to college, right?"

"What do you mean by that?"

"I'm talking about you. About what you'll do then. About that responsibility that you have now but you won't have forever. I know you've got the tuition and the apartment for her, but it's not the same. You can take back part of your life. And if she starts painting again…"

"She won't," Oliver cut me off.

"If it does happen…" I went on, remembering the promise I made to Douglas one night lying on my porch, "I'll help her figure out her path."

Oliver finished his drink. "She's not going to do it. Don't you see that? She's a different person."

"But she is doing it," I said softly, and for some reason, I felt weird sharing it, as if I were betraying her, her trust, our bond. But shit, he was her brother; he was worried.

"Are you serious?"

"Yeah. She's not doing a lot. And no colors."

Oliver sat there thinking. "Why didn't she tell me?"

The question I didn't want to hear. "Maybe you're too close. Why are there are people who can open up and talk with a psychologist about things they can't tell their own family? I guess sometimes being so close to someone makes things harder. And I think...I think she feels guilty with you, because of all the changes..."

He stared into his empty glass and ignored the loud music around us.

I felt an unknown pressure in my chest.

"I'll do it, I promise." I stood up. "Come on, let's have some fun."

41

Leah

I RUBBED MY EYES AND sat down on a stool next to Oliver in front of the bar in the kitchen where we often had breakfast. I drank a bit of orange juice.

"Leah, you know I love you, right?"

I looked at him. Surprised. Timid. Scared.

"You're the most important person in my life. It doesn't matter what you ask me for, I'll always say yes. We're alone now, you and me, but we'll find a way to get ahead and stay together. I want you to trust me, okay? And if you ever feel like talking, no matter what time it is or if I'm in Sydney, call me. I'll be waiting on the other line."

I breathed, breathed, breathed deeper...

June

—

(WINTER)

42

Axel

"HOW WAS PAROLE? YOU HAVE fun?" I asked when Oliver left. I followed Leah to her room and crossed my arms while she set her suitcase next to the closet. "What's up?"

Leah looked at me, on edge. "I want you to help me."

My heart started pounding. "I'm here. You can trust me."

"Thanks." She looked away. "I'm going to put my clothes away."

I noticed how she wiped the sweat from the palms of her hands on her jeans, how her nerves shook her, the stiffness in her shoulders.

"What would you like for dinner? Don't prisoners have a special day when they get to choose their menu or something?"

She smiled a little and the tension dissipated.

"Come on, it's your chance; pick the menu."

"Between broccoli and chard? Hm."

"Vegetable lasagna? With lots of cheese."

"Perfect," she said and opened her suitcase.

I put on a record, and music filled each corner of the house while I started chopping the vegetables into little pieces. I thought about that *I want you to help me* that had almost been a plea, and the mixed bravery and fear and how it was hard to tell where one sentiment began and the other ended.

"Can I help you with anything?" Leah asked.

"Yeah, grab the tray."

We ended up making it together, but I wasn't sure if it was really a lasagna or just a scramble of vegetables, pasta, and ridiculous quantities of cheese. While it was baking, we cleaned the kitchen and washed up—I soaped, she rinsed.

We had dinner in silence on the porch.

When we were done, I went inside to get a pen and paper.

"This is the plan. We're going to do things this month. New things. Things that make us feel. The other day I was thinking of all those people who live sort of automatically, without really being aware of what they're doing; you know the ones I'm talking about?"

Leah nodded slowly.

"Right, so that's what I was thinking of…and whether it's possible to forget how to be happy, to look back one day and realize you've been dissatisfied for years, empty."

"It's possible, I guess."

"I was thinking about what I would do if that happened to me. What things would make me remember that feeling of fulfillment. And I don't know, the stuff that popped into my head was so basic. But also weird things. Like eating spaghetti, for example." She laughed, and I held on to that sound, so vibrant, so alive. "I'm serious; shit, it's a pleasure. And I regret all those times I finished a plate without really tasting it, because I think now, being aware, I would really enjoy it. Stop laughing, ba…"

I stopped talking and sighed, a little annoyed at not being able to call her *babe*, the way I had before, ever since she was a child.

"Food. You're right," she admitted. She was still smiling as I wrote it down.

"Something you used to do. Dive, for example."

"I could try it," she said doubtfully.

"Of course. We'll do it together one day."

"Okay." She breathed deeply.

"Listen to music, breathe, paint, dance without rhythm, or talk to me to reinforce the idea that I am the most incredible person you've ever known," I joked. Leah nudged me softly. "Walk barefoot and feel it. See the dawn…" I paused. "But none of this has a point if you don't feel it, Leah."

"I understand…"

"But…"

"It's going to be hard."

"Tell me what makes you most afraid."

"I don't know."

I held her chin between my fingers so she'd have to look at me, because I was starting to know those new layers covering what had been there before. I knew when she was lying, when her pulse was racing, when she couldn't breathe. "Don't hide from me. Don't do that, please."

"What if it doesn't work? What if I can't be happy again and I'm like this for the rest of my life, all empty and dull? I don't like it, but I don't like the other way either, just acting like nothing ever happened, because it did happen, it happened to me, Axel, and it's still there, but I am incapable of paying attention to it because when I do it hurts. It hurts too much, I can't control it, and that makes me feel bad, makes me feel guilty for being so weak, for not accepting it the way other people accept worse things, even more fucked-up things. So everything is like a spiral and I'm walking in circles and I can't find the way to get out, to...breathe."

"Damn, Leah."

"You asked me to be sincere."

She didn't cry, but it was worse. Because I saw her crying inside, biting her lower lip, holding on, holding on...

"Live me," I whispered without thinking.

"What?" She blinked, still trembling.

"Just live me. Let yourself go. Come on."

I held out my hand. Leah took it. I pulled her up.

43

Leah

"LET'S DO SOMETHING ON THE list. Let's walk barefoot."

"It's nighttime," I said, still confused.

"Who cares? Come on, Leah."

I stopped talking when I realized Axel wouldn't let go of my hand as we left the porch steps behind and walked onto the trail. In theory, I should have been concentrating solely on the little stones I felt on the bottoms of my feet or the delicate sensation of the grass when we went a bit further, but in practice I couldn't ignore his hand, his fingers, his skin. My heart skipped a beat, as if inside my chest there weren't enough space for it, as if it were longing for something at the same time as it was shouting for me not to do it.

"Tell me what you feel," Axel whispered.

I feel you, I wanted to respond. "I don't know..."

"What do you mean, you don't know? Leah, don't think. Just try to concentrate on this moment."

We walked slowly. He was a little ways ahead, pulling on me softly, not letting go of my hand.

What was I feeling?

His fingers, long, warm. The carpet of damp grass tickling my feet. His skin against mine, rubbing softly with each step. A rougher section of trail, dryer. His soft nail under the skin of my thumb. And finally, sand. Sand everywhere, heels sinking into the warm surface.

Only then did I understand what Axel was doing. For those minutes our walk lasted, I had felt everything. Being present. I felt the reality of this moment, not through the broken window of a car that had left the road.

I sat on the sand. Axel too.

The sound of the sea embraced us and remained with us awhile, until he sighed and started to play distractedly in the sand. "Tell me something you've never told anyone else."

One day I told you I loved you, but all you heard was "We all live in a yellow submarine."

The memory stunned me, as if it had been asleep for years and was trying suddenly to break through, dragging with it countless instances I had tried to forget. And sometimes, when we find boxes covered in dust, we discover photos that still rouse old feelings, that stone shaped like a heart that used to mean everything, that special wrinkled note, that song that would always be ours even if he didn't know it.

I sank my fingers into the sand, trying to ignore that memory, and sank into another, harder, more painful one, as if all of them were connected, and awakening one was like pushing a domino and making all the ones next to it fall.

"You want to know what I felt when I got outside after it happened?" I asked, uncertain, and Axel nodded. "It was sunny. I remember it as if it were yesterday. I stood in front of the door to Oliver's apartment, looking at everything and trying to absorb it. A man passed by me smiling, tripped, and excused himself before continuing on his way. Out front there was a woman pushing a baby carriage with a shopping bag in her hand. I know because I couldn't stop staring at the carrots sticking out of it. There was a dog barking far away."

I don't know if Axel was aware that just then I was sharing something I hadn't shared with myself, hadn't even thought over in solitude. Because it was easier like that, with him, with those feelings welling up when he was near me mingling with others, more complicated ones I didn't even want to look at.

"Go on, Leah. I want to understand you."

"I just...I just saw all that and asked myself how it was possible that nothing had changed. It didn't seem real. It was like a joke. I guess that's what happens when the world stops, not just because of something like that, but with a breakup, an illness... It's like feeling frozen while everything else is moving. And I think...I think that all of us are living in a bubble, all focused on our own thing, until one day that bubble bursts and you want to scream and you feel alone and no one's protecting you." I swallowed to try and get rid of the knot swelling in my throat. "It was like seeing things from another perspective, distant, blurry, with everything just black and white."

"And you always paint what you feel," Axel whispered, and I liked how he could get inside me, understand me, decipher me even when I didn't know why I was doing things. Like that, like that absence of color, my need for it to be that way.

44

Axel

AFTER THAT NIGHT ON THE beach, Leah closed up again. She didn't want to tell me why, and I didn't push it. Instead I let her be for a couple of days. In the morning before school, she still went surfing with me. And in the afternoon, when I was done working and she was done studying, we would spend a while together on the porch, reading, listening to music, or sharing the silence.

We weren't avoiding each other, but we hardly talked.

Leah started painting on Friday night. I was taking my last sip of tea with a book in my hand when I saw her stand up slowly and approach the blank canvas. I watched her out of the corner of my eye, lying in the hammock a few feet away.

She grabbed a brush, opened the black paint tube, and took a deep breath before letting whatever was in her head come out. I was amazed as I watched her, attentive to the soft movements of her arms, the strength with which her fingers grabbed the brush, her tense shoulders, her furrowed brow, that energy that seemed to push her to paint one line, then another, then another. I held back my desire to get up and see what she was doing as I saw her mixing paint to come up with different tones of gray.

I had felt that way before too, but so long ago I was incapable of recalling the exact occasion. It had been in Douglas's studio, on the afternoons that I spent there with him, feeling...feeling everything, maybe because back then I didn't think too much and the final result didn't matter much to me, whether I did a good or a bad job. It was enough to talk with him for a while, drink a beer, and let it all flow.

When Leah finished, I got up.

"Can I see it?" I asked.

"It's horrible," she warned me.

"Okay. I'll try to deal."

A smile pulled at the edges of her mouth as I came over and looked at the painting. There was a dot in the center, round and alone, frozen in the midst of an eddy of paint that spun around it., the bubble and the rest of the world following its course. For once, I didn't just notice the content, I also saw the technique, how she had captured the circular movement. So real, so her.

Once Douglas told me that the complicated part of creativity isn't having an idea or an image in your head you want to reproduce; the hard thing is getting it out, making it exist, managing to find the thread that runs through the imaginary and the earthly so you can manage to express your thoughts, your sensations, your emotions...

"I like it. I'll take it."

"No! Not this one."

"Why?" I crossed my arms.

"Because…I'll make a different one for you. One day. I don't know when."

"Fine. I'll hold you to it." I stretched my arms up high. "We should get to bed soon if we want to go diving tomorrow."

"You didn't say anything to me about that," she replied.

"No? Well, I am now."

Leah wrinkled her nose, but she didn't complain. She cleaned her brushes and put her things away. I told her good night, left her there, and went inside.

Julian Rocks is one of the most famous places to go diving, and it was just twenty minutes from home. We packed some of our stuff into the back of the pickup. The rest we would rent at the diving center. I started the engine and turned up the volume on the stereo. It was a nice day; the temperature was pleasant and warm for wintertime. While we left behind the almost-wild beaches and the tropical woods, I remembered why I felt so bound to that part of the world.

"You're going fast," Leah whispered by my side.

"Sorry." I braked a little. "Better?"

She hardly said anything when we arrived and started getting ready, but I liked seeing her concentrated and resolute. There were surfers on the beach when we got into the boat along with several other people and pulled away from the coast. Leah stayed pensive beside me, and I talked to an old acquaintance who was the diving instructor. We stopped shortly.

"Are you ready?" I looked at her.

"Yeah. I...I'm excited."

After working out the last-minute details, I looked over her gear. "You first, all right? I'll follow you."

When her turn came, after two other young people dove in, she sat on the edge of the boat, her back to the water, and let herself fall in. I felt something strange as I watched her sink. Uncertainty. A fucked-up, anxious feeling. I liked it and didn't at the same time. It was strange and not quite rational.

"I'll go now," I told the instructor.

I saw her right away, just a few yards from me. The sea was calm. Julian Rocks is a marine reserve with immense biodiversity thanks to the mix of warm and cold currents. We quickly saw a leopard shark and manta rays. Leah stretched out her hand to a school of clown fish that dispersed when we approached them. I followed her when she stopped to delight in a huge turtle and when she floated there in the midst of thousands of fish, surrounded by an explosion of color in the middle of the ocean. The image was engraved in my mind as if I had taken a mental photograph, the peace it gave off, the blended tones, the beauty of something so wild...

Back on land, we ate at a Thai place. We ordered noodles, rice with vegetables, and the soup of the day.

"What time are we going back?"

"Why do you ask? You in a rush?"

"I told Blair that maybe...maybe I could have a coffee with her this afternoon."

"You didn't tell me. Sure, I'll take you wherever as soon as we finish eating. What about the diving? Did you like it?"

Leah smiled, a real smile, still excited and content. "I almost didn't remember what it was like. All those colors..." she said as she stirred the noodles they had just served to us with her chopsticks. "Yellow and orange and blue fish...and the turtle, that was amazing. I love turtles, their little faces..."

"Goddamn this is good," I said, licking my lips.

"You're always like this, aren't you?"

"This cool?" I raised an eyebrow.

"You enjoy every moment."

"Yes and no. I've had my bad times."

"Have you ever really suffered?"

"Of course. Lots of times. Like everyone. It's inevitable, Leah. And it's not a bad thing. There's no reason why it should be; life is like that. There are good times and bad times. I think the secret is trying to push through the bad ones and enjoy the good ones. There's not much else."

"Aren't you going to tell me what happened to you?"

"Depends. What do I get in exchange?"

"From me? I doubt I've got anything that interests you."

"What is that, some kind of compliment?"

"Fine, we'll make a deal."

I liked watching her joke around even though we both knew we were talking about something serious. I stretched my legs under the table and they almost touched hers. The Thai place was very small; there were just five wooden tables, and we were in one in the corner.

"There's something I've been asking myself for months." I rubbed my chin. "How is it possible that you're still listening to the Beatles every day? It's a direct connection to them, to your parents. And you've been doing it from the very first day, when you used to spend the whole afternoon in your room with your headphones on."

Leah looked away, slightly nervous. "I needed it. I couldn't...I couldn't leave them behind; I had to take them with me. I don't know, Axel. I don't have a rational answer; I don't even see the logic in half the things I feel or do. I contradict myself all the time."

"We all do now and then."

"I guess. I just know I need those songs, need to hear them." She fell silent, hesitating, and added, "All of them but one."

"Which?"

"'Here Comes the Sun.' Not that one."

"Why not?"

Leah slid her finger over the veining of the wood in the table, stroking it slowly, following the trajectory of that small imperfection. She looked at me and sucked in a breath. "That's the song that was playing when the accident happened. The song I asked my mother to put on."

"I didn't know, Leah." I stretched out a hand to put it on top of hers, but she pulled hers away before I could.

"Talk to me about you, about your bad times."

"There have been a few. The worst was when your parents died, but there were others. Moments when I felt a little lost, you know, like everyone when you don't really know what you want to do. And then I had to figure out how to handle the frustration when I realized I didn't want to paint; I had to make a choice...

Sometimes you hope for things in life and they don't come. Maybe it's our fault for planning too much, for marking out paths that we never end up taking. I guess that disappoints us."

We didn't say anything while we finished eating. Then, unhurried, we returned to Byron Bay, and Leah asked me to drop her off on Blair's street.

"Should I pick you up later?"

"No. I'll walk back."

"You sure?"

"Yeah."

"You got your phone on you?"

Leah sighed and opened the car door. "Axel, don't treat me like a baby."

"Hey!" I lowered the window to call to her. "Remember to brush your teeth if you eat something! And don't take candy from strangers."

She knitted her brows and flipped me the bird.

I shook my head, laughing and happy to see her that way.

45

Leah

BLAIR CAME OUTSIDE SOON AFTER I rang the doorbell, and we walked down the street together under the sun. A soft wind was blowing and we decided to sit on the patio of a café we used to go to before. I used to always order a coffee and a banana-chocolate muffin that was almost as tasty as Georgia's cheesecake. Blair was more for savory foods, and sometimes would get a small order of fries while we chatted away. We used to spend the whole day together, just the two of us.

"I didn't think you were coming," she said.

"I went diving with Axel and it got late."

"Diving?" She smiled. "Sounds wonderful."

"It was all right," I admitted.

Actually, it had been much more than that. Stimulating. Intense. Floating in the middle of the ocean, feeling weightless while the fish whirled around me like dots of light dancing in random patterns. And Axel there by my side.

"I'll have some fries and a soda," Blair said when the waitress came over. "What about you?"

"A banana muffin and a decaf with milk."

"Sure thing, ladies, I'll be right back."

"You know what? This reminds me of that day we played a joke on Matt and filled his locker with glitter, and we ended up here laughing about it, and then we saw him in the distance and we took off running…," Blair said. "But he caught us because I turned around to grab the last bit of muffin I'd left behind. I remember. Also his books were sparkly for weeks."

Blair started laughing and I ended up doing the same. She had a way of making all those moments add something to laugh about rather than subtract it. She had been my best friend in the world, and I had struggled for months to keep her away from me because somehow I knew, if I kept her close, I'd wind up hurting and disappointing her.

"How's school?"

"A lot better than before."

"You going to go to college, then?"

I shrugged. I didn't want to talk about it. "You happy at work?"

"Yeah, I love it. It's exhausting though."

"You've always liked kids."

They brought us our order, and I started breaking off pieces of my muffin and eating it, distracted. I savored it slowly, thinking of Axel's words, enjoying the contrast of the banana and the soft bitterness of the chocolate.

I looked up at Blair, uncertain. "I think I've got feelings for him."

"You mean Axel, right?"

"Yeah. Why…why is this happening to me?"

"Because you like him. You always have."

"I'd like to be able to fall in love with someone else."

"We can't choose these things, Leah..." She gave me a gentle look. "How is living with him?"

I thought it over. I'd been in that house in the middle of all that nature for four months. I didn't remember much about the first two months, which I spent shut up in my room. March had been chaos. I got mad at him, I lost control at Bluesfest, and I started actually painting again. When April arrived, Axel had tightened the reins, forcing me to make a decision. And sometimes, being the way you are is easier, more comfortable, than facing change.

"Up and down. It's good right now."

"Be you, Leah," she said.

"What do you mean?" I grew tense.

"In everything. With Axel too. Be like you were before. Let yourself go; don't think about things. Don't you remember? I used to laugh when you said your breath stopped when you saw him or you'd die for a kiss from him, but I was used to it because you've always been a little over the top."

I brought my hand to my chest. Blair was right, but I still felt very far away from all that, even if sometimes a memory flared up, even if it vanished as quickly as it arrived. These were peaks, but they were unpredictable. I still had on my raincoat, despite all the holes in it, and it was hard for me to recognize myself in that girl I'd left behind, the one who wasn't scared to take a leap without asking how far it was to the ground.

I pushed that image and the nostalgia from my mind. "Talk to me about you. You going out with anyone?"

"I wanted to talk to you about that, but I wasn't really sure how." Blair shifted, uncomfortable. "Last month I went out a couple of times with Kevin Jax."

I smiled almost from inertia. Kevin hadn't only been the boy who'd given me my first kiss in front of the golden trellis at my home; I had also lost my virginity to him a couple of years later, when I decided the time had come to be realistic and admit that Axel would never look at me like a woman instead of a girl.

"So how was it?"

"Nice. Too nice."

"How can something be too nice?" I put a bite of muffin in my mouth.

"Leah…" she grimaced. "I told him I couldn't keep going out with him until…until I'd talked to you. You all were together for a while. And we're friends. That always comes first."

I felt a slight tingle in my nose and blinked to keep from crying. I looked at Blair, so transparent, with her dark hair tousled and that sweet expression on her face. I didn't deserve her. I didn't deserve a friend like that, so loyal even though I had ignored her calls for months and had pretended I couldn't see her every time she came to my house to see me, telling Oliver to open the door and make up some excuse.

"You can go out with Kevin. He's a great guy, he really is. I think you will make a perfect couple because you're both so generous." I rubbed my nose and took a deep breath. "I'm really sorry about how I've been these past few months. I'm trying to change. To be better."

"It's working," Blair said.

I went back to Axel's house walking slowly, observing my

surroundings as I hadn't for a long time. The rocky path was surrounded by leafy vegetation in infinite tones of green: olive green, moss green, bottle green, lime green on the younger leaves, mint green, jade green...

Recreating every color had always been one of the things I liked most. Mixing paint, trial and error, mixing again, brightening, darkening, looking for the exact shade I had in my mind and wanted to transmit...

I walked faster when it started to rain. The drops of water were big and the rain intensified as I kept going, as if telling me it was time to hurry home. By the time I closed the door, it had transformed into a storm.

"I didn't know if I should come get you," Axel said.

"I arrived just in time."

The sound of the rain echoed through the walls.

"I think there's still hot water if you want a shower," he said, and then I watched him walk toward the surfboard leaning against the wall by the back porch.

"What are you doing? Going surfing?"

"Yeah. I'll be back in no time."

"No! Don't go..."

"The waves are perfect, it'll be fine."

"Please..." I begged again.

Axel mussed my hair and smiled. "I'll be back before you know it."

Frustrated, I watched him depart, walk down the three steps of the porch, and take off into the rain headed for the beach. I wanted to shout to him to turn around, to beg him not to get into the water, but I just stayed there, frozen in place, my pulse racing.

The rain was plinking against the wood roof over the porch when I walked outside with my easel and opened it. I looked anxiously through my paint tubes, my heart pounding to the rhythm of the raindrops splashing on the ground. I opened them with quivering hands, grabbed a brush, and stopped thinking.

Then I just felt.

I felt every line, every curve, every splatter.

I felt what I was painting in my stiff fingers, in the vulnerability that shook me because I was so worried about him, in my shifting pulse, and in my chaotic thoughts.

I don't know how long I was in front of that canvas spilling out everything I couldn't put into words, but I only stopped when I saw Axel in the distance, his board under his arm, through the rain that was still falling.

He was soaked when he climbed onto the porch and set his board aside.

"The current was great, there were waves that..." He fell silent when he saw my expression. "What's up? Are you mad?"

I wanted to control it. I wanted to swallow my feelings and shut myself up in my room as I had during those first months. Not react. Not let it go.

But I couldn't. I just couldn't.

"Yes, god damn it! Yes!" I exploded. "I didn't want you to go. I didn't want to have to worry about whether something would happen to you! Or be anxious or afraid or wanting to shout at you like I am now!"

Axel looked at me, surprised, and understanding filled his eyes. "I'm sorry, Leah. I didn't even think about it."

"I realize that," I replied and put down my brush.

How could he not know? I was scared; no, worse, I was in a panic, horrified that something could happen to the people I cared about. I couldn't even stand to think about it. There, in front of him, I felt angry and relieved at the same time, knowing he was here.

"What's that? Did you paint something in color?" Axel pointed at the picture. It was dark, like all the rest, but on one side was a single intense red point, vibrant, the only thing in the whole image that caught the eye.

"Yeah, because that's you! A zit on someone's ass!"

I left it there and went inside, hearing him cackling further and further off. I wrinkled my nose at what I was feeling and brought a hand to my chest.

Breathe...I just needed to breathe...

46

Axel

I HADN'T EVEN STOPPED TO think about how scared Leah would be when I told her I was going surfing in the storm. I was used to it. Actually it was one of my favorite times: the sea wild, the rain breaking the surface, the chaos around me, and the currents throwing up taller waves than usual.

But that red dot, that zit on someone's ass... Well, I almost think it was worth it.

Leah didn't leave her room till dinnertime. I made a salad and two of those soups my mother brought every time she came to visit, as if she wanted me to squirrel them away in case the rapture came and we were trapped or something.

It was still raining, so we ate in the dining room while we listened to a Beatles record. She concentrated on her dish until she finished it and answered all my questions with monosyllables.

She washed the dishes while I made tea.

Once we were back on the sofa, I grabbed a piece of paper.

"We need to do more things," I said. "Like, I don't know,

what's up with the strawberry suckers? You used to love them, right? You used to always have one in your mouth."

"I don't know. Not anymore," she replied.

"Well, what would you like us to put on the list? You've got carte blanche right now. That's fun, right? You and me together doing the first thing that pops into your head."

"I want to dance to 'Let It Be' with my eyes closed."

"Brilliant. Done." I put it on the list.

"And I want to get drunk."

"Who am I to tell you not to? You're an adult. All right. I'm glad you're participating. What else can we do?" I put the pen in my mouth. "Let's see, things that make you feel, that make you stop thinking…"

"A kiss." Leah looked at me. "From you," she clarified.

"Leah…" My voice was a hoarse whisper.

"It's not a big deal. Just another feeling…"

"We can't. Let's think of something else."

"Weren't you the person who didn't try to make things seem more important than they are? It's just a kiss, Axel. No one will ever find out, I promise. But I want…I want to know what it's like, what it feels like. What do you care? You'll kiss anyone…"

"Exactly. You're not just anyone."

"Fine. Forget it." She sighed, giving up.

I toyed with the pen in my hands. "What was that about, Leah?"

She looked up. Took a deep breath. "You already know, Axel. I… Years ago…"

"Drop it. Don't tell me. I'll be right back." I got up to go have a smoke.

It was still raining buckets when I leaned on the wooden railing and blew out my first drag. The darkness enveloped everything and seemed to soften the noise of the storm. I sighed, tired, rubbing my chin.

I thought of the girl in my house. How complicated she was. All the knots I had untied little by little without grasping how many there still were to discover.

And at the same time, I liked that.

The challenge. It was almost a provocation.

I snuffed out the cigarette just as the cat appeared on the porch. It looked at me and meowed.

"Well, one time can't hurt. You can spend the night." I opened the door, and it shook off and went inside as if it had understood me.

"Poor thing!" Leah came over.

"I'll go get a towel."

We dried her off, rubbing her while she snorted and pawed at us.

"You know who she reminds me of?"

"Very funny," Leah replied.

"You've got a lot in common."

"I'm going to get her some dinner."

She served her a dish of leftover soup, and the cat finished it while we sat on the wooden floor in the living room watching her. I lay down, falling backward with my hands behind my head. "Day Tripper" started playing, and I mumbled along distracted while she smiled and relaxed. The tension from fifteen minutes before had dissipated.

"I'll look for some old clothes she can sleep on top of."

"No, I'll take her to my room," she said.

"Are you joking? I wouldn't trust her. She seems nice when she wants to, but she could reveal her claws at any moment. Have we never talked about what makes cats so awesome?"

"No, it's not one of our regular topics of conversation."

"Well, we should. They're independent, curious, and they sleep a lot. The three keys to a happy life. They're wild and solitary, but they'll let themselves be domesticated in exchange for comfort. This is how it must have been at first: 'Hey, human, I'll pretend to be civilized and you stuff me with food, protect me, and take care of me. Deal.'" Leah started laughing and I stretched out more on the floor, just as a lazy cat would do. "Don't laugh. It's true."

"I think I'll try and sleep with her."

"Okay," I said, standing up. "If she attacks you and you need help, shout and I'll come for you."

She rolled her eyes. "Good night, Axel."

"Good night."

47

Leah

THAT WEEK, I CONCENTRATED ON school. I tried to pay attention in class, finish my homework during the day, and study in the afternoon while Axel was working. On Wednesday, I had coffee with Blair. On Thursday, when the math teacher asked me a question and the whole room was silent, expectant, I managed to answer without my voice giving out on me. When it was time to go, I pedaled fast, leaving my nerves and insecurity behind.

"Do you have a lot to do today?"

"Lit and Chemistry," I responded.

"What record should I put on?" Axel got up.

"Whatever you like. I don't care."

I opened my books, sat on my side of the desk, and started to do my work. We didn't talk again all afternoon. Now and again, I would look up a bit and watch him draw. He was my exact opposite. He didn't let himself go; there was no emotion, nothing to pour into what he was doing. He was delicate, with well-planned, subtle lines and little room for improvisation. But there was something captivating in his movements, so contained, so willing to maintain a line between himself and the paper.

"Stop watching me, Leah," he murmured.

I blushed and looked quickly away.

When Friday came, I had the feeling this had been the most normal week of the past year. I had studied, I had hung out with a friend, I had exchanged a few words with a classmate after lending her an eraser, and Axel's presence still gave me a tingle in my stomach.

That was how my life used to be. Or pretty much.

When I got home, I had left my bike next to the wooden railing and my backpack on the porch when I saw the cat sitting there giving me a serious look.

"You hungry, pretty girl?"

She meowed, then followed me into the kitchen, as if she were perfectly in her rights to spend another night at the house. I looked in the pantry.

Axel appeared ten minutes later, still wet.

"What's the cat doing in the house?" he grunted.

"She came in on her own. What's for lunch?"

Axel grimaced. He grabbed a T-shirt he had left on the back of the sofa and put it on, stretching his arms. I tried in vain not to look at his torso, his golden skin, his defined muscles...

"What are you in the mood for?" he asked.

"Anything would be fine."

"Spinach egg scramble?"

I nodded, and a little later, we were eating on the porch.

The afternoon was calm, and since it was a Friday, I put off my homework for the next day and fell asleep in Axel's hammock. I didn't really know how I felt. Sometimes good. Sometimes horrible. I could change from one mood to another in the blink of an eye.

In the evening, while Axel was cooking, I painted awhile. Brush in hand, I hesitated and looked over at the little suitcase full of colored paints, all of them still unopened except for the red from the other day, all of them so pretty, so impossible to reach...

"The tacos are ready," Axel said.

"Okay. Coming."

I cleaned my brushes and helped him get the dishes out.

When he finished, instead of making tea, he told me to come inside and he brought down the bottles from the cabinets. Rum. Gin. Tequila. He leaned on the bar in the kitchen and raised an eyebrow mirthfully. "What are you in the mood for?"

"A mojito?"

"Done. Crush some ice."

Axel grabbed sugar and a couple of limes from the fridge, then went outside to pick some of the mint growing near the porch. We made a pitcher and he shook it to mix the ingredients.

"I present you with the finest mojito in the world."

"Let's see if it's true..."

He watched me go out onto the porch with a grin. "If at any point I see you're about to wind up stripping naked in the middle of the living room, I'm stopping you, okay?"

I could feel my cheeks burning. "You said it never happened."

"And it never did. I'm just giving an example." He took a sip and licked his lips without taking his eyes off me. I felt a shiver. "Be good and satisfy my curiosity. Did you used to get drunk a lot? Is that why you put it on the list?"

"No way. Just a couple of times."

"So what happened at the festival?" he asked, serious.

"Nothing. I drank three beers and obviously I didn't digest them very well."

"Okay, well, take it easy. Little sips, like a baby."

That hurt, and I tried to strike him dead with my stare. It seemed like he was constantly pointing out I was just a girl to him on purpose. And this wasn't the best time to show him he was wrong, not when I was so dependent, when I hadn't been able to get over losing my parents the way everyone else does.

I drank half my mojito in one sip.

"I wasn't kidding, damn it. Baby sips."

"I didn't ask for your advice," I replied.

"Still, I'm going to give it to you: don't disobey me."

I finished the rest. Axel clenched his jaw while I went and served myself a second one. I came back a few minutes later. He was standing up with a cigarette in his hand, leaning on the porch railing.

He turned around and crossed his arms. "What's with you? Come on, spit it out."

I took a nervous breath. We were close. "I hate you treating me like a child. I know sometimes I might seem like one and you think I am one, but I'm not. I didn't feel that way before, and I don't like feeling that way now."

"All right."

Axel snuffed out his cigarette and went for another mojito. We sat together on the cushions and talked without stopping for more than an hour. About him, about me, about things that didn't matter and others that did.

"You think I should go to college, then…"

"It's not that I think it, Leah; I know it."

"I don't want to be alone."

"You'll meet new people."

"That's easy for you to say."

"You need experience."

"Of what?" I took a drink.

"Everything. You need to experience life."

"That sounds horrifying…"

Axel laughed and shook his head. "Wait here, I'm going to put on some music."

48

Axel

I PUT ON A BEATLES record.

Leah smiled at me when I came out onto the porch with two more mojitos in my hands and passed her one as the music filled the night. I lit another cigarette, staring into the sky full of stars that seemed to tremble with the notes.

"Is this what you hoped for?"

She stretched. "Yeah. Thanks, Axel."

I liked seeing her that way, so centered on the moment, not thinking about anything else, her head free of the chaos that normally filled it. Her hair was long and wild, and when she stood up, it shifted a little. I grabbed her around the waist.

"I'm a little dizzy." She laughed.

"You've drunk a fair bit."

Her eyes were shining like a turquoise sea. I got lost in them for a few seconds as she moved slowly closer and closer. "Let It Be" started just then, and I let her wrap her hands around my neck. I let myself go. I raised my arms and let my fingers glide down slowly till they reached her hips, pulling her close to me, dancing slowly, dancing under the stars in that house so far from the rest of the world.

She stood on her tiptoes and I felt her warm breath on my cheek. I quivered before I grasped her tighter and held her still against my body, frozen in that moment.

"Leah, what are you doing?" I whispered in her ear.

"The kiss… Just give me that."

"You're drunk."

"You too. A little."

"You don't know what you want…"

"I do. I always have."

She rubbed against me, and when I felt that prick of desire, I thought, *Shit, I did drink too much*. And I was a real bastard. I sucked in a curt breath.

"Forget that. It's a bad idea."

"It's just a feeling, Axel."

"Why don't you ask one of your friends?"

"I'll bet no one kisses like you."

"Check…" I whispered, looking at her lips.

"Meaning I'm right?"

"I'm just being sincere. It's a fact."

"Well, I guess I'll never know."

I didn't like the sound of that *never*; it seemed like a long time. We moved together. I tried to keep my distance from her, but I couldn't. When the chorus came, Leah closed her eyes and let me guide her. I don't know if it was because we had both been drinking or because having her so close clouded my thinking, but I let go of the reins and let me be me, the person who didn't think about rules and consequences, the one who just lived in the present, period.

"Fine, just one kiss. One."

"Are you being serious?" She looked at me.

"But tomorrow we won't remember."

"Of course not," she murmured.

"Close your eyes, Leah."

I took a deep breath and bent down toward her slowly. It was just a brief touch, but it warmed me up inside. I left that kiss on the corner of her mouth and pulled away while Leah knitted her brows, disappointed.

"That's it? That's all?"

"What the fuck did you expect?"

"An actual kiss."

"Come the fuck on," I groaned.

Then, frustrated, I kissed her again.

This time for real. Not a fleeting touch, not a trembling caress. I grabbed her face in my hands, held her cheeks, and dove in. I caught her lower lip in my teeth before I let it slip between mine. Leah moaned in response. A moan that went straight to my crotch. I closed my eyes to try to ward off the excitement. She tasted like lime and sugar, and in the middle of that madness, I decided sinking my tongue into her mouth was a good idea. Something quivered in my stomach when it touched hers, knowing I was kissing Leah and not just some girl, that I was feeling her, that I was making a big mistake...

I jerked away.

Leah watched me while I grabbed the glasses and the pack of cigarettes I'd left on the railing.

"You going?" she asked.

I nodded and walked off.

My heart was still pounding when I got into the shower and ran the cold water to try and clear my head. I thought about how stupid it had been to drink and let my defenses down. Kissing her should have been unpleasant, I thought. I shouldn't be getting a hard-on over her. I should have seen it coming, I thought. I thought...so many things.

And none of them made sense or explained anything.

I lay in bed, still confused.

I spent hours tossing and turning without being able to sleep, trying to figure out what had happened. It was ironic that I was trying to get into Leah's head and she had managed to get into mine.

I sighed as I remembered the taste of her.

I had never understood why people thought kissing was such a big deal. It's just two mouths coming into contact. I felt more of a connection with sex. Pleasure. An ending. An act with a beginning and an end. That doesn't happen with kissing. When is it supposed to end? When do you stop? It's not instinctive; it's emotional. She was everything I had never managed to be, and when I kissed her, I realized I had been spent half a lifetime being wrong. A kiss is... intimacy, desire, trembling inside. A kiss can be more devastating than an orgasm and more dangerous than anything words can say. Because that kiss...that kiss was going to stay with me forever, I knew it as soon as I closed my eyes after our lips touched.

49

——

Leah

AXEL HADN'T STOPPED THE RECORD player, and "Can't Buy Me Love" started playing while I leaned against the railing with trembling legs and my heart in my throat.

Because I had my answer. The one I had been dodging for months.

When our lips touched, I realized the effort had been worth it. The pain. I had taken off my raincoat. I had accepted fear. I had felt. Feeling. Feeling. I saw before my eyes the way emotions achieve a balance through highs and lows, because if sorrow didn't exist, no one would have bothered to invent the word *happiness*. And that's what kissing him had been. A spark of happiness, the kind that lights up and explodes like a castle of fireworks. There had been a tickle in my stomach. The taste of that explosive night on his lips. The scent of the sea absorbed in his skin. His fingers rough on my cheeks. His eyes stripping me naked. Him. Him again. Always him.

Giving that up...was impossible.

50

Axel

I GOT UP IN A rotten mood, still mad at myself, at her, and at whatever was in front of me. I downed my coffee in one sip, grabbed my board, and took the trail to the beach.

The water was colder at that time of the year, but I was almost grateful for it. I concentrated on the waves, on dominating my own body as I rode them, on the sun rising slowly past the line of the horizon, on the sound of the waves…

And when I was exhausted in the water, arms resting over my board, the thoughts I had tried to bury came rushing back.

Her. And those lips that tasted like lime.

I closed my eyes and took a deep breath.

What the fuck had happened to me?

I got out of the water even angrier and went home. I left my board on the porch and saw Leah up and about, pouring herself a coffee in the kitchen behind the bar. I swallowed, tense. She looked at me from the corner of her eye.

"Why didn't you get me up?"

"We were up late last night."

Leah pushed a strand of hair behind her ear. "Yeah, but you always get me up."

"Not today. Any coffee left?"

"A little, I think."

"Good."

I served myself my second cup of the day and opened the fridge to find something to munch on. As I'd feared, I heard her voice behind me. And that tone...that tone told me she wasn't just going to let it go. I hadn't wanted to hear that tone.

"Axel, last night..."

"Last night was a fucking mistake." I exhaled the breath I had been holding and leaned against one of the cabinets. I looked into her eyes. I was firm. Hard. As I had to be.

"Leah, you asked me for that, for me to give you a kiss. I did it, even if now I know I shouldn't have. I guess I ought to have known you would get confused, and I don't blame you. You're having a hard time. And you...you..."

She stepped forward. "I what?"

"You're a girl, Leah."

"You know that hurts me."

"With time, you'll realize the hurt sometimes cures other things."

And she needed to cure herself of me, of whatever it was she had in her head. I wasn't really sure what she was feeling, and just as on that day years ago when I saw the heart in her day planner, I didn't want to know. There are things it's best to just ignore and let disappear. Avoid. Look away from.

It was easier like that. Much easier...

I grabbed a carton of orange juice.

"I don't believe you, Axel. I felt it. I felt you."

She stepped toward me. And every step made my stomach turn. I saw her as the girl she used to be, the one who jumped without thinking, who didn't know the word *consequences*. The passionate girl. Intense. The one who let her feelings well over because they didn't scare her. The one who might do anything. Who painted with her eyes closed and let her feelings carry her away, without analyzing every line, without knowing she was creating magic.

"I know I asked you for it. But it was real. That kiss."

"Leah, don't make things complicated," I grumbled.

"Fine, but admit it. And I'll stop."

"I'm not going to lie to you to make you happy."

I put away the OJ and slammed the door to the fridge as I thought about what a fucking mess I'd made over something so silly. I left her there and went outside.

When the fuck did I decide it was a good idea to get drunk with her? When did I give in and let my impulses carry me away? When...did it come to this? I didn't understand what was happening. How this girl, the one I'd known forever, had watched grow up, could be here asking me to admit that kiss had been real.

If Oliver found out, he'd kill me.

And what would Douglas Jones think of this shit?

When I felt the force of that question, I scowled. It was the first time I'd thought of him that way, as if he were still somehow here. I rubbed my face. I had never understood people who, when something good happened to them, acted like it was some kind of gift or disposition from their deceased loved ones or, when the opposite occurred, reprimanded themselves, imagining they had disappointed them. It was an illusion. Holding on to the hope of survival.

The half-empty glass told me that, if the situation of the first months had been hard, with her shut away and not talking, the one starting now was going to be far worse. The half-empty glass shouted to me that in some twisted way, Leah was feeling. Yes, she was feeling what she shouldn't, but that was better than the alternative: the void.

But not even that thought calmed me down when, a while later, she walked out onto the porch and looked at me like I was a fucking knight in shining armor.

I realized I had to do something drastic. Something that would cut this off at the roots.

51

Leah

AT THE BEGINNING OF THE day, I felt a knot in my stomach.

I didn't care what Axel said. I had felt it. In his look. On his lips. It had been real, very real. And I had been dreaming of a kiss from him for so long... So many nights in bed, looking at the ceiling in my room and asking myself what it would be like...

I held my breath when he came out onto the porch without looking at me. I suppressed my desire to say something, because I was starting to taste the disappointment, and I didn't expect anything more from him. I understood the situation—but still, I was surprised he was such a coward. He had always seemed so solid, so open, so brutally honest, even if that turned out to be the wrong thing.

Later on, when I grabbed a little fruit, I noticed Axel wasn't going to have lunch at the normal hour. I spent the rest of the day in my room with my headphones on listening to "Let It Be" with my eyes closed while I remembered how we had danced on the porch, how delicately he had let his hands slip down to my hips and waist, relaxed, looking at me under the stars...

And then his lips—demanding. The hoarse moan that entered

my mouth. His hot breath. The butterflies in my stomach. The soft feel of his tongue. That moment. Ours alone.

I turned over in bed and fell asleep.

When I woke up, night was falling.

Axel was in the living room, sitting at his desk looking over his work even though it was Saturday. He was dressed. Since he always went around in a bathing suit or track pants with a plain cotton T-shirt, I was surprised to find him in jeans and a printed button-down with the sleeves rolled up to his elbows.

"You going out?" I asked nervously.

"Yeah." He stood up. "Don't wait up for me. You think you can figure out dinner, or you need me to make you something before I go?"

I wanted to ask him why he was dressed that way. Or rather, who he had dressed that way for. But I was scared because I didn't want to hear the answer. I couldn't.

I watched him leave a few minutes later.

I stayed there in the middle of the room looking around the house as though I hadn't been there four months. I stared at the oldish furniture, the records Axel had left on top of the trunk the night before, the plants growing almost wild without anyone pruning them or pulling off the dead leaves...

When I could react, I decided not to have dinner.

My stomach was upset, and my feelings were pounding in my head and telling me to let them out. I took a deep breath. Over and over. Finally, from inertia, I looked for the one thing I knew how to do. I grabbed a blank canvas, put it in the middle of the room, and let myself go.

I painted. And felt. And thought. And went on painting.

In my head, I had the image I was trying to represent. I could see every line and every shadow before the brush touched the canvas. I didn't know another way to do it. I felt something. I felt it intensely until that feeling overflowed and I had to release it.

My mother told me one time that all the women in the family were like that. She told me my grandmother fell in love with a rebellious guy that her father wouldn't let her hang out with. Apparently she ran into him one day, looked into his eyes, and that was it; she knew he was her soul mate. When they forbid her to see him, she ran away from home one morning, took off with him, and returned three days later with a ring on her finger. Fortunately, it was a long and happy marriage.

She was like that. So was my mother, Rose.

She was always running off at the mouth. Saying the first thing that came into her head, whether it was good or bad. Dad used to laugh at how transparent she was and watched her tenderly while she ranted and raved walking from one side of the kitchen to the other, opening and closing cabinets with her wild hair in a bun and that energy that seemed to never give out. When he thought it had gone on long enough, he would go over and hug her from behind. Then she'd calm down. Then…Mom would close her eyes and let herself sway in his arms.

Remembering that, I grabbed another shade of gray.

The lines started coming together and gathering meaning bit by bit while the night grew darker and the clock crept toward one in the morning. I could hear nothing. I was alone, accompanied by those tangled feelings.

Then I heard the door creak...

Axel entered. I looked at him. And I hated him. Hated him...

"You're still up?" he grunted.

"Do I need to answer?"

He stumbled forward and tripped over a flowerpot, holding himself up on the sideboard. I noticed his strange smile as he came over. All I wanted was to take off running for my room. Axel's eyes were glassy from drinking, a cloudy blue, a blue that wasn't his. And his lips were red from someone else's kisses.

I was breathless, asking myself who she might be, why her and not me. I looked down at the marks on his neck.

Maybe I wanted to hurt myself. Maybe I wanted to punish myself for being unable to control my feelings. Maybe I wanted to hear it from his lips.

"What is that?" I pointed.

He rubbed his neck with that same idiotic smile. "Ah, Madison. She's wild about me."

"Did you sleep with her?"

"No, we played Parcheesi."

"Fuck you," I said, exhausted.

He came up behind me, pressing his chest into my back. One of his hands descended to my waist and pulled me into him while he bent over to whisper in my ear. "Maybe you think I'm a fucking pig, but one day you'll realize I did this for you, babe. A little favor. You don't have to thank me for it. If you thought you knew me...well, this is me; this is what I am."

"Let me go." I pushed him.

"See? Now you don't like me touching you so much. You know

what your problem is, Leah? You're stuck on the surface. You look at a present, and all you see is the shiny wrapping paper, and you don't think about how there might be something rotten inside."

I couldn't even look at him as I walked past him and slammed the door to my room so hard it reverberated through the house. I fell into the bed, sank my face into the pillow, and clenched my teeth to keep from crying. I heard that *babe* again, and ironically, for the first time, it didn't sound paternalistic on his lips. It was different, dirty. I grabbed the sheets, feeling…feeling hate and love and frustration all at once.

52

Axel

MY HEAD WAS GOING TO explode.

It had been hours since the sun had come out when I got out of bed and left my room for a coffee as if I needed it to survive. I rifled through the drawers in the small kitchen looking for an aspirin or something that would quiet the fucking drum pounding in my head that kept me from thinking clearly.

Although perhaps better...

I took a pill and sucked in a breath, remembering slightly disjointed events from the night before. I had gone to Cavvanbah, had drunk with some friends until I'd forgotten my worries, then had fucked Madison between the bar and the back room. I think she asked me if I wanted her to take me home, and I said no, I preferred to go walking.

Then, well, the whole thing got out of hand.

I gathered my courage later and knocked at her door.

Leah jerked it open and looked at me as if I were a stranger and she was waiting for me to introduce myself. When she realized I wasn't going to say anything, she turned around and went on packing her suitcase, the way she did every Sunday at the end of the month. When she finished, she zipped it up.

"Can you move? I need to go."

I stepped aside, a little confused, and Leah dragged her wheeled suitcase over to the front door. "About last night…"

"You don't need to explain it to me." She cut me off.

"I wasn't going to." *Shit. Shit shit shit.* "I just…"

"You know what? Sometimes it's better if you don't say anything."

There was a knock at the door, and before I could respond, Leah opened up anxiously, as if she wanted to get away. That irritated me, but I covered it up, smiling at Oliver, who hugged his sister before saying hi to me.

"How's it going, dude?" He clapped me on the back.

"Same as always. Want a beer?"

"Sure. You got a Victoria Bitter?"

"No. Will a Carlton Draught work?"

"Sure. How's work?"

"Wait, Oliver," Leah called to her brother, not meeting my eyes. "I told Blair I'd try to stop by her house soon…"

"Sure, we can go now." He grabbed Leah's suitcase. "Axel, I'll take a rain check on that beer. Tomorrow?"

"I'll be here." I held the door while they walked out.

Leah was wearing a dress with a blue floral print. Very short. I looked away from her legs and shut the door quickly before going out the back and grabbing my surfboard.

Only when I got back an hour later, tired and a little calmer, did I notice the painting that was still in the middle of the dining area. I shook off my wet hair and stood there in front of it.

The dark lines formed two silhouettes. In the foreground was a girl looking at herself in the mirror. Her reflection had on a dress of straight gray lines that seemed to hug her body. The other, the real figure, was in a kind of raincoat that hung to her knees.

Her two faces. Past and present looking each other in the eye.

53

Axel

IT WAS A COMPLICATED WEEK.

I wasn't there. I was behind, still kissing her, on Saturday morning, in her pained stare. I focused on trying to catch up on work and take care of some commissions, but I couldn't manage to relax. And her absence kept feeling bigger and bigger, filling the nights I spent on the porch reading alone, or the mornings watching the dawn on my surfboard in silence, or the scent of paint that started to awaken as the days passed and I missed her more and more.

It frightened me. So much that I ignored it.

54

—

Axel

FOR THE FIRST TIME IN a long time, I got to my parents' house early on Sunday. Actually, I was the first one there. My mother asked me as she was drying her hands on a rag in the kitchen, "Is everything okay? Did something happen?"

"Don't be ridiculous!" I gave her a kiss.

"I'm not! Daniel, am I being ridiculous with your son?"

My father pretended he hadn't heard her.

"For three years you've never made it on time on Sunday."

"I must have read the clock wrong. What's for lunch?"

"For you, peas. For everyone else, roast beef."

I helped my father set the table while she followed us from the kitchen to the living room, telling the story of a customer at the café who'd been diagnosed with a tumor.

"They've given him three months to live," she concluded.

"Fucking hell," my father said.

"Daniel, the phrase is *how sad*," my mother corrected him. "By the way, Galia broke her hip again; that woman has the worst luck."

"Can we stop talking about death and disaster?" I asked.

She ignored me, walked over to the plate I'd just set on the table, arranged it properly (one more inch to the left), and wrinkled her nose.

"How long has it been since you've gone to the doctor, Axel?"

"I go as little as I can. I'm trying to set a record."

My father pursed his lips, trying not to laugh.

"How can you joke about something like that? You know how many times your brother goes into town for a checkup?" She crossed her arms.

"No idea. Every time a mosquito bites him?"

"Every three months. You should learn from him."

"If I follow his example, I'll die from boredom."

At that moment, the doorbell rang, and I felt something unknown in my chest. But it wasn't her, it was Justin, Emily, and my nephews shouting and making noise like a herd of elephants. I mussed their hair before taking the plastic pistol Max held in his hand.

"Give it back!" he said.

"You'll have to catch me first!"

I took off running. My mother shouted something like "Careful with the vase," but neither of us was really listening when we took off down the hallway at top speed. Max cornered me and asked Connor to help him get the pistol back. I held it high and they tried to climb my body like monkeys to get it.

"Don't tickle me, you little snot-noses!"

"We're not snot-noses!" Connor said.

"Of course you are. What do you think you have in your nose? Snot."

"Mamaaaaa!" Max shouted while continuing to jump and try to get the pistol.

Emily came into the room and started laughing. "I wouldn't know which of the three of you was the bigger baby."

"Axel, obviously," Justin answered, turning around.

"So who's the baldest one of all?" I asked, giggling.

"Son of a…"

"Shhh!" Emily said.

Her children were perplexed when their father, normally so proper, leapt at me and threw me onto the bed. That was my gift. I was the only person on earth capable of driving my older brother nuts. The boys and Emily disappeared when my mother announced that she'd brought candy.

"Fucking dickhead!" Justin punched me on the shoulder and I started laughing.

"What the fuck's wrong with you? Did you not get your regulation fuck in this week?"

"Very funny." He pulled away from me and lay on his back. "Axel, do you think our parents will ever retire, or is it all just hot air?"

"I don't know; why, what's up?"

"I took the job at the café because they were thinking they'd retire soon, but years have passed. I'm starting to think they only hired me so I wouldn't find another job and leave."

"That sounds like something Mom would do."

"I think I'm going to talk to them. I'm supposed to be running the café, but they still treat me like an employee. I'm going to give them an ultimatum. Either they do what they promised or I try to set up something of my own. I want to do things my way without Mom calling the shots. Will you take my side if things get ugly?"

"Of course, I'm with you."

He breathed a sigh of relief I didn't understand, because Justin's never needed my approval or support. I punched him in the shoulder to relieve the tension.

The doorbell rang again.

"I'll go," Emily shouted.

We got up and walked to the living room. I took a deep breath when I saw Leah at the end of the hall.

Fuck, what is going on with me?

I greeted her as always, with a kiss on the cheek, and the usual racket started up. Plates right and left, my mother examining Oliver to be sure he hadn't gotten some infectious disease during his weeks in Sydney, Emily ordering the twins to go wash their hands, my father softly humming the popular song of the moment.

I sat down in my usual spot, next to Leah.

"You want peas?" I offered her the dish.

She shook her head without looking at me.

"Max, don't grab the food with your hands!" Justin shouted. "Damn it! Emily, pass me a napkin. Or two."

"How's everything going, dude?" My father looked at Oliver.

"Good, it was a good week, actually, right, Leah?"

She nodded and took a sip of water.

"Yeah? Any news?"

"Well, we went out to surf a little in the afternoon. I don't remember when we last did it together." Oliver looked at Leah with pride. "She got an A on her last exam, didn't she tell you?"

"That's great, honey!" my mother exclaimed.

"Thanks," Leah said softly.

"You want any more sides?"

"No." Leah got up. "I'll be right back."

I did the same thirty seconds later. "I'm going for dressing," I said.

I walked through the kitchen to the bathroom. I waited in front of the door until she opened it, then took a step forward, got inside, and closed it behind me. Leah looked surprised, then uncomfortable, when she found herself trapped.

"Now you don't talk to me? You want everyone to realize something's up?"

"Oh, is something up? I thought you made it clear that it was nothing."

"Don't fuck with me. You know what I mean."

"I don't, but they'll start thinking something if they find you in here."

I was mad. But I didn't know if it was at her or at myself. "Leah, don't make my life complicated..."

She got tense. Her eyes stared through me.

And she had a deadly look... Deadly, captivating, and electrifying.

"I won't. From now on, I won't make anything complicated. I won't bother you; you can rest easy. Let me out, Axel. I want to go back to the table."

I stepped away, relieved and disappointed at the same time. As if this were possible. As if it made sense...

Leah exited like a hurricane. I washed my hands and passed

through the kitchen to get my dressing. In the dining room, my mother was upbraiding Justin for something to do with purveyors.

"I promise you, it's under control," he said.

"No one else would say so," Mom said, clicking her tongue.

"The boy's doing all he can, Georgia," Dad intervened.

"Why are you calling your son *boy*?"

"He's only thirty-five."

"The way he manages things, I'd have thought he was younger."

I don't know why I reacted. If it was because I saw Emily biting her tongue to keep from defending her husband or because the girl beside me had pissed me off a few minutes before, but I interrupted my mother.

"Let my brother be." I sounded dry, brusque.

Everyone looked at me. Everyone. Even Oliver raised an eyebrow in surprise from the other side of the table. My mother looked perplexed, but she ended the meal in silence. When she got up for dessert, I followed her. I watched her lean on the counter before she started sobbing.

"Shit, Mom, I didn't…"

"It's not your fault, dear."

I hugged her and waited for her quietly while she wiped away her tears with the back of her hand. She grabbed the pile of dirty plates she had brought and set them in the sink.

"What's with you?"

"It's not the time, dear."

She passed me the cheesecake and a knife, and asked me to serve it, and I left her alone with those thoughts she still didn't want to share. My brother looked at me gratefully from the other side of the table. I started cutting the cake into pieces. I gave Leah the biggest one, even though I was pissed at her. Or at myself for how I was acting with her. Who knows.

Anyway, when I left that afternoon after saying goodbye to everyone and was walking through Byron Bay away from my parents' place, I found myself waylaid by all the problems brought together between those walls with all the people gathered there. Emily, suppressing her reply. My brother, frustrated and insecure. My mother and her demons. My father and his conformism. Oliver and the burden he was dealing with. And Leah...

Maybe I was too used to the easy life.

Maybe I had spent half my life avoiding problems.

Maybe being alone looking at your belly button was the easiest way of surviving.

55

Leah

"YOU WANT US TO BUY some takeout for dinner?"

"I'm stuffed," I told Oliver.

"Too stuffed for ice cream?"

"That's different." I smiled at him.

I grabbed my jean jacket before we left, because it was getting chilly on those winter nights. I walked down the poorly lit streets with my brother, and I felt good. I felt like me. Like before. I felt the same when we sat on a patio close to the water and I ordered a chocolate pistachio ice cream.

In theory, it should have been the other way around...

I should have felt bad for what happened with Axel. Because he had disappointed me and disappointment always tastes bitter and is hard to swallow, but when you do, and you digest it, you can face up to things more easily, with a cooler head. Probably he wasn't even aware of why I was upset. And realizing that in some way I was being faithful to myself made me feel stronger.

"I don't want you to go," I said. And it was true. For the first time, I wasn't indifferent about who was at my side. I wanted my brother close to me.

"Three weeks will pass in no time."

"Yeah, I can tell you're dying for it to..." I looked at him, amused, and licked my spoonful of ice cream.

"Why do you say that?"

"Uhh, what's her name, Bega?"

My brother nodded, slightly tense. "Don't get ahead of yourself. It's complicated."

"I can imagine..."

"And you?"

"Me?"

"What happened to that guy you were going out with a while back?"

"Kevin? Nothing. He's a friend. He's with Blair now."

"Wow. Are you cool with that?"

"Yeah, I was never that into him."

My brother arched his brows. "Wasn't he your boyfriend?"

I hesitated with my spoon halfway to my mouth. I ended up sticking it back into the bowl and leaning back. "The problem is I like another guy more."

"You never told me..."

"We didn't used to talk much."

Oliver was thoughtful for a few seconds.

It was true. We had always loved each other. He had been the perfect brother, protective, gentle, and flexible when he needed to be. I had idolized him as long as I could remember, and I loved being around him, but the ten years dividing us had always been an issue. We had never talked about this kind of thing because before I had friends to empty my heart to and it would never have even occurred to me to bring those issues up with him. We just joked and had good times with our family when he came home to eat or stay with me for a while in Dad's studio.

"So...another guy," he continued.

"Yeah, but he's kind of out of my reach."

"That means he's not the right one."

"Why do you say that?"

"Because you're special. And I'm not saying that because you're my sister, even if that's a point in your favor." He leaned forward. "I'm saying it because it's true. You're the kind of girl that would make a guy lose his mind."

I picked my ice cream back up without much enthusiasm. "I doubt that's going to ever happen with this guy."

"Then forget him, because if he can't see how amazing you are, he's an idiot." Oliver drummed his fingers on the table. "Did you ever talk about it with Mom?"

I grinned remembering, remembering her...

It was the first time I ever smiled as I did so.

"You can't hide anything from Mom," Leah said.

56

Leah

THE YARD AT HOME WAS decorated with garlands between the branches of the trees that lit up the rectangular wooden table. It was my seventeenth birthday. I had already celebrated with my friends the week before, but Mom wanted to do something with just the family and the Nguyens, and she invited them over for dinner.

They had already seen each other that afternoon, but when they showed up, there were hugs and kisses before they went to the kitchen to get the dishes ready. I stayed in the yard because Emily came with a smile to hand me a present from her and Justin. I unwrapped it quickly, tearing the paper. It was several books about drawing. Precious. Perfect.

"Thanks, Emily!" I hugged her.

"Hey, I picked them!" Justin complained.

I hugged him too.

"Let the king through," Axel said boastfully. "Now it's time for her real present."

Oliver rolled his eyes next to him. "I still don't know why I'm your friend."

"Here." Axel handed me an envelope. No wrapping.

I turned it around. On the back was a drawing of his under the message *Happy birthday, Leah*: a girl with a baby face and long blond hair painting on a canvas, her clothes stained with colored paint. Me.

"Go on, open it. The gift is inside."

I couldn't stop looking at the drawing. There was something intimate in the idea of his fingers drawing me, those long masculine fingers I had drooled over so many times. That he had made every line thinking just about me...

"Leah, either you do it or I will."

I looked up at him nervously.

"Yeah, sorry." I opened it. And for the first time, I did so slowly, not wanting to ruin the paper, wanting to keep the drawing, the one I would store in my wallet for so long, looking at it until it was tattered. "They're...concert tickets! I can't believe it!" I jumped when I saw the logo of a band I had been following for months. "Thank you, thank you, thank you!"

"What's this I just heard? A concert?" My mother put the plates down on the table. "Where?"

"In Brisbane..." I whispered.

"And you think you're going by yourself?"

"No, there's two tickets, I'll give one to Blair."

"At what time?" she asked, worried.

"I'll take them, Rose." My father gave her a kiss on the cheek, and she calmed down right away, closing her eyes and nodding.

I smiled when Dad winked at me.

We sat down at the table. Daniel opened a bottle of wine and told us a story about something that had happened that morning at the café. My birthday dinner was calm but exciting. Emily and Justin put the twins down in my parents' bed until it was time to go. They were dead tired after spending the evening running all over.

My mother brought out a cake and everyone sang "Happy Birthday" in chorus. She put it down in front of me, with that smile of hers so full of pride that made me feel so fortunate and loved.

And then I made the wish that I would remember for a long time. I wished for a kiss from Axel while I blew hard on the candles.

"The timer's already running down," my father said, putting his camera on the porch railing. "Quick! One, two, three, cheese!"

The flash clicked and the moment was immortalized.

But the one after was only recorded in my memory.

"So you're going to go to the concert with your friend." Axel licked his spoon after a bite of cake. "You're not going out with that guy anymore?"

"What guy?" Daniel furrowed his brows.

"His name's Kevin Jax, isn't it, honey?"

"We're not together anymore," I said.

"The boy who cut the grass? What happened? Did he mess up and leave one blade of grass longer than the rest, and his parents grounded him?" Axel joked.

"Shut that mouth of yours," Georgia said and took the bottle from him. "Don't pay any attention to him; he's had too much wine. You're still young; you'll meet someone better soon enough."

"What she needs to do is study and forget about boyfriends," Oliver added while getting up and helping my father with the dishes.

I hated everyone talking about me as if I were a little girl and they had a right to say what they wanted about my life.

In the background, I could hear the Beatles playing softly. I imagined the record spinning and spinning...

"Don't pay any attention to your brother." Axel's eyes were gleaming. "What you need to do is have fun. Study too, sure. But the rest of the time, go out, meet boys, have se..." He bit his tongue. "Have fun with them, and don't limit yourself or get tied down."

"What's wrong with being tied down?" Justin asked.

"Well, it's like it sounds; you're tied."

Axel and Justin spent the next twenty minutes arguing, despite Georgia's attempts to make peace. I looked at him under the light of the garlands on that summer night: the five o'clock shadow on his square jawline, and his hair, shaggier than usual, the tips of it almost brushing his ears.

When everyone left, I went up to my room, put on my pajamas, lay in bed, and looked at the envelope with the concert tickets Axel had given me. I slid my fingers over the drawing, imagined him at his desk composing it, his desk with all the junk all over it...

"Can I come in?" Mom was calling at the door.

"Of course. Welcome." I left the envelope on the nightstand.

"Did you have fun?" She tucked back in the colored sheet that I always shrugged off halfway through the night. Then she sat on the edge of the bed.

"Yeah, thanks, Mom. It was wonderful."

"I came to give you something…"

"But you already did."

"A different kind of gift, Leah. Advice." She brushed a bit of hair out of my face. "Give Axel time, dear."

"What do you mean?"

"You know. In life, everything has its moment; you understand that, don't you?"

"Mom, I don't know what you're…"

"Leah, I'm not expecting us to talk about this like I was one of your friends. I'm just giving you advice because I don't want you to suffer. I know you. And I know how you feel. We're more alike than you realize, okay? Maybe you don't realize it, but Axel is…complicated. And you're very impatient. It's not a good combination."

"It's fine. He'll never look at me the way I want."

"Don't blame him for that, Leah. You're still a girl…" Mom had the prettiest, sweetest smile in the world. "My little princess… every time I look at you, the only thing I can think is *How is it possible that seventeen years have passed since you were an adorable little ball of joy?*" Her eyes were damp. She was like that, so emotional, so fragile… "Rest, honey. Tomorrow we can do something together if we get up early enough, okay?"

I nodded and she leaned over to give me a kiss before putting out the light.

July

—

(WINTER)

57

Axel

LEAH RODE HER BIKE HOME from school on Monday. Oliver had left a day late. That same morning, he'd come by the house to drop off his sister's suitcase. We hugged goodbye. I didn't want to think of anything while I clapped him on the back. Not of her, not of anything that had happened in the past month.

"Can I help you with that?" I offered to take her backpack on the porch, but Leah shook her head and came in. I followed her to the kitchen. "Don't greet me with such enthusiasm; confetti might start raining down from the ceiling."

"Sorry. Hi." She grabbed one of the instant soups my mother had left and started reading the instructions, leaning on the counter. She was wearing one of those T-shirts that tie behind the neck and are so short they leave your belly button visible. I looked away and cleared my throat.

"I already made lunch."

"Thanks, but I want soup."

"I didn't even tell you what it is."

"Yeah but this is what I want most."

Our eyes drilled into each other.

"As you wish." I opened the fridge, grabbed my lunch, and went to the living room.

We didn't speak anymore.

Not then, not on Tuesday, not on Wednesday.

At first, I tried to bring up some topic of conversation when we got lost in the waves at dawn. Back at home, she'd grab an apple from the fridge, put it in her backpack, and go off on her bike to school.

I couldn't decide whether to demand an explanation or let it go, because for the first time in ages, Leah seemed whole, awake. I wasn't sure what that meant, but the rest of the time, she was focused on her things.

She did her homework in the early afternoon, sometimes next to me on the desk, sometimes sitting on the living room floor or lying in bed. Then she'd kill time with her headphones on or painting. She painted for herself, in a notebook she often kept under her arm, always within reach, as though she were afraid of leaving it out and having someone find it.

That fucked me up.

It fucked me up that she was denying me her magic, the feelings she was portraying, the secrets in her mind. I knew I didn't have a right to be bothered, but I couldn't keep a handle on my resentment. Selfishly, I wanted things to be like before, but they never could be because she shed her skin before my eyes every month, growing and choosing her own path.

When Friday came, I was so frustrated I couldn't even concentrate on the book I was reading as the crickets chanted through the night.

Leah came out onto the porch. She was wearing a very simple light blue dress that revealed each and every curve of her body, along with colorful sandals that matched her earrings. She had on lipstick and black eyeshadow. I don't think I'd ever seen her like that, so…different, so…womanly. Or I hadn't noticed that side of her before. And damn the moment that I did, because there was something addictive there, that mystery, those emotions, that unpredictable nature. Her. "I'm going out with Blair. I won't be late."

"Hey, wait up." I stood before she could turn. "Why didn't you tell me earlier? Didn't it occur to you I might want to go out for a while?"

"Who's stopping you?" she replied.

"I thought you'd be here."

"If memory serves me, that didn't seem to be a problem for you last week."

"Leah." I grabbed her arm and stared into her eyes. "Don't try me. You live under my roof, so before you do something, tell me. Is someone picking you up?"

"No, I'm walking."

"No, you're not."

"I feel like taking a walk."

"Forget it. I'll drive you."

I watched her bite her tongue while I went for my keys. I didn't care if it hurt her that I treated her like a child, because that's what she was, in the end. She was nineteen fucking years old. I repeated that to myself as often as I could, but I don't know if that was some kind of reproach against her or a reminder to myself.

Neither of us said a word on the way to Byron Bay. I drove to a large two-story house near the beach. I stopped in front of it. Music was coming from inside, and I don't know why, I had the urge to step on the gas and take her far away so we could be alone. To spend that night somewhere walking on the sand, or sitting on our porch, listening to music, talking, dancing, painting, or sharing the moment in silence.

I clutched the steering wheel. "What time should I pick you up?"

"You don't need to, thanks."

I locked the door before Leah could open it. She turned toward me with knitted brows and a tense mouth in a horizontal line. A look of defiance...

"I don't care if you stay here till the crack of dawn. That's fine, have a ball. But tell me a fucking time. And I'll be here at that time, waiting at the door. And you better be too. Have I explained myself?"

"I can't have a friend bring me...?"

"No, not unless you want me to come in, meet everyone, and talk to them about how pissed I'd be if any of them gets the idea to drink and then let you get in the car with them. And believe me, they don't want to see me pissed off. Anyway, I suspect you don't like the idea of me presenting myself as your personal babysitter, so let's make things easy, Leah."

"Three," she said.

"Done. I'll be here. Have fun."

I don't know if she heard me before she slammed the door.

I stopped by the sea before driving awhile longer. I could have gone home, but I left my sandals in the car and walked down a path to the beach. I heard the roaring of the waves close by. I lay down in the sand, my hands folded behind my head, and observed the stars scattered across the sky.

And I thought of her. Of me. Everything.

58

Leah

THERE WERE LOTS OF PEOPLE in the house and music playing in the background. The voices coming from the living room shook me a bit. I stopped at the door, trying to decide whether to go in. I knew some of the guests from school, from the year I failed and was now repeating.

I felt the urge to turn around and run after Axel's car. My mouth was dry. I had told Blair I'd come to the party because a part of me wanted to be normal again, do the things I used to do, show that I was the same girl as always. But my heart was pounding out of my chest...

"Leah? You're here. Blair told me you were coming." Kevin Jax smiled at me from the other side of the threshold.

"Hey." I had a knot in my throat.

"Come on, I'll get you a drink."

"No. I better not." I was shaking.

"Not even a soda? Something without alcohol?"

"Yeah, that'll work," I said.

My anxiety was like an uncontrollable insect living inside me.

It could go weeks without appearing. According to the psychologist my brother took me to the year before, that was common. Lots of people suffered brief attacks of it in their day-to-day lives, even those who hadn't experienced any trauma. Anxiety could stay there sleeping in a corner and awaken without warning, stretch its arms and legs, and make even saying something coherent turn into an insurmountable task.

I followed Kevin to the kitchen, which was full of half-empty bottles and plastic cups. This was the boy who had given me my first kiss and to whom I had given my virginity two years later. But still, I didn't feel anything. Not even a slight tug in my stomach. I took a sip of the soda he handed me.

"Thanks. Is Blair here yet?"

"Yeah, she's in the living room. Speaking of...I wanted to talk to you about something. I wanted to be sure us hanging out isn't a problem for you. I know you've had a tough time and I don't want to add to that..."

I restrained my desire to hug him.

Kevin, with his sincere smile and good humor. Kevin, so loyal, so ready to put himself in someone else's shoes. I remember how honest he was when I confessed I was in love with someone else and I didn't want to hurt him. He nodded, he understood, and after a few tense weeks while he got himself together, he came back into my life as though nothing had happened, the same friend as always.

"I'm really happy you two are together." I exhaled the breath I'd been holding in.

"Thanks, Leah."

"You want to go to the living room?"

There were a few people standing, but most were on the two long sofas. Blair got up and ran toward me. We hugged. Then she introduced me to a couple of guys I didn't know and made a space for me to sit down. Nervous, I gave her a sip of my drink.

"Long time, no see," Sam said.

"Yeah, I've been... I don't go out much."

"You don't have to explain yourself." Maya nudged Sam with her elbow.

I slipped a lock of hair behind my ear and managed to say, "No worries. It's fine."

Blair squeezed my hand. That calmed me down.

No one paid me any more mind, so I relaxed and tried to enjoy the evening, the trivial conversations and that feeling of not thinking of anything deep or important, just hanging out with people. I finished my soft drink, taking little sips, and when some people started to play a drinking game, kind of like Truth or Dare, where you had to either answer a question or take a shot and strip off a piece of clothing, I opted out, staying close to Blair.

"You sure you don't want to play, Leah?"

I shook my head and Sam shrugged.

"Fine. We're going to get started. Maya, have you ever been in a three-way?"

She blushed.

"Drink and strip."

Blair asked me if I wanted to take a walk and get some fresh air. I said yes, and we stepped out on to the porch. The night wind was pleasantly cool.

"I'm glad you decided to come. How does it feel to be here?"

"Good. It's all...like things were before."

"Some things, anyway. How is it with Axel?"

"Not so great, honestly."

"You want to talk about it?"

I pulled a leaf from a creeping vine on the wall and started to tear it into tiny pieces the wind carried away. I ended up telling her everything that had happened two weeks ago. I talked to her about the kiss, the next night, the meal at the Nguyens' house, and how hard the week had been without us talking to each other. And how the situation hurt me, but... Axel had disappointed me. I wasn't mad; I was disappointed. That was worse.

"So what do you think you're going to do?" Blair rubbed my arm. I watched her, the way her hand comforted me.

"I don't know. I never do when it has to do with him."

"You know what? This reminds me of the old days. Talking about Axel."

"God, I must be unbearable." I laughed.

Blair did the same, and we cracked up for a long time for no apparent reason until my stomach started to hurt.

"It's...it's amazing," I said, trying to regain composure. "I've spent half my life anchored to the same spot. Him, always him. If only I knew how to avoid him and not feel...feel everything, when it comes to Axel." I turned serious. "What do you think?"

"Unfortunately, I think that even if years have passed since you fell in love with him, for Axel, it's been different. They are two different perceptions of the same story, Leah. It could be that up to a few months ago, he never even would have thought of looking at you in that way, and you're pushing too hard."

"I know. But at least I got something out of it."

I didn't need to say out loud that I wanted to continue. At that moment, I knew what path I was taking. I was aware of how hard it would be and that feeling does not only imply doing it in the good things; it can also refer to bad things, to sorrow, but still, I was going to try.

"Tell me about those dates with Kevin."

Blair's eyes twinkled. "The best ever. Remember when I used to think no one could top Frank? I have to admit, the bar wasn't that high ever since I said I'd take him out and he ordered half the menu, but still, with Kevin, everything...everything's been perfect. I don't know how I never noticed him. Why are we so blind sometimes?"

"I think we often just don't know how to look."

"And it's funny, because you miss the most obvious things, the stuff that's right in front of your nose every day. I hope everything works out with Kevin; sometimes I get scared..."

"Why?" I asked.

"Because he could hurt me."

I nodded, with a knot in my throat. It was something instinctive, avoiding pain. "Everything will be great, you'll see. By the way, what time is it?"

"A quarter after three."

"Shit!"

"What's up?"

I didn't answer before going back inside and taking the stairs two by two down to the first floor. Just as I'd feared, Axel was there in the middle of the dining room with his arms crossed, waiting for me.

"What are you doing in here?" I hissed angrily, but he didn't take the bait.

"Do I need to answer?" He turned to my friend. "Hi, Blair. Nice to see you again."

"Same."

"I'll call you tomorrow." I waved goodbye to her. Then I waved to everyone else and followed Axel to the car, walking quickly. I didn't open my mouth until we were far away.

"Are you trying to embarrass me?"

"It's not my fault if you feel that way."

"It would be nice if you hadn't gone in like that."

"Is there a right way to do it?"

"Yeah, one that doesn't say you're acting like my big brother."

Axel stopped at a red light. "I'm glad you're starting to get it, Leah."

And I would, if his face didn't say something very different.

I know he was waiting for a reply, but I also know nothing bothers Axel more than silence, so I bit my tongue and looked out the window at the houses we left behind. I heard him huff a few times, but I ignored it.

When we got home, I went to my room.

59

Axel

THERE ARE SOME THINGS IN life you see coming and others that catch you by surprise. I had no idea that Saturday would be the day when I would be doomed to say words…words that I couldn't erase.

I got up early, as always.

I didn't call to Leah before going to the beach. I guess I was tired of her *no*s and her ugly expressions, her silence, her complications. I wanted to go back to that simple life I'd struggled so hard to make a reality.

Hours later, I saw her eating one of those packets of soup.

We spent the whole day avoiding each other. But I couldn't get her out of my head, I couldn't…

It was almost night when I decided the time had come to resolve this issue, because it was getting out of hand. When she went out onto the porch, I got up from my desk, leaving a commission half-done, and followed her.

"Are you going to stay mad forever? I hope you realize that you don't have any reason to and that you're acting like a fucking little girl."

That pushed her button. Leah tensed up. "You don't get a damn thing."

"Really? Surprise me then."

"You think I'm mad because I thought that kiss meant something and the next night you banged some other chick, right? But it's not that, Axel. It isn't."

I tried to process, to understand her...but I couldn't. Leah kept her each and every thought under lock and key. Or else I had just gotten stuck on the surface and couldn't see any further.

"Then what the fuck is it about?"

She leaned one hand on the railing. "What it's about is, you're a coward, Axel. And that pisses me off. Pisses me off and disappoints me." She looked up. "I've...I've always been in love with you. And it's stupid for the two of us to keep acting like we don't know."

"Leah, shit, don't say that..."

"But I fell in love with a guy I thought I knew. A brave guy, sincere, even if that meant being politically incorrect. A guy who never held back. Everything about you fascinated me, how you live for the day..." She licked her dry lips and I looked down at them. "I'm not going to say it didn't hurt me that you slept with someone else, but I can bear that. I have before. What pissed me off was how you acted like a coward, because that kiss meant something, and you thought you could nip the problem in the bud just like that. That's what I can't forgive you for."

I stayed rooted to the spot while she walked inside.

Fuck. I had gooseflesh. A part of me wanted to go back in time and not ask the damned question, because leaving the windows closed was almost better than letting her strip me bare that way, so viscerally, so sharply.

I walked down the porch steps, running away.

I walked on the beach, away from that house that was turning into a place almost more hers, more ours, than mine. With every month that passed, more and more stones seemed to be bearing down on the roof.

I don't know how long I walked. Emotionally blocked. Angry. Repeating her words over and over: *I've always been in love with you. You're a coward.* That reproach had struck my soul. Because Leah was right. I had always thought you have to face things head-on. But with her, I couldn't.

Night had fallen when I returned.

Leah had her back turned, facing the microwave, listening to music. I walked over to her, and when I was right behind her, I grabbed her around the waist and pulled her into me. She flinched. I took off her headphones and bent down, grazing her earlobe. I felt her quiver and swallow. I was tense. Very tense. I smelled the soft aroma of her skin.

"Don't move." I held on to her. "You're right. It did mean something. It meant that I got hard and I had to stop myself from tearing off your clothes then and there. It meant that I had to take a cold shower and go the whole night without sleeping. It meant that I didn't know a kiss could be like that, and since then, I can't stop looking at your mouth. But Leah, it can't happen. It can never happen, understand, babe? I can't stand being here, with you so far away like this. Please don't make it so hard."

I let her go. Because it was that or ignore everything I had just said and throw myself on her and kiss her all over… I took a deep breath and walked off, shutting the door to my room. I fell onto my bed, my heart in my throat. What had I just done? I was like her. I'd leapt without thinking. Without looking first to see if there were sharp rocks or water at the bottom.

So it is. In life there are some things you see coming and others that catch you by surprise, and those words I'd just said in her ear…those words would be my perdition.

An hour later, she knocked on my door. I told her to come in, and she opened it slowly. Our eyes met for a few seconds, and it was like an electric charge had shot through the room. Something new. Something throbbing.

"I was coming… I made tacos. I thought we could have dinner together."

I smiled and stood up.

I looked at her from above and murmured a soft *thanks* as I walked past her to the kitchen, which smelled of spices and grilled vegetables. I put the food on plates, turned on the record player, and followed her to the porch.

That's how Leah and I became friends again.

60

Leah

ONE DAY I THOUGHT, SINCE the red tube was open, I should start using it before it dried up. So I grabbed the alizarin crimson. It was an intense blue-red color, a dark tone like the wax seals of letters.

I put a little oil paint on my palette and looked askance at the other colors, all intact, all pretty, with thousands of possible combinations...

I grabbed a soft-haired brush, and when I touched the surface with its tip, I let myself go, not thinking about anything. Two diffuse profiles against the shadows. Two faces breathing the same air. Two pairs of red lips almost touching, but not. And a kiss, almost, frozen in time.

61

Axel

THAT AFTERNOON, I'D HAD TO go to a nearby town to talk to a few clients. When I got home, Leah was gathering her paints. She looked at me from the other end of the living room and grabbed the piece she was working on.

I left my notebooks on the desk. "Hey, what are you doing? Can I see?"

She stopped me short with her words. "No. This... No. It's mine," she said.

Damned Leah. She knew I was a curious cat and couldn't stand not knowing everything. I stood there, fascinated, staring at her face. She had a spot of paint on her right cheek, and it was all I could do not to wipe it off with my fingers. I went to the kitchen, telling her I would make dinner.

It had been a week since we'd made peace.

Leah hadn't brought the kiss back up, but that didn't make me think about it any less. It was complicated because she kept getting prettier, fuller, more herself. Either I was seeing things, or every day she wore shorter shirts and dresses that made me want her even more. Plus, I wasn't used to holding back, to restraining myself. I had gone through life doing whatever I wanted without overthinking it. Hitting the brakes was frustrating.

Necessary, but frustrating.

I relaxed while I made dinner, but I couldn't get the thought out of my head of what she'd been painting in my absence. I liked knowing she was feeling the need to express herself. I envied it. She had so much to show the world, and I so little. Her emotions ran over, and it was hard for me to even find mine, and then I kept them locked away.

"What are you making?" she asked.

"Fried tofu and tomato sauce."

"I guess it could be worse," she joked.

She took out the plates, and I served the food before we went out on the porch. She said it was good, and we didn't talk much more while we ate. Then I made tea, put on music, and lay in the hammock with a book in my hand.

Leah broke the silence after a while.

"What are you reading?" she asked.

"An essay. About death." I suppressed the impulse to get up, kneel beside her, and embrace her. That's what I would have done during the first two or three months. Now the idea seemed so distant, almost impossible.

"Why are you reading that?"

"Why not?"

"It's not something people like to talk about…"

"Don't you think that's a mistake?" I'd been thinking about it for months…

"I don't know."

I put the book aside. "I've been reading about death in other cultures. And I'm wondering if the way we face things is a matter of how we're raised or if it's instinctive, inborn. You know what I mean?"

Leah shook her head.

"I'm talking about the different ways human beings have of channeling and feeling the same thing. Like some aboriginal people in Australia put dead bodies on a platform, cover them with leaves and branches, and leave them there. When they have an important celebration, they rub the liquid from the corpse on themselves, or they paint the bones red and use them to commemorate the people they love. In Madagascar, the Malgache take bodies out of the grave every seven years, wrap them in cloth, and dance with them. Then they spend a while talking to them or touching them before they bury them for another seven years."

"Jesus, Axel, that's gross." Leah furrowed her nose.

"That's where I have questions. Why does something that seems horrible to us comfort other people and make them feel better? I don't know, imagine if since we were children someone taught us that loss isn't sad, it's just a goodbye, something natural that we have to talk through."

"Death is natural," she agreed.

"But we don't see it that way. We don't accept it."

Leah's lower lip trembled. "Because it hurts. And it's scary."

"I know, but it's always worse to ignore something and pretend it doesn't exist. Especially when it's something we're all going to experience, right?" I got up and crouched down next to her. I held her chin in my fingers. "Are you aware that I'm going to die?"

"Don't say that, Axel."

"What? The most obvious reality there is?"

"I can't even think about it."

I opened my mouth, ready to go on tensing the cord, but when I saw her face, I stopped. I got lost in her frightened eyes, and couldn't keep myself from bending over and kissing her forehead. Then I pulled away quickly. I went back to the hammock and opened my book again. I stayed there reading until late, after Leah had said good night, thinking, thinking about everything...

It was so strange, so illogical that for years, they taught us math, literature, biology, but not how to deal with something as inevitable as death...

62

Leah

I HAD TAKEN A DECISION, a path.

To turn back. Find myself. Get myself together.

It was a Friday afternoon when I opened the kitchen cabinet and looked through the bags there until I found a heart-shaped sucker. They had been my weakness for years. My father always bought them for me. I took off the wrapper and looked at it slowly, focusing on its intense color. I put it in my mouth and savored the strawberry flavor. I closed my eyes. Then I saw him, Dad, always smiling and in a good mood.

Memories are like that. Sparks. They come when you least expect them. *Sssss.* The slightly harsh feel against your cheek, so similar to that sweater your grandmother knitted for you from thick wool, with a Christmas design in the middle. *Shhhh.* That word your father used to address you and you alone, no one else, that *Sweetie, give me a good night kiss. Shhhh.* The sun. Light. A certain light. The light of midday, of Sundays on the porch at home right after lunch, when it seemed like the beams were lazy and hardly heated you up. *Shhhh.* The scent of fabric softener, the soft scent of roses, the feeling of bringing clean clothes to your face and inhaling slowly. *Shhhh.* The hoarse sound of familiar laughter. *Sssss.* An entire life in images, textures, scents, and flavors passes before your eyes in a second.

63

Leah

I READIED MY SUITCASE ON Saturday afternoon to have it ready when Oliver came to pick me up the next day. When I finished, I put on the clothes I had left out, a peach dress and flat sandals with brown straps. I grabbed a matching bag and walked out. Axel was in the living room. He was wearing jeans and a ridiculous-looking shirt that would have looked awful on any other guy, but simply made him stand out more.

His eyes traveled over me, and I shivered.

"I see you're ready. Let's go."

Axel had said we should go out for dinner and walk around for once. It was all I could do not to jump for joy and throw myself in his arms, but I managed it. Because he had asked me to. Begged me, actually. I couldn't get out of my head his whispering to me that it couldn't be, and I wanted to shout to him that it wasn't true, but I couldn't bear the idea of us being upset and distant with each other again. I accepted that he had admitted there was something there, even if that made things harder.

We went to a nearby town, twenty minutes away by car, and had dinner at a restaurant Axel liked that served vegetarian dishes of all kinds. We ordered a few things to pick at and then chose a few more dishes to share. He looked at me as he chewed.

He was so handsome under that orange light.

And I was so fucking hooked on him...

"I was thinking one day we could go to Brisbane."

"What for?" I took a sip of water.

"I don't know, just to go around, check some places out, see the university, maybe."

I put aside my glass and a silence enveloped us. "I don't even know if I want to go."

"Why not? Spit it out."

"I...I've just got the feeling I'm starting to breathe again. And I'm terrified of drowning, of being there all alone and having to meet new people. I don't know if I can. A year ago, that was my life's dream, but now...I'm scared."

"But fear isn't a bad thing, Leah."

"I don't want to talk about this today."

Axel leaned back in his chair. "Okay. What do you want to do?"

"Just be normal, for one night. Without thinking about the future. I don't want to talk about death either, or feelings or anything related to painting."

He leaned his head to one side without taking his eyes off me.

"Just be here in this instant. Isn't that what you told me to do a long time ago?"

"Yeah. Let's go have fun."

We left some cash on the table and went outside. We walked through poorly lit streets to an area near the coast where most of the cocktail bars were. We picked one with low tables and colored cushions. I ordered a piña colada and Axel a glass of rum.

"I came here a few times with Oliver."

"I like the place." I smiled. "I like this."

Axel didn't take his eyes off me until the waiter arrived and served our drinks. I grabbed mine and relaxed, talking with him, looking at him, wanting to be closer, to have him, to take another moment of his…

"Lost Stars" played in the background.

"Can I ask you a question?" I said.

"Knowing you, I should be prudent and say, 'It depends.'"

"It's nothing really personal."

"Okay. Shoot."

"What did you used to do when you lived alone?"

"Before?" He shrugged. "Same as now. Just without you."

Something about his tone in those last words gave me goose-flesh. I put my straw in my mouth and took a sip of my drink. I tried not to blush. "Was it better?"

"No." He sounded certain.

"Will you miss me when I go?"

"Leah…" He sounded irritated.

"Come on. Be honest."

Axel exhaled a breath. "I even miss you on the weeks you're not here."

My heart beat faster. I took another drink. I shouldn't have... but the words got away from me. "Axel, why can't it happen?"

He understood me without any need to say more. "You know. It's just how things are."

"What if they weren't?" I said.

"What are you getting at, Leah?"

"I don't know. Knowing what everything would be like in a parallel reality. If nothing stood in our way and we were two strangers who just bumped into each other here in this bar, would you notice me?"

Axel nodded slowly. His intense stare told me there was desire there, and more.

"What would you do?"

Axel shifted, nervous, discreet. "Sometimes it's better to let things lie."

"I'd rather know. I need to know," I whispered.

He leaned back and let his defenses down. The wall crumbled at his feet and his words emerged from behind the cloud of dust that trapped us. "I'd talk with you. Ask you your name."

"That's all?" My lips were moist.

"Then we'd dance, and I'd kiss you slowly."

"Sounds romantic," I admitted uncertainly.

A muscle tensed in his jaw and he leaned his forearms on the table between us and came close to me. "Then without anyone noticing, I'd push you against a wall, put my hand under that dress you've got on, and fuck you with my fingers."

"Axel..." My heart skipped a beat.

"And I'd make you say my name while I did it."

I opened my mouth to say something, but nothing came out. We stayed there in silence, both of us breathing hard, not noticing the music or the people around us. Axel sighed and rubbed his face with his hands.

"We should go," he said.

"Already? It's early, and…"

"Leah, please."

"Fine."

64

Axel

OLIVER GRABBED HIS PONY OF beer and smiled, relaxed. We were sitting on the porch steps, and the sea breeze was whipping through the surrounding brush.

"So things are happening with Bega."

"That's how it looks. I like her. I like her too much."

"I can see that…" I took a sip of beer.

"I didn't think I'd ever feel this way…"

"I never thought I'd witness it." I laughed.

Oliver ran a hand through his hair. "I don't know, at first I just liked her, but things got complicated. She's…different. I know you think I'm not making sense, but it's true, Axel. You think it'll never happen, and then one day there's someone you can't get out of your head."

"I need to grab a smoke."

I went to the kitchen for my cigarettes. When I came back, he was uncomfortable, like when you've got a tiny stone in your shoe and it doesn't hurt, but you can't help noticing it's there. I lit my cigarette.

"How are things around here?" Oliver clapped my back and I coughed up a cloud of smoke.

"Good. Like always, I guess."

"I wouldn't say that. Leah's changed. A lot. For the past two months, she's seemed like the girl I used to know."

I swallowed the words burning in my throat because, from my point of view, she wasn't at all like the girl of before. There were things that would never change, but lots of new ones too. The Leah who lived with me was more complex, more intriguing, and unfortunately for me, a lot more of a woman. She had her cold, distant side, the one that painted in black and white and spent hours shut up in the room with her headphones on or a piece of charcoal between her fingers. Then there was the other one, the unpredictable one who caught me by surprise and fucked up my life, stripping naked in the middle of my living room on a random night. I liked both of them, damn it, in some twisted way I couldn't quite work out.

"Yeah, a little at a time." I took a long drag. "Hey, when they gave you the job, didn't you say maybe you'd be able to cut your time there short?"

"I was thinking about it, speeding things up..."

"Can you still?"

"Why, is Leah giving you trouble?"

"No, it's not that." I rubbed my face. "Forget it."

"Come on. Spit it out."

Oliver was impatiently awaiting a response. I could feel my heart beating faster. We had spent our whole damn lives together. Until a few years ago, I didn't know how to do anything without him. He was the only true friend I'd ever had, almost a brother. And I was acting like a bastard.

"I was just saying, because of the dates. The idea is she's going to go to college, right? So depending on when she starts, we'll have to look at dorms. And so that made me think maybe I could take her one day to Brisbane, show her the campus... Maybe that would motivate her. I wanted to talk to you about it first."

"Sounds fucking brilliant to me." I said.

"I figured the end of next month. You think it will work out okay?"

"What do you mean?" I gave Oliver a close look.

"That this was worth it. The Sydney thing. That Leah will go to college and not drop all the plans she had before...before the thing happened."

"The accident," I said.

"Yeah, you know what I mean."

"Why don't you just do it?" I demanded.

"What?" Oliver furrowed his brow.

"Stop beating around the bush. Do you talk to Leah about your parents?"

"No." He took one of my cigarettes. "I don't really see it as the best thing right now. She had a really bad time, Axel; she couldn't deal. It was difficult..."

"If she never faces it, she'll never get past it."

Oliver shook his head, a little angry. "What the hell do you want me to do? I spend three weeks a month hundreds of miles from here, and now she's better and the last thing I want to do is bury her in shit again. Months ago, she couldn't even stand to be around anything that reminded her of them. So no, I don't feel like mentioning them. I don't want to make her feel bad or see her suffer more."

"But Oliver..."

"You weren't in the car."

"You weren't either."

"Exactly. That's the difference. She was."

He stood up and I followed him around the porch. I wasn't used to arguing with him. At least, not about anything serious. Once, when we were drunk in college, we had come to blows and we both ended up with bloody noses. The next morning, we didn't even remember why. I think it was over a girl or something to do with one of the coasters at the place where we were partying. Anyway it wasn't important or else we would have figured it out.

"Wait, Oliver!" I grabbed his shoulder.

"Sorry. It's just, I don't know..."

"What's up?"

"Everything's so different..." He ran a hand through his hair. "Not just Leah. My life too. I don't even know what I'll do when I finish the job in Sydney and come back here..."

"What are you trying to tell me?"

He bit his lip. "That Bega's there. And if everything goes as it should, Leah will live in Brisbane. I don't know if it makes sense to come back to Byron Bay like nothing ever happened. I don't know if I can be the same person I was..."

I wanted to tell him, *We're your family*, but the words got stuck in my throat. I understood that feeling that maybe you didn't belong anywhere. Before I could say anything, Oliver clicked his tongue, hugged me quickly, and said goodbye after stealing another of my cigarettes and tucking it behind his ear.

I was tense and just as edgy as before. I sat back down on the steps and lit another. I watched the smoke, self-absorbed, remembered what I had told his sister a few days before. That I'd fuck her with my fingers. That all I could think of was her mouth. I closed my eyes and took a deep breath. I was losing it. No doubt.

I was losing my head over her.

65

Leah

IT WAS A WARM AUTUMN night, and I couldn't stop thinking about the talk we'd had that day at school about making decisions, choosing a path, mapping our future. The whole school year was ahead of me, but I'd already known what I wanted to do for years.

My father looked at me with a smile from his colored chair. "You sure you know? If there's anything else you might like to do…"

"Like what?" I laughed.

"Astronaut, maybe?"

I sucked on the lollipop in my mouth. "Or candy sampler. That would work for me."

"Diving instructor, you'd like that, right?"

"Yeah, I love diving. But I've decided. I want to paint. I'm studying art."

My father took off his glasses and cleaned the lenses with his shirt edge. I could see a glint of pride in his small vivacious eyes. "You know better than anyone that the world is a tough and complicated place. But you're amazing, Leah, and your mother and I will support you in whatever you want to do. You know that, right?"

"I know." I got up and gave him a big hug.

66

Axel

SILENCE. TOTAL SILENCE. SO MUCH silence that it seemed like a different house. I felt tired and I set aside the commission I was working on. And I don't know why, I knew it was wrong, but still...still, I got up, opened the door to Leah's room, and looked around for the notebook she'd been carrying under her arm those past few weeks. I wanted, needed, to see it.

I ignored the guilty feelings in my chest as I went through her drawers. But I didn't find anything. Just a wrinkled piece of paper. I grabbed it and sat on the bed looking at the drawing of Leah I had made years before on the envelope for the concert tickets for her birthday. It was one of the few times I'd drawn something without anyone hiring me, without it being work. I looked at the round red cheeks, the enormous eyes, the braid that fell over the shoulder of the caricature, and the paintbrush she had in her hand while she smiled.

Perplexed, I put it back in the drawer.

August

—

(WINTER)

67

Axel

LEAH CAME BACK. AND WITH her, the fleeting looks, the silence full of words already pronounced that seemed to weave a net around us, the tension, the prudent distance. Or that's how it felt to me. Unsettled. Alert. Trying to understand what I was feeling, what was happening....

The problem was that, though I might have spent half my life viewing her as a girl, almost as a little sister, I couldn't ignore the fact that she wasn't that anymore. That if I'd bumped into her on the street one day, I would have gawked at her or flirted with her without caring about the ten years that separated us. Because that wasn't the real barrier. It was something else, something higher: how we knew each other, the life we'd shared up to then, the fact that wanting her made me feel guilty.

Because I couldn't deny it. I wanted her. And I loved her. I always had loved her, since the day she was born. Leah could have asked me for anything and I would have done it with my eyes closed. It wasn't something just physical, an impulse. It was more. I missed her when she wasn't there and I wanted to know the girl she was now, not just the memory I had of her in the years past us. I struggled to separate my feelings: My desire to bite her lips versus the calm I felt on those nights we spent on the porch talking or listening to music. Leah's naked silhouette and the curve of her hips versus the image of her as a little girl running through the yard, shouting my name in her high-pitched child's voice…

When had all that changed? When was the exact second she stopped being invisible to me and invaded every nook and cranny of my mind?

"You all right?" She had sat down in the hammock.

No, I wasn't all right. Not at all. I took a deep breath. "Yeah. I'll be right back, I'm going to make a tea. You want one?"

She gave me an amused look and raised an eyebrow. "When are you going to stop asking me? It's been almost half a year now."

"I don't know. Maybe when you finally say yes."

"Fine. Make me one. Let's get this over with."

I went into the house smiling and shaking my head. I put the kettle on and waited for the water to start to boil. I came out calmer, more myself, and sat down in front of her on the ground. Leah wrinkled her nose when she noticed the distance between us. She took a sip of tea.

"It's okay. A little bitter."

I lit a smoke. "How's school?"

"Fine. Same old, same old."

"Good."

"What's with you? You're being weird."

"I'm just a little tired. I'll go to bed soon." I took a long drag and finished my tea. "What about you? You seem…different."

"Maybe so," she responded.

"How?"

"Remember months ago when I told you I was afraid I wouldn't want to live again?"

Of course I remembered, because I was on the verge of emotional suicide telling her *Live me, Leah*, as if it wouldn't bring trouble. I nodded.

"Well, I'm not afraid of that anymore. And that's liberating. As if everything is falling into place."

I furrowed my brow. She noticed.

"What? You don't like that?"

"Yes and no."

"Why?"

"Because it's a step, but you can't stay there. Answer me a question, Leah. What do you think is easier? Ignoring something that hurts and pretending it's not there so you can get up every day with a smile on your face, or confronting that pain, internalizing it, understanding it, and still managing to smile eventually?"

I lit another cigarette just to keep my hands still and not run over and console her like I used to when I'd hug her.

"You're harsh," she whispered.

"It would be worse if I was the other way, if I said, 'Sure, everything's fine now...'"

"What do you want, Axel?" She raised her voice.

"You know..."

"That's not true."

"For you to accept it."

"What?"

"That they're dead, Leah. But that even if they're not here, we don't have to act like they never were here with us. We can go on talking about them, remembering them. Don't you think so?"

Leah held back her tears and got up. I was quick and I grabbed her wrist before she could make it into the house.

"Remember that notebook where your father painted a field full of flowers and life? In the corner there were these beetles cut open with daisies inside. I wondered why for years. One time I asked him to explain it to me and he started laughing. We were right here, you know? On this porch, drinking a beer on one of those nights when he came to visit me and chat."

"Why are you telling me this?"

"I don't know. Because I remember them a lot; I think about them every day, but I don't have anyone to talk to about it. And I would like you to be that person, Leah, to be able to tell you anything that passes through my head without having to watch every word."

Her lower lip trembled. "Why does it still hurt so much?"

"Come here, babe."

Then I hugged her.

I hugged her while she sobbed against my chest. I told her to cry, to let it all out, to not swallow her pain. She shared it with me, holding me tight. I closed my eyes and thought how that was one of the realest moments of my life.

68

Leah

ONCE AT SCHOOL A GIRL a few years ahead of me tried to kill herself because some of her classmates were making fun of her, and her ex-best friend started calling her *slut* in the hallway and writing it on her desk. I remember it hit me, maybe because of her age, maybe because they got all the kids together in the auditorium to tell us what had happened. That day, while the principal talked about respect, camaraderie, and empathy, I heard the girl behind me say it wasn't such a big deal. I turned and scowled at her. She looked down, she was too scared to face me, and that made me realize that lots of people who spend their time judging others do so to make up for their own insecurities.

Years later I thought about that. About the different ways human beings channel the same realities. There were girls who responded to teasing by flipping the bird or blowing it off. Others cried or tried to be invisible. Some couldn't handle it and changed schools.

I guess it's impossible to know how to manage an emotion until it hits you and you're living it in the flesh. If I had asked myself before, I would have said I was strong, that I would have a normal process of mourning, that I would never be one of those ghosts who barely talks and wanders around with headphones on seeing the world in black and white.

But sometimes we're wrong. We fall.

Sometimes we don't know ourselves as well as we think.

Sometimes…sometimes life is so unpredictable…

69

Axel

THE FIRST WEEKEND IN AUGUST, Leah met with some friends to take an evening walk. She asked me if I could run her down to the boardwalk. I stopped in front of the ice cream shop she pointed out and sized up the three guys waiting for her with Blair. Two of them had the acne typical for their age. I watched her get out of the car and walk up the street. I stayed there like an imbecile staring at them until I realized I looked more like a kid than they did, then I pressed the gas hard.

I stopped at my family's café. Justin greeted me.

"Why the long face?"

"You talking to me?" I muttered.

"No, to the invisible customer who came in behind you. Yes, Axel, I'm talking to you. You look like you're constipated or something. Everything okay?"

"Yeah. You gonna serve me a coffee?"

"Depends on your tone."

"Please, Justin."

"That's better."

He walked over to the machine and passed me a coffee a minute later, along with a slice of cheesecake. I grabbed my spoon and brought a bite to my lips.

"Well, look who's here. Nice to see you, dude." Dad came out of the kitchen and squeezed my shoulder. "How's work? Lots of commissions?"

"Don't ask; he's in a bad mood," Justin said.

"You want to shut your mouth for once?"

"Hey, come on now, positive energy." My father smiled.

He was wearing a shirt that said, *I'm a virgin, I swear on my children.* I had to struggle not to laugh as he sat on the stool next to me and wrapped an arm around my shoulders.

"You've got bags under your eyes. Did you sleep badly?"

"I've had a couple of rough nights."

"You want to talk with your old man?"

"Dad…" I rolled my eyes.

"Okay, dude. No problem."

He got up, his smile still on his face, and told Justin he was going shopping and would be back in a few hours. The doorbell chimed as he left.

"Mom's not here?"

"Fortunately, she's got a meeting about the fair in two weeks. Obviously she offered to make twenty or thirty cakes and take them there. The usual."

"Have you tried to talk to her?"

"Yeah, but it's pointless. She doesn't listen."

"And Dad?" I finished my cheesecake.

"Dad…he'll just do whatever she says."

"I don't get it."

"You will someday, Axel." Justin wiped the bar down with a rag and took away my empty plate. "He loves her. He adores her. When you're in love with someone, you can do things for that person even if you know they're not right; you'll even put their desires before yours. It's hard."

"Why are you taking that for granted?"

"What?"

"That I've never been in love."

"Because I know you. And you haven't."

"What the fuck do you know? I've been out with tons of chicks, and…"

"And none of them has got you to stop staring at your own belly button." He cut me off. "It's different, Axel. Being with someone, commitment, going through fucked-up times, what do you know about that? Marriage is complicated. Lots of stages, you know. Not everything is that first year when you fall in love and life seems perfect."

"Are you having problems with Emily?"

"No, of course not." He hesitated. "I mean, the usual. Too little time alone. Lots of stress with the kids. The normal stuff, I guess."

"You can leave them with me one day if you want."

"So you can let them paint the walls?" he joked.

"I'm the cool uncle; what can you do?"

Justin turned serious. "By the way, you need to pay more attention to Dad."

"How so?"

"You really haven't realized it? He's been trying to get your attention forever. When Douglas was alive... I mean, he accepted the situation and just sort of stepped aside."

"Accepted what situation?"

"The fact that you seem to get along better with other people. That you treated Douglas like the father you wished you had."

That wasn't true. Not exactly. I felt my hair stand on end. With Douglas, all it took was a look to understand each other, that's how well we got along.

"I'll never replace Dad."

My brother frowned and told me he had to go to the kitchen to prepare some things. I stayed another minute, taking in his words, then went to the car. I rubbed my fingers over the seams of the steering wheel, thinking about Justin's expression, one that I hadn't seen before. I pushed it out of my head when I turned the key and the motor started up.

I drove slowly through the streets of Byron Bay and returned to the ice cream shop where I'd left Leah a while before. She was still there, sitting on one of the patio tables. She seemed to be concentrating on the words of the boy next to her. I watched her for a minute before honking the horn. She turned when I did it for a second time, and smiled. A huge smile, the kind that used to cross her face all the time. Now it filled me with some strange, incomprehensible emotion.

"Did you have fun?" I asked when she got into the car.

"Yeah, I love pistachio ice cream."

"Think about what you want to do this weekend."

"Hm, plans... The waves in the morning, then a nap. Yeah,

that would be good. I want to paint in the evening with the music on, on the porch, and then relax before my exam Monday. What do you think?"

It struck me as the best damn plan in the world. "Great. We'll do that."

70

Leah

THE REFLECTIONS FROM THE SUN blinded me, and I had to bring a hand to my forehead to see Axel moving among the waves, sliding through them before leaving them behind and falling into the water. He surfaced a few minutes later and remained floating on his back with his eyes closed. I watched him. It warmed my heart. Him out in the middle of the sea under the warm light of dawn. He looked so right there. It was as if everything were created for him: that place, the house, the wild vegetation that surrounded the beach…

I swam over, still on my surfboard. "What are you doing?" I asked.

"Nothing. Just…not thinking."

"How do you do that?"

"Leave your board and come here."

I went closer to Axel. Very close. Closer than we had been that week in which he had simply avoided me and I had allowed him to do so by giving him space. Water droplets glimmered in his eyelashes and on his lips, which were half open.

"Now lie back like you're dead."

I obeyed and floated there in front of him. The sky was an intense, cloudless blue.

"Just think about everything around you, the sea, my voice, the movement of the water... Close your eyes, Leah."

I did. I felt light, ethereal.

I felt calm, the absence of fear...

At least until Axel touched me. Then I shivered, lost my concentration, and moved in the water. It had just been a brush on the cheek, but it was impulsive, unexpected.

Axel took a deep breath. "You want to go home?"

I nodded.

We didn't do much the rest of the day. Just as I had planned, I took a nap after lunch, lying in the hammock. I woke up when I heard the insistent mewing of the cat, who was sitting on the porch staring at me. I got up, yawning, and went to get her some food. I kept her company during her afternoon meal, after which she licked herself and marched off through the shrubs around Axel's house.

I took my painting things out onto the porch. The black, gray, and white tubes. And the red.

Axel woke up not long afterward, when I was already concentrating. He watched me awhile, sitting nearby, smoking a cigarette and yawning, with bed head and pillow marks on his cheek. I wanted to kiss him just then. Erase those lines with my lips, and then...then I looked away because he said it couldn't be, and I understood, but I was getting more and more afraid that I would wind up doing something I shouldn't, because I wanted to... I wanted him.

"What are you painting?" He took a drag.

"I don't know yet."

"How can you not know?"

"Because I just...I just let myself go."

"I don't get it," he whispered, looking at the aimless lines I was tracing out slowly, just thinking about how nice it was to move the paint, mix it, feel it. He crossed his arms in frustration. "How do you do it, Leah?"

"It's abstract. There's no secret."

Axel rubbed his chin and, for the first time, he seemed not to like what he saw. I don't think it was the image; I think it was his own hang-up, because he couldn't understand himself. I stayed there painting awhile longer, with no limitations and no aims, just doing it and enjoying the sundown and the darkness spreading across the sky. When the crickets started chirping, I cleaned my brushes and went inside to help him with dinner.

We prepared it side by side. A casserole of potatoes, soy, and cheese, one of Axel's favorite dishes. We ate sitting at the surfboard-shaped table in the living room, talking now and then about pointless stuff, like how the cat had come by that afternoon or what we needed to buy at the store that week.

I took away the plates while he made tea.

That night, instead of going out onto the porch as we usually did, Axel sat on the floor in front of the record player and pulled out a big pile of records. I sat down next to him, cross-legged and barefoot like him.

He set a few records aside, then smiled. "This is the best cover in the world."

He picked it up so I could see it, and I gulped when I saw the color illustration of the four members of the group standing over the title printed in yellow: *The Beatles Yellow Submarine.*

Axel put it on, and as the childish rhythms began, the voice amid the sound of waves, he tapped his fingers. He smiled, entertained me, and sang part of the chorus, not knowing what that song meant for me, that every time I heard, "We all live in a yellow submarine," it was an *I love you* that got caught in my throat.

It felt like my heart was going to leap out of my chest, but I couldn't help laughing when he lay on the floor, still belting out the chorus.

"You're a god-awful singer, Axel."

He was still smiling when I lay back on the floor. He turned his head toward me. We were so close that his breath tickled me. His eyes descended to my lips and remained staring at them a few tense seconds. He sat up quickly and looked back through his records, showing me one.

"*Abbey Road*?" he asked.

"No! Not that one! It's…"

"It's my favorite."

I looked with new eyes at the mythical cover where the Beatles appeared on a crosswalk. I loved it too, but track number seven…I hadn't listened to it again, and I didn't want to, not then and not ever. I always skipped it, always. Finally I nodded, saying it was fine, and "Come Together" filled the living room, followed by "Something."

We chatted for a while, lying there close to each other. I was fascinated as he talked about Paul Gauguin, one of his favorite painters, with his synthetic style and his swaths of color. His masterpiece was *Where Do We Come From? What Are We? Where Are We Going?* and he painted it just before attempting suicide. He also liked Vincent van Gogh, and while "Oh! Darling" was playing, he fooled around and sang, and I realized that neither of those artists had achieved success while alive and that madness had united them.

"What about you? Who do you like?" Axel asked.

"There's just so many."

"Come on, name one."

"Monet transmits something special to me, and there's a phrase of his I love."

"What?"

"'For me, the motif is something completely secondary. What I want to represent is what exists between the motif and me,'" I recited from memory.

"A nice phrase."

"But you always want to know the motif! You spend the whole time going, 'Leah, what does that mean?'" I imitated his gravely voice. "'What's this red dot here? Why did you do that line?'"

"I can't help it; I'm curious."

I didn't reply. I was relaxed, my eyes focusing on the wooden beams in the ceiling, thinking how perfect it was to be by his side, to spend a Saturday by the sea, painting, listening to music, cooking together, doing whatever we felt like... I wanted it to last forever.

And just then the first chords started. They were weak, soft, but I could have recognized them anywhere in the world: "Here

Comes the Sun." I tensed up instantly. I leaned on my elbow to get up as soon as I could and take the needle out of that groove, but Axel got in my way. I was scared when he put his hands on both sides of my body. I tried to escape, but he hugged me close and stopped me.

"I'm sorry, Leah."

"Don't do this to me, Axel. I won't forgive you."

The notes rose up and whirled around us.

His hug squeezed me tighter.

I wriggled, trying to get away...

71

Axel

I HELD HER DOWN ON the ground, and I trembled when I saw her that way, so wounded, so broken, as if those feelings were somehow penetrating me, as if I could feel her in my skin. Leah tried to push me away with all her strength as the song seemed to spin around us. A part of me wanted to let her go. The other, the one that thought I was right and I was doing this for her own good, squeezed her hard against my body. I pushed her hair out of her face, and she shook and sobbed.

"It's over. Relax," I whispered.

The notes proceeded to the finale and Leah cried her soul out. I had never seen her like that, as if the pain were born inside her and finally emerged.

"*Here comes the sun. Here comes the sun.*"

I relaxed my embrace when the song was over. Her body continued to tremble beneath mine, and the tears slid down her cheeks. She wiped them off and closed her eyes. I didn't know how to explain to her that she couldn't go on hiding away her painful memories instead of confronting them, how to convince her that you could learn from pain and sometimes you had to...

I pulled away and Leah stood up.

I heard the door shut.

I stayed there by myself while the record she hadn't managed to stop kept spinning. I probably should have gone outside to smoke a cigarette and calm down before going to bed. Or stayed there awhile until I felt sleepy.

But I didn't.

I got up and went to her room. I entered without knocking. Leah was in her bed, balled up beneath the tangled sheets, and I went over and slid in beside her. Her soft sweet scent rattled me. I ignored my common sense, wrapping a hand around her waist. I squeezed her against me, hating that her back was turned and she wouldn't let me see her.

"I'm sorry, babe."

She started crying again. Fainter now.

My hand remained on her stomach and her outspread hair tickled my face. I just wanted her to stop crying, but at the same time, I wanted her to keep on, to let it all out...

I remained next to her in the darkness until she calmed down. When her breathing settled, I knew she was asleep and thought I should let her go and leave. I thought about it...but I didn't do it. I remained by her side, awake for what seemed like hours, and I must have fallen asleep at some point too, because when I opened my eyes, the daylight was pouring in through the little window.

Leah was holding me. Her legs were intertwined with mine, and her hands were on my chest. My heart skipped a beat. I looked at her, asleep in my arms. I gazed at each detail of her peaceful face, the round cheeks and the freckles softened by the sun on her button nose.

I could feel a knot in my stomach.

All I wanted was to kiss her. That was all. And I was scared because it wasn't lust. I imagined doing it. Bending over her, brushing her lips, covering them with mine, licking them slowly, savoring them…

Leah shifted as though troubled. She blinked and opened her eyes. She didn't pull away. She just looked up at me a bit. I held my breath.

"Tell me you don't hate me."

"I don't hate you, Axel."

I kissed her on the forehead and we remained there in the morning silence, holding each other in bed, her cheek on my chest and my fingers sunk into her hair while I struggled to maintain control.

72

Leah

IT WAS A SUNNY DAY, despite the presence of a few tangled clouds. I know because, as we drove down the highway to Brisbane, I kept my forehead pressed into the window in the back seat, thinking about how beautiful the cobalt blue of the sky was. I tried to imagine what paints I would use to recreate it, what the exact tones would be...

"How are your nerves, dear?" my mother asked.

"Good." I brought my hands to my neck and remembered I had left my headphones at home. Then I slid my fingers down my seat belt. "Dad, can you skip this one?"

He did, and "Octopus's Garden" started to play.

We were on our way to the gallery belonging to a friend of my parents who had come to our house two weeks before and had taken an interest in one of my paintings that was hanging in the living room. He had said they were thinking about setting up a small exhibition of young talent free of charge, and said we could go to Brisbane and meet with him and his partners to see if any of my work clicked for them.

"We can have lunch when we're done. I know a place near the gallery that makes the best scrambled eggs you can imagine, with everything: mushrooms, shrimp, bacon, asparagus…"

Dad started laughing when Mom said, "Yeah, I get it, everything."

I asked him to skip to the next song.

Here comes the sun. Here comes the sun.

"I love this song." I sang along, excited.

"Good taste. It's in the genes," Dad responded.

I smiled when he looked at me in the rearview mirror and winked. And a second later—just a second—the entire world froze and stopped spinning for me. The song cut off suddenly and the deafening sound of the car's frame tearing apart bored into my ears. It turned over and over, and with a scream caught in my throat that never made it out, I managed to glimpse a green stretch that told me we'd run off the road. Then…just silence. Then…a huge abyss.

My entire body hurt, and I had a busted lip and the metallic taste of blood in my mouth. I couldn't move. I swallowed. It was like I had a stone in my throat. I couldn't see my mother, but I could see Dad's bloody face, the cut on his head…

"Dad…" I whispered, but no one responded.

73

Axel

THAT WEEK, I LEFT HER with her pain, licking her wounds.

Leah was hushed. She would go to school in the morning, and I would stay there leaning on the porch railing, watching her ride off until she disappeared at the end of the road. Then I'd have my second coffee, work, and count the minutes until her return. We ate without saying much, her slightly absent, me focusing on her every gesture.

The problem with Leah was that I didn't need to talk to see more and more of her every day, to see how she was putting herself back together, picking the pieces up off the ground, storing them in her pockets, struggling to put them together again. I would have helped her if she had asked me, but I knew that sometimes there are roads you have to go down alone.

74

Leah

IT WAS LIBERATING. AND HARD. And painful.

It was going back to that moment, remembering it, confronting it, no longer letting myself see it as something unreal, something alien, accepting that it had happened. To me. To us. That one day a woman fell asleep behind the wheel after leaving her twelve-hour shift at the hospital and ran into our car and knocked it off the road. And my parents died when it happened. And they would never come back. That was the reality. That was my life now.

75

Leah

"YOU FEEL LIKE GOING TO Brisbane Saturday?"

"Why?"

"We already talked about it. We could go to the college, see the campus, walk around…"

"I don't know… Plus I'm leaving Sunday."

"We won't be back late. Come on, say yes."

I smiled. I couldn't refuse, so, three days later, the two of us were in his car headed to the city. The trip was almost two hours, so I relaxed, taking off my sandals and turning the radio to a local news program. Axel drove slowly, one arm leaning out the window and the other on the steering wheel. He was wearing dark sunglasses and a cotton T-shirt with the image of a palm tree in the center. I remembered how it felt to sleep there, leaning against him, embracing the warmth he emanated. If only…

I looked away and noticed the colors we were leaving behind: the green of the leaves of the trees, the blurry gray of the asphalt, and the snatch of sky reflected in the rearview. The world was too pretty not to want to paint it…

"What are you thinking about?" Axel turned down the radio.

"Nothing. The colors. Everything."

"That's ambiguous enough." He laughed. I loved the sound of his laughter.

We didn't talk much before reaching Brisbane. The city greeted us with its wide streets and ample vegetation. Axel drove toward the university, and I felt something strange in my stomach, because it made me nervous to see all that and think that in half a year I might be there alone and far from everything I knew and loved.

"You ready?" He had just finished parking.

"I don't know."

"Come on, I know you are." Axel got out of the car, walked around, and opened the passenger door. He reached out his hand. I took it and pulled softly. "Open your mind, Leah. Just think of everything you used to want to do, okay? You owe that to yourself."

I followed him in silence. We walked around the campus. Axel's eyes gleamed when he started to remember his student years there. He showed me the place where he used to sit with his friends to have lunch in the cafeteria and the grassy spot beneath a tree where he'd escape to read awhile with a cigarette between his lips when he skipped class. He told me anecdotes about his professors and what happened in that place full of stories.

The people we came across seemed easygoing. There were lots of students with art materials entering and leaving the classrooms and walking down the halls. I swallowed remembering the times I had imagined myself there, learning, wanting to do it all, feel, reveal, represent the world…

"You all right, Leah?"

I nodded.

"Let's go grab a bite."

We sat down in one of the cafeterias and ordered two vegetable sandwiches and two sodas. We ate in silence. I couldn't stop looking around, soaking everything in, the laughter at the next table over, the boy drawing in a corner with his headphones on, lost to the rest of the world, the independence that seemed to envelop us.

"I would have loved to be here ten years ago," I whispered, "living here with you, sharing everything... Why is life so unfair?"

Axel smiled and turned his head. "You can't imagine how much you seem like a little girl right now."

"You don't have to make fun of me; it's just a thought."

Axel grabbed my wrist over the table, and his thumb traced circles on my skin. I got goosebumps.

"That's not how I meant it. Hasn't anyone ever told you you've got to keep alive the child you carry around inside you throughout your life? Don't ever lose that child, because the day you do, part of you will be gone." His eyes descended to our joined hands. "I would have liked to...to have shared this with you too. But it would have had its bad sides."

"Like what?"

"You'd be the bookworm, the teacher's pet. I would have tried to copy off your tests after skipping class for a month, and you'd probably have told me to go fuck myself."

I laughed. I moved my fingers and they grazed his. He breathed harder, but he didn't move away. His skin was soft, his fingernails short and masculine. "It's not true. I'd have let you copy."

"How considerate. Is that all? Would you have agreed to a date?"

I had a knot in my throat and couldn't stop looking at him. "Depends on what your intentions would have been."

"You know they're always bad, babe."

"Sometimes bad things are worth it."

A muscle tensed in his jaw and he let me go. He slid his hand under the table and then rested it on the back of his chair.

We got up soon afterward and took away our trays. We walked a bit more of the campus and then took a stroll through South Bank. We walked by the river, leaving Victoria Bridge behind, arriving at GOMA, the biggest modern art gallery in Australia. The building was designed to harmonize landscape and architecture, taking advantage of the nearness to the river. It was spectacular.

I don't know how many hours we spent inside, but they flew by. I looked at each work, admiring them, noticing the colors, the textures, and the volumes, every tiny detail. Axel would disappear or I'd find him sitting in a gallery further off, pensive, patient. He didn't rush me. Finally, I told him that was enough for the day and that it was time to go.

We walked back to the car. Once inside, he rested his hands on the wheel. "You feel like a drive, or you want to go home now?"

"What are you proposing?"

"Just going with the flow."

"Nothing bad can come of that, right?"

"I hope not," he whispered.

His eyes roved my face and then got stuck on my lips. My

pulse started rocketing. He shook his head and started the car. I thought of something I had read some time back in an article about words that express concepts our own language doesn't contain. *Mamihlapinatapai* means, in Yaghan, "a look between two people, each of whom expects the other to undertake an action that both want, but that neither is ready to perform."

76

Axel

I DROVE IN SILENCE THROUGH that city I knew so well where I'd had so many experiences. Memories washed over me. Oliver was in all of them, the best friend I could ever hope for, who never judged the dumb things I did, instead ignoring them or acting like they didn't matter.

And there I was. With his sister in the passenger seat trying to suppress my desire for her, for more, for the feeling I had when I was beside her.

Night was starting to fall when I stopped in the busy Stanley Street Plaza area, where there was a flea market on the weekends, stands with exclusive and eclectic clothing made by emerging artisans, with handmade jewelry, art, antiques, photos...

A group was playing as Leah and I walked through the streets. She seemed happy to stop at each stall, looking at any knickknack that caught her eye. I was too taken with watching her to think about anything else.

I couldn't stop asking myself how it was possible that I hadn't seen her before. Her. The girl she'd become. Or was it...was it that I hadn't wanted to see her?

"You like?" Leah tried on a ring.

"Yeah, buy it."

She paid and we walked around awhile longer, until my stomach started growling and we decided to eat. We went to a restaurant that made the best veggie burger in the world.

"It really is good," she admitted as she chewed.

"Of course it is. Now tell me. What do you think about all this?"

"The university? Brisbane?"

"Yeah. What's your impression?"

"I've always liked it, but..."

"You're still scared."

"I can't help it."

"Listen." I set my burger down on the plate. "You think this doesn't happen to other people, Leah? We all have our issues. There will be a ton of students just like you starting university next year, and they'll be frightened because it'll be the first time they're away from home, and they'll have to be independent and learn to take care of themselves."

She didn't argue, she just ate, looking absent, thoughtful. "Why is it you used to paint, Axel? When you were a student?"

"You still haven't figured it out?" I tensed up.

"No, I don't get it. You...you had talent."

"But that's it. That was the problem. It still is the problem."

"Explain, please."

I bent toward her. "The day you understand me, you'll see yourself better."

She blew out a breath, irritated, and I wanted to laugh. I waited patiently while she finished her dinner, and then we passed by a packed bar that served gigantic drinks. It was late, but the idea of getting in the car and putting an end to the day didn't please me. So I didn't think twice; I just walked in like she was a regular girl and not Leah. We sat down at two stools by the bar. I ordered a beer, since I was going to drive, and told her to pick a cocktail. She chose one with strawberry and a bit of lime.

The lights were soft on the dance floor, and the blue LED bulbs at the bar didn't shine on the people dancing.

I took a sip of my beer and licked my lips. I looked at her until she started to blush.

"What's up?" she asked, embarrassed.

"I was thinking…"

"About what? Surprise me."

"About you. Me. Our differences."

"I think we've got more in common that you believe," Leah whispered.

"Could be. But we understand the world in different ways. You look at a cloudy sky and see a storm. I look at a cloudy sky, and for me it's clear."

Leah swallowed. I could see her throat moving. "So which of the two is better?"

"Funny enough, neither, I guess."

She laughed and two dimples appeared. I wanted to bite them. I took a long sip of beer, because it was that or succumb to temptation, to lust…

"Dance with me?" she asked.

"Are you serious?"

"Why not? I don't bite."

You don't, but I do.

Leah extended a hand and I accepted. We got lost on the dance floor, surrounded by strangers. It was a strange sensation. No one there knew who either of us was, and the anonymity made it seem like nothing mattered.

Leaving a proper distance between us, I slid my hands down her waist to her hips. A slow song came on, one I would often remember when I thought of her years later, "The Night We Met." It almost hurt me caressing her with my gaze alone. It wasn't enough anymore.

"Axel, just give me this moment." Leah wrapped her arms around my neck and pulled me in close. I held her against my body, moving slowly, almost still in the middle of the dance floor, feeling her breath tickle my neck and her hands weave through my hair.

I lowered my head slightly and kissed her ear, almost on the lobe, then slowly followed her jawline to her cheek. I closed my eyes, feeling the softness of her skin, how good she smelled, the heat of her breath, how perfect that embrace, that moment, everything was.

I was about to kiss her. I was. Fuck the world.

When I brushed against her lips, I knew it would be a disaster, but also the best disaster of my life.

I held the back of her neck before pressing my lips into hers. It was a real kiss. No doubts, no stepping backward, just my tongue sinking into her mouth and looking for hers, my teeth trapping her lip, my hands rising to her cheeks as if I was afraid she'd pull back. I savored every touch, every second, and that taste of strawberry.

That moment was worth whatever the consequences were, I thought.

Leah stood on tiptoe and rested her head on my shoulders when I pulled her tight, as if she needed to hold on to something solid. I pressed my lips into hers again. I thought kissing her would calm me down, but it was the opposite, like throwing the floodgates open. I needed to touch her all over. My hands went down to her ass and grabbed it, pulling her into me, grinding.

"Axel…" Her voice was almost a moan.

And it was just what I needed. That fucking erotic sound in my ear.

I sucked in breaths between kisses, starting to move through the room without letting her go until we'd made it over a few yards and were against the bathroom door. I pushed it open, ignoring the guy who was coming out, and we were soon inside. Leah's eyes were closed. She trusted me blindly, she was mine, and she trembled every time I touched her. We locked ourselves in one of the stalls. She groaned when I grabbed one of her breasts in the palm of my hand and squeezed it, drawing in her panting breath with a long, wet kiss.

What was I doing? No idea. I had no idea.

I just knew I didn't want to stop. That I couldn't.

"I'm losing control," I grunted.

"Sounds good to me," she panted, wild, reaching for me.

If I was hoping she'd put on the brakes, I was dead wrong.

Leaning against the tile wall, Leah wrapped her hands around my neck and pulled me into her, closer and closer, until we were grinding against each other through our clothes. It was the same way we would have fucked if we had no pants on. I had never been so hard. I tried to find some part of my mind that was still reasonable, but I gave up when she bit my lower lip until it hurt.

"Damn, Leah." I stepped back to slide a hand between her legs and rub her through her jeans. Hard. And fast. Because all of a sudden, I needed to see her expression when she came and preserve that memory forever.

She moaned and I held her around the waist with my free hand while she arched her back and let herself go, eyes closed, lips slightly open.

I closed them with a kiss. Then I released her, slowly...

Leah looked at me, still breathing hard. Her cheeks were inflamed and her eyes full of questions I couldn't answer. I took a breath, trying to calm down, and held her, resting my cheek on her head. The sounds outside came back, as if before that moment the music and voices of the people around hadn't existed.

"Let's go home, Leah."

I took her hand and dragged her out of the bathroom. The cool wind roused me slightly as we walked down the street. I was still hard, and my heart was still pounding loud and nervous, warning me about what had just happened, the line I had crossed. I knew there was no going backward, that this couldn't be fixed, not for her and not for me.

When we got in the car, the silence was dense. I rested my hands on the wheel and took a deep breath.

"You're regretting it," she whispered. There was pain in her voice.

I held her cheeks in my hands and kissed her slowly, taking away the flavor of her tears on my lips. I pulled back to wipe off her face. "I swear I'm not. But give me a few hours to get my head straight."

"Okay." She smiled. At me alone.

I kissed her again before starting the engine.

Absence accompanied me the whole way back: the absence of lights on the highway, the absence of voices except for Leah's calm breath by my side as she slept. I had time to be alone with my thoughts, but I was just as confused and fucked up when we arrived and I parked on the side of the road. The only thing I knew was that I felt something for Leah, and denying it at this point was ridiculous.

Maybe that's why I opened the door to the house, then went back to the car, took off her seat belt, and picked her up. Leah opened her eyes and asked where she was. I just said to keep sleeping and laid her in my bed. I went back to the car, grabbed her bag, and left it on the sofa before looking for my cigarettes and going out onto the porch to smoke. I looked at the sky and then went back to her when I was done.

I lay down beside her and embraced her. Leah woke up again and turned to lean her head on my chest. I stayed there for minutes, hours, who knows, caressing her hair and looking at the ceiling in my room, convincing myself that this was real, that my life was going to change. Some risks were worth it. Some...

77

Axel

POUNDING. POUNDING ON THE DOOR. I opened my eyes.

Fuck fuck fuck. Leah was holding me. I shook her. She awoke on the third try. She looked at me confused, still groggy.

"Get up. Now. Fast!"

She obeyed when she realized what I was saying.

"Go to the bathroom."

I prepared myself mentally before opening the door, but there was no point, because when I saw Oliver there smiling at me, I felt nauseated. I stepped aside to let him in. He seemed happy. He went to the kitchen and served himself a cup of coffee.

"Is this from yesterday?" he asked.

"Yeah. We were asleep."

"What's up with that?" He looked for the sugar.

"We got back late. We went to Brisbane, didn't we tell you?" I rubbed my chin, but then I stopped when I remembered that was a common gesture among liars: touching the face, gesticulating.

"We went to the university and the museum." *And then I mastur-bated her in the bathrooms in a bar at the end of the day to put the icing on the cake.*

"Right. So how was the trip?"

"Good."

Leah appeared in the kitchen.

"What did you think of the college?"

"Interesting." She stood on her tiptoes to kiss her brother on the cheek, and he hugged her before she could get away. "I need to go pack my bag."

"You didn't yet? Un-fucking-believable. I've come straight from the airport. I need a shower or I'm going to mutate into something weird."

"I didn't have time yesterday. I won't be long."

Leah disappeared into her room, and I tried to stay calm, even though I was about to have a heart attack. Oliver leaned on the counter, and I connected the last two neurons I had to make fresh coffee for myself. I needed it right in the vein.

"How is Brisbane nowadays?"

"Same as always. Hasn't changed much."

"Where did y'all go?"

"We had dinner at Getta Burger."

"It's still open?" He smiled. "What memories. I'll never forget that time we got drunk there and tried to get into the kitchen. The owner was nice about it."

"I don't know if it's the same dude..."

"Sure. What about campus? Same?"

"More or less. What's up with you?"

"I'm good. It was an easy month."

"There's got to be some perks to banging your boss."

Oliver tried to punch me in the shoulder, but I dodged it, and for a second, I felt everything was the same between us. The feeling vanished when Leah came dragging her suitcase out of the bedroom. Her brother stepped forward to take it.

I held the door frame after opening it. Oliver was already on his way to the car when I bent over and gave her a kiss on the cheek. A kiss that lasted a few seconds longer than usual. She looked at me doubtfully before turning around and leaving.

I shut the door, leaned against the wall, and rubbed my face.

I tried to lose myself in my routine to keep from thinking too much. Surf, spend a little time in the sea till I got exhausted. Then work. And later in the afternoon, when I felt like I was going to climb the walls after thinking the same thing over and over, I went out for a walk. I ended up at Cavvanbah and had a few beers with Tom, Gavin, and Jake. I concentrated on their words to keep from hearing myself think. It was almost morning when Madison came over and asked me if I was waiting for her to get off, and I shook my head, grabbed the keys I'd thrown on the table, and walked home.

I don't know why, I don't know why I did it the time before, but I went into Leah's room. I stood at the door, paralyzed. She'd left for me, carefully laid out on the bed, the sketch pad that had intrigued me months before. And next to it, a sheet of paper, I assumed the one she was working on when she refused to show it to me, saying it was just for her.

It was two silhouettes, two mouths, two sets of lips.

A kiss. Ours. Depicted for eternity.

I held my breath, sat on the bed, leaned into the wooden headboard. I grabbed the notebook and started to flip through the pages. Leah was on every one of them. Her anger. Her pain. Her hope. Her excitement. I looked at the outlines of some of the drawings, all of them done in charcoal, some melancholy, even those that showed close-ups of lips breathing, joined hands, timid touches.

And when I'd seen her, nude in that visceral way, all I could think was that love tasted of strawberry, was nineteen years old, and had a gaze the color of the sea.

78

Leah

LYING IN BED, I CLOSED my eyes and remembered that kiss. His soft anxious lips, his warm mouth, his hands traveling my body, pulling me into him. It was blue and red and green. Breathing sped up, the taste of him, his gruff, sensual voice in my ear. And then sky blue, magenta, and yellow. We were somehow the perfect pairing, like when something seems chaotic, but then there's a kiss and it all falls together. It didn't matter if I saw stormy skies and he saw clear ones.

Then we, everything, turned white. Us.

79

Axel

I SPENT THE WHOLE WEEK shut up at home working, trying to recover the routine I'd had six months before, before she set foot in there and everything changed forever. I finished most of my commissions. And even though I didn't have anything to do, when Oliver called me on Friday night to go grab a drink, I said I didn't feel well. Was I a coward? Probably. But telling him what was going on wasn't an option unless I wanted him to kill me.

There was an alternative.

Not going any further. Stopping it.

But I couldn't. I could have tried if I didn't live with her, if I didn't want her more and more every day, if I hadn't started needing her. Because when the sun rose and Leah wasn't there, the charm of it was gone, and the nights without her on the porch were cold and silent.

On Saturday, I called my father.

I did it for no particular reason. Maybe because I hadn't stopped thinking about what my brother had said. Maybe because I felt confused and alone, and I wasn't used to it.

We agreed to meet for dinner at an Italian place. He was there when I arrived, sitting at a corner table with an absent expression, but he lit up when he saw me and gave me a hug.

"Hey, dude. Come on, sit down."

"You order anything to drink?"

"No. You feel like a glass of wine?"

"Better a bottle," I said and grabbed the menu.

"Everything okay?" For the first time in a long time, my father let down his smile. "Your mother was worried when you called me. She says there can only be three reasons why you might want to see me alone."

"Really? Let's hear those three."

"You know how your mother is," he said before starting. "Maybe you've gotten a tourist pregnant, or you're in trouble with the law, or you're dying from a disease and you don't want to tell her so as not to worry her."

"Mom's nuts," I said and laughed.

"Yeah, but you've got to admit, you don't call me often," he said, slightly anxious.

I felt a little guilty. I sighed. "I should do it more."

The waiter returned with a bottle of wine and we ordered dinner.

"Axel, if something's up…"

"I'm fine, Dad. It's just that the other day, Justin made me realize some things. Things I didn't like." I furrowed my brow, discomfited. "Did you ever…feel pushed aside because of my relationship with Douglas?"

My father blinked, surprised. "Your brother told you that?"

"Yeah, more or less."

"Axel, when you hear something, don't just take it at face value; dig a little deeper. Words can deceive you; they cover up things. I never felt pushed aside because of your relationship with Douglas. He wasn't the one who had to chew you out when you were bad, he wasn't the one who had to punish you. He wasn't your dad."

They served me a dish of spaghetti.

"So why did Justin say that?"

"I told you, dig a little deeper..." My father wiped his mouth with his napkin and looked at me before deciding to speak. "Maybe he hasn't absorbed the fact that you view Oliver as a brother, your real brother. You've said that more than once."

"Shit, I didn't...I didn't mean that..." Or did I? I shook my head.

I remembered Justin's grimace the other day when he told me he had things to do and went into the kitchen. And how much he seemed to care when I supported him over my parents the month before. His failed attempts to get close to me and how I made fun of him for it. It was never on purpose; some relationships just start to have a certain pattern as the years pass.

"I love that tight-ass bastard," I said.

"I know, son, I know. Let me try your spaghetti." He reached out and stuck some of it with his fork.

"Dad, can I ask you a question?"

"Depends on whether or not it's sexual."

"Fuck! I don't even want to imagine."

"Good, because I don't know if you could take it. Truth be told, your mom's a firecracker."

"I'm begging you, don't say another word."

"My lips are sealed. What do you want to know?"

"Why do you put up with her?"

My father gave me a grave look. "Axel, your mother is having a very hard time. When something like that happens, something unexpected, it's like dominoes, understand? One falls. Or in this case, two. And that provokes a chain reaction, sometimes a big one."

"Why doesn't she talk to anyone?"

"She does. To me. Every night."

I nodded, distracted, and looked down at my food. "You love her..." I whispered. It wasn't a question.

"You boys and she are my world."

There was a hint of pride in my father's voice that I didn't understand because I didn't know the feeling, having a family of your own, with your rules, your traditions, choosing the person you want to spend the rest of your life with, good years, bad years, and hard years. Watching your children grow up, growing old... All of it seemed so strange to me, maybe because I'd never imagined it for myself.

But I had considered lots of things that my father overlooked, because you never understand a situation from the inside the same way as from without.

I tapped my fingers on the table. "I think I know how you can help Mom."

He looked at me with interest, but I shook my head and said I'd tell him soon. Dad nodded, agreeable as ever, and we finished eating and talked about a little bit of everything. I looked at the braided leather bracelets on his right wrist, the kind you buy at a craft stall and the surfers in the area wore.

"Looking good," I said, trying not to laugh.

"They're sweet. You want one?"

"Nah, actually..."

"Come on, son. We'll match."

I smiled while he took one off and put it on my wrist. Then he placed his wrist beside mine.

"Crunk."

"Excuse me? What did you just say?"

"Crunk. Sounds like you're not up on the latest slang."

"Crunk. Amazing," I repeated.

"Now you're getting it."

———

The family meal on Sunday was hell. My nephews tried to get me to play with them, but I was so exhausted I ended up sitting in an easy chair waiting for Oliver and Leah to get there. My mother asked me again if something was up, because this was the second time in my life I hadn't shown up late. Emily settled down next to me while her kids played in the room with Justin.

"How are things at the café?" I asked.

"The usual. Justin's too impatient."

"I thought the opposite."

"I wouldn't say so. He's got his bad days, even if it doesn't seem like it. He told me he talked to you about the problem."

"Yeah, a little bit. It'll get worked out."

I got up when the doorbell rang.

I stared at Leah when I opened the door, gawking like an imbecile, until Oliver got in the way, hugging me and clapping me so hard on the back I almost coughed up a lung.

"You left me hanging Friday, you son of a bitch!" he shouted.

"Shh, the kids are here. No curse words," Emily warned him.

"I had a cold," I lied.

"You should have grabbed a tissue."

"Very funny," I grunted.

I avoided greeting Leah with the usual kiss on the cheek so I wouldn't have to get close to her... I wasn't sure it was a good idea.

From the corner of my eye, I could see her disappointed expression.

My mother came out with the food and asked us all to take our seats at the table. I sat down next to Leah. I spent the entire damned meal wanting to grab her hand under the table. Or worse, slide my hand between her legs. It was fucked up, and it didn't help having Oliver right in front of me, talking and telling stories nonstop. I barely took a bite before getting up before dessert and telling them I was going.

"So early? Why?" Mom asked, horrified.

"I've got...an assignment I need to turn in tomorrow."

My brother was the only person who grimaced when I lied, as if he knew it wasn't true. I said a quick goodbye after setting a date with Oliver for that afternoon so he could drop Leah off before going to the airport.

Hours. That was all. A few hours.

I grabbed my surfboard and got lost in the waves.

September

—

(SPRING)

80

Leah

OLIVER WAS RUNNING LATE TO the airport, so he only got out of the car to take the suitcase out of the back seat. I kissed him goodbye and promised I'd call at least twice a week. I ran down the path to Axel's house as his car pulled away. I called at the door, but since there was no answer, I took out my keys. I went inside. It was all silent. I went to my room and saw that Axel had been in there and had leafed through the sketchbook I'd left out for him.

I smiled, but I was trembling inside.

Trembling because I was scared Axel would tell me again there was nothing between us. Trembling because I could no longer pretend I wasn't in love with him. Trembling because I had started to feel like the person I'd been before, in all her magnitude, and I couldn't stay in that house another night if he was kissing another woman.

I left my suitcase on the bed and started taking out my clothes and storing them in the closet. I wasn't done when I heard him coming.

My nerves made my stomach upset. I came out and held my breath as I looked at him in his swimsuit putting his surfboard aside. He looked up and his eyes saw through me.

"Hey," I managed to whisper.

"Hey." He stepped toward me.

"I...I just got back."

"Sure." He came closer.

I bit my lip. "You want to talk?"

"Talk?" He stopped in front of me and his eyes descended to my mouth. "Talking is the last thing I'm thinking about."

"So what is it then that you're..."

I couldn't finish. His lips covered mine and it was an implacable kiss, a kiss unlike any other in the silence of the house. Real. Intense. Hard. I closed my eyes, memorizing that moment I had dreamed of so many times. His skin was cold, and his hair and swimsuit were still wet, but I didn't care and I embraced him as though I would never let him go. I just wanted to be closer and closer to him. Despite the difficulties, it was as natural as breathing, the way his lips fit over mine...

Axel picked me up and I wrapped my legs around his waist. He walked to his room and we hit the door frame. I knew no one would ever kiss me that way again, so savage, so emotional, without another thought in their head.

He lowered me slowly to the floor, sliding his hands over every curve of my body. I twitched. From lust. From possessing him like that. From love. And then I felt brave enough to take off my shirt. Axel took in a deep breath through his nose when the garment fell to the ground. He stood still, not touching me, while I removed my bra.

His eyes got lost in my skin…

My knees went weak. I almost asked him to do or say something, but his stare mingled with mine and I didn't need any words; I could see it all. I saw the fear, but also the determination. The longing.

He took a step back. Our torsos met when he leaned his forehead against mine. His hands caressed my stomach, rose to my chest. His thumb rubbed my nipple with a soft movement, and I had to grab his shoulders, I was so shaken.

"Open your eyes, Leah. Open them."

I obeyed. Axel unbuttoned my shorts and let them fall. He slid an index finger around the waistband of my panties, killing me slowly, and lowered them until they were around my feet. Maybe it wasn't the first time he had seen me naked; I went around in a bikini all the time anyway, but I had never felt so exposed before his eyes, so open. If he had wanted, Axel could have reached out and taken whatever he wanted from me. I would have been incapable of denying him anything because it would be as though I were denying it to myself.

"Now you. Please," I asked.

He gave me an intense look before embracing me. He grabbed my hands softly and guided them down to the knotted string of his bathing suit. I had a knot in my stomach as I untied it. He watched me with his head low and tension in his jaw. When I got it off, we stood there naked in front of each other.

Axel kissed me. His tongue intertwined with mine while we bumped into the bed and I let myself fall back. He leaned down with his hands on either side of my body and looked at me for seconds that seemed eternal.

"I want to touch you," I said.

"I want it to last longer than a minute."

I laughed and he kissed me, muffling that sound.

"Axel, please, let me."

I looked for his erection and stroked it. Everything about him was perfect to me. Axel breathed through his teeth while I felt him. Then he closed his eyes tight and pulled away. His hand grazed my stomach softly, tickling me, before getting lost between my legs. He kissed me and sank a finger inside me. I tensed up. He spoke, close to my mouth. "You want to know what I was thinking about before?"

I nodded. I wanted him so bad my heart was going to jump out of my chest.

"I grabbed my surfboard to calm down, because I wanted to talk to you like a normal person. But when I got home, when I saw you, I short-circuited. Then all I could think about was fucking you real slow, licking you and you licking me, and how I couldn't spend another second without touching you."

"Do it, Axel," I told him, my mouth parched.

He stretched his hand out to the nightstand to grab a condom and got on top of me. His lips found mine and merged with them into a deep, moist kiss. I could feel he was holding back. Trying to be delicate. Doing it softly. I wanted to tell him to let himself go, but the words got stuck in my throat when he plunged inside me, slipping in until his hips locked with mine and I was breathless.

He kissed me all over, on the cheeks, the eyelids, the nose... then he started to move slowly, and I grabbed his shoulders and held him so tight I thought I might hurt him. I had started to take it for granted that he would never see me for who I was. I had almost given up. Now I knew what it was to feel his hands on my skin, and I realized it had been worth it to wait all those years, feeling invisible.

I took a breath of air when a shiver of pleasure ran through me. Axel felt my tension and went faster, biting my lips, breathing on my neck, grabbing my ass as if every thrust needed to be deeper, quicker, more intense. Everything more. I didn't know making love could be like that. Devastating. More.

"Axel…" I finally whispered his name.

He grunted and thrust one more time before letting himself go, and I drove my nails into his hips. Then we stayed there holding each other in silence, panting. Axel bit my earlobe and I shook, still hyperventilating.

"You're going to be the fucking end of me," he whispered.

81

Axel

I OPENED MY EYES SLOWLY. The sunlight poured through the window and Leah's hair was tickling me. I rubbed my nose against her cheek before giving her a kiss. She stretched out slowly, so adorably that I had to hold back to keep from grabbing a camera.

"Come on, shake it off. We fell asleep."

"Hmm…" She turned around.

"Leah, you're going to be late to school."

She turned around and wrapped her legs in mine. We were still naked. I was hard. Her skin was so soft, I wanted to kiss her all over.

"I could skip," she whispered.

"I'm supposed to be the one who thinks bad thoughts, and you're supposed to stop me."

"The world won't end if I skip one day."

"Sorry. Breakfast and you go."

"Breakfast?"

She laughed when I turned her around and got on top of her.

I grabbed one of her nipples in my lips and pulled softly until she gave off a muffled moan.

"Axel, what are you...?"

Before she could finish the question, I responded by pulling her knees apart and going lower and lower. I sank my tongue in her sex and licked and caressed her, feeding on her.

I held her legs when she got nervous and started to tremble. And I kept rubbing my lips against her with firmer intensity. Her eyes were closed, and she didn't look at me as her body tensed, her hands clutched the wrinkled sheets...and I kissed her with my tongue, panting over her body. I don't think I'd ever wanted to give another person pleasure that badly, make her melt in my arms.

She shook and shouted when the orgasm came.

I savored her taste in my mouth before climbing her body, and when she looked at me, I licked my lips slowly. Leah blushed. That amused me, and I smiled.

"Does that embarrass you?" I caressed her cheek with my thumb.

"No. Yes. I never..."

"Bullshit."

Leah looked away, but I grabbed her chin, forcing her to look back at me. I kissed her softly.

"Well, you're going to be my breakfast every day. And next time I do it, you'll watch me."

She nodded, her cheeks glowing.

"Come on, get up and go learn something good and useful before you come home and I teach you all the bad stuff I know." I pinched her butt while she stood up and slapped me away, laughing, as she headed to the shower.

I suppressed the impulse to follow her, because at that rate, she wouldn't even make it to her last class. I had an unfamiliar feeling of fullness in my chest, and I got up to make coffee. When she came out, already dressed and with her hair in a ponytail, I passed her a cup of coffee, which she drank in one gulp, and an avocado toast.

"You don't want me to take you?"

"Nah. I like going on the bike."

"Wait, your snack." I passed her an apple. "You're not forgetting anything?"

"My backpack!" she shouted.

"And a kiss, damn it! Come here."

She blushed again. I grabbed her by the nape of the neck to give her a long slow kiss before letting her go and walking out onto the porch to tell her goodbye. I watched her ride away on her bike with her ponytail bouncing in the morning sun. I took a deep breath, calm and not calm at the same time, if that was possible. Because I was happy, really fucking happy, but I couldn't ignore the fact that I was stepping into shifting sands, danger, and even still, I couldn't stop walking forward...

I lit a cigarette and made another coffee.

After a lazy morning full of tangled thoughts, Leah returned, and when she climbed the stairs of the porch with a smile on her lips, I felt that everything clicked again. The doubts and mistakes disappeared with the first kiss, and I was just there, in the present, with her.

When night fell, after dinner, I lay in the hammock and she got in beside me, curling up against my body while we swung back and forth. We were nothing but the music coming softly from the living room, glimmering stars, and the scent of the sea borne on the breeze.

"You know we need to talk, right?"

"We don't have to," I said.

"I want to know what it is that most worries you." She looked at me, reached up, and smoothed the space between my eyebrows. "See? I don't like that. You being so tense."

I pushed a hand inside her dress and squeezed the right side of her ass before kissing her. "I know a way to get rid of the tension."

"Axel, please. No jokes right now."

Her face turned sad and I wanted to die. Because I never thought I could get that hooked on another person that fast. Because I wasn't used to feeling that or to silly gestures melting my heart. Because I thought I didn't go for romantic bullshit, but just then, I could have written a love song about her. The last girl in the world I thought I'd lose my head over. The one I'd known my whole life. The one who had always been there, invisible before my very eyes.

I rubbed my chin and sighed. "Fine, let's talk."

"What are we going to do?"

"No fucking idea."

"You...you must have thought of something."

"Wait. I need a cigarette."

I went to the kitchen to grab the packet. When I returned, Leah was sitting on the hammock, swinging shyly and watching me. I lit a cigarette and took a long drag before finding the right words, if they even existed.

"I think we should take some time. You know, to see how everything works. And then, I don't know, I don't have a plan; it's not like I saw this coming. I'm just making it up as I go along and trying not to think too much."

"Fine. We won't think about it." She said this with a furrowed forehead.

"Come on, don't make that face." I put out my cigarette and walked over to her. I stood between her legs and drew a heart on her face with my fingers before tugging at her cheeks. It worked; she laughed.

"Leah, you know how fucked up this is for me, right? It makes me feel guilty. Bad. It's not a normal situation. It's tough."

"Sorry," she whispered and rested her head on my chest.

We stayed like that for a while, kissing slowly. I don't know how I had never noticed before how magical a kiss could be. How intimate. Something so little, so lovely. With her all I wanted to do was close my eyes and feel every touch and every breath.

82

Leah

BEFORE THEN, I THOUGHT LOVE was like a match that catches fire and then trembles as it burns. But no. Love is that soft series of sparks before the fireworks go off. It was his cheek against my chin when I woke, when the sun still hadn't come up. It was that feeling I got in my stomach when I touched him. It was his slow movements when we made love and his deep voice whispering my name. It was the taste of the sea on his skin. It was my desire to freeze every moment we spent together. It was his intense, mirthful look.

Love was feeling everything in a single kiss.

83

Leah

BLAIR CRACKED UP WHEN I told her the latest news. We were lying on her bed in her room looking at the fluorescent stars on the ceiling that glowed in the dark.

I nudged her. "What are you laughing about?"

"I don't know. You. the situation."

"Very funny." I turned around, grabbed a stuffed bear, and cuddled with it. "I'm scared, Blair."

"Don't be. You should be enjoying this moment. It's what you've always wanted, right? And now you've got it. The boy forever out of reach, the one you always said would never notice you."

"I thought he never would."

"Life is unpredictable like that."

"Right. But..." I slipped a lock of hair behind my ear and thought about what I wanted to say. My nerves were killing me. "It's too good to be true. And too complicated too. No one knows, just you. I don't like that, having to hide it, but I understand...I understand it could be a problem. I can't even imagine how my brother would react if he found out."

"You're grown up, Leah."

"I guess."

"So fuck it. Maybe he's right to wait and see how everything goes before getting your families involved. Don't overthink it; you'll figure it out when the time comes."

The doorbell rang and Blair got up to answer. She reappeared in her room with Kevin a few minutes later. I smiled and said hi to him.

"Is it girls' night? Am I missing any good gossip?" He sat at the chair by her desk.

"If we told you, we'd have to kill you." Blair kissed him before sitting next to me cross-legged on the bed.

I laughed, pleased to see them so happy together. And because it seemed like just another afternoon in the old days.

I said goodbye to them after a bit and walked home. I stopped at the Nguyens' café and greeted Justin from the door. He was surprised to see me.

"Well, look who's here."

"I was just passing by."

"Who is it?" Georgia emerged from the kitchen and smiled when she saw me. She wiped her hands, which were coated with flour, on her apron and gave me a hug so tight she squeezed the air out of me. "You look so pretty, dear."

"You want anything?" Justin asked.

"Not for here, but I was thinking of taking a piece of cheese-cake home with me."

"Sure. I'll pack it up for you to go."

She ran her fingers through my hair and rubbed my cheek as if I had a spot on it.

"Something wrong?" I asked, worried.

"No, just a scratch."

I hugged her again, without warning, catching her off guard. Her and me. It was an impulse. I don't know if it was because of the way she had always worried over me, over all of us. Even if she was sometimes wrong to do so, I liked that warmth and familiarity. When I let her go, I saw she had tears in her eyes and was trying to wipe them away.

"Sorry, I just...I don't know..."

"Don't say you're sorry, dear. You know? I really needed a hug. Especially one from you, sweet as you always are. Come on, give me another cuddle."

And she let me hug her again and closed her eyes, content. We pulled apart when a customer came in.

"Here, come with me to the kitchen."

I stayed there awhile with Axel's mother, just keeping her company, though we didn't talk much. It made me remember the afternoons I used to spend with her and my mother in the kitchen at home, sitting on a stool while they cooked and I listened to them talk about their things, their day-to-day lives, the silly stuff their husbands did sometimes, and their plans for the weekend. I loved how they let me listen to their grown-up conversations, because it was like opening a window to a world different from the one Blair and I shared at school.

84

Axel

I KNEW BY THE SOUND of the door Leah was home, but I didn't move. I stayed there on the porch, elbows on the railing, a cigarette between my lips, watching the smoke twist before the wind drove it away.

Then I felt her arms wrap around me from behind. I closed my eyes. I felt like shit those days every time she left the house and the weight of guilt came down on me. But I was happy again when she came back and greeted me with one of those huge smiles that took up her whole face.

"How was your afternoon?" I asked.

"Good. I was with Blair and Kevin for a while. Then I went to the café and I brought you a piece of cheesecake," she said, standing beside me and kissing me. "Your favorite."

I pulled her in, devouring her until I was breathless. I stroked her tongue slowly with mine, as if it was our first kiss, because with Leah everything was like that, as if every kiss I'd ever had was just a rehearsal for when she arrived. I didn't want to think why or when or how, because I was afraid of what I might discover, that maybe I'd always felt something for her. Not love. Not desire. But a connection, as if that halo in her pictures that drew me in was an invisible thread that somehow tied me to her.

"What's up?" She looked at me with worry as we separated.

"Nothing. I missed you."

"Missed you, too."

"Let's go make dinner."

I stopped thinking about anything. Just about her being there, the dimples in her face when she smiled, the finger she brought to her mouth when she tasted the sauce, which made me hard right away, the shimmer in her eyes every time she looked at me.

We had a relaxed dinner on the porch, and she washed the dishes while I heated up water for the tea. I sat down on the cushions and Leah sat between my legs with her back to my stomach. I lit a cigarette and held my hand at a distance so the smoke wouldn't bother her. The music was audible from the living room. It was perfect, and I had the feeling it was not the first night we were that close, that there had been many others, but with different forms, colors, and textures. It was natural to me to wrap my free hand around her waist and pull her closer to me. She took a deep, calm breath.

"I can hear your heart from here," she said.

"What's it sound like?" I took a drag.

"I don't know. You. Things. I wish I could paint it."

"Paint a sound..." I whispered. "Good luck with that."

Leah laughed softly and we fell silent again. I didn't need to talk when I had her close. I closed my eyes while "Pepperland" played. I thought how that night was like all the ones I had spent alone on that porch through the years, but just more...just more, period.

"What do you like about me?"

"Everything." I smiled because I couldn't remember anyone asking me something so girlish. But I liked it.

"Come on, don't be shy."

"Your ass, your tits, your..."

She pinched me on the arm, grumbling, then I spoke into her lips.

"I like the sound of your laugh, I like your contradictions. How intense you are, almost overwhelming. I like the way you feel and trying to guess what you're going to say, even if I'm always wrong. I like this house when you're in it..."

She hushed me with a kiss. I separated her legs, sat her straddling over me, and slid my tongue into her mouth. Leah sank her fingers in my hair while we dry-humped. A wave of heat passed through me and I could only think of being inside her, as if that was where I belonged forever.

"You're killing me," I panted.

"You're killing me. You have been for years."

I was blinded. All I could perceive was how good she smelled, how soft her skin was, how sweet her voice was whispering my name. I put my hands on her thighs, and pulled down her cotton shorts and her underwear before doing the same with mine and plunging inside her. Without a condom. I held my breath and clenched my jaw, trying not to move. I moaned when she did, dancing over me, sinking her nails into my back.

"Wait...fuck, wait..."

But she didn't seem to hear me, and I lost all sense of reason when she looked me in the eyes as she fucked me on that porch where I had started to fall in love with her. I held her hips, listening to her breath, wanting to tear off what clothes she still had on to caress every inch of her body with my fingertips.

I was out of breath as I saw her orgasm under the stars. So powerful over me, so committed to that instant without thinking of anything else. I clenched my teeth when a lash of pleasure struck me, and pulled out before coming in my hands with a groan.

She hugged me. I tried to catch my breath.

"Leah, this isn't... Never again..." I managed to say.

"I've taken precautions," she said, shaking.

"You should have told me."

"I...I couldn't think about anything else."

I calmed down and kissed her on the cheek. "We need a shower," I said, picking her up.

I took off my dirty clothes as we walked through the living room, and I stripped her naked after putting the plug in the bathtub and running the hot water. I looked at her from every angle, noticing every line, every curve, every mark on her skin.

Leah blushed. "What are you doing?"

"Nothing. Go on, get in the tub."

Memorizing you to draw you, I told myself, but I pushed that thought out of my mind, because I would never do that, would never paint her; there was no way I could capture her.

I sat behind her, hugging her, and turned off the water when it was near the edge. We got into the bath with the music still playing in the living room. I leaned my chin on her shoulder and closed my eyes.

"Yellow Submarine" started playing. She moved.

"Remember the night you asked me if I heard a song in my head when I met my soul mate, and I said yes?"

I nodded against her cheek.

"It was with you. And this was the song. Years ago."

The notes milled around us.

"Tell me the story," I whispered.

"I had just turned sixteen. You didn't come to my birthday because you'd been in Melbourne with some friends, and you gave me a nib pen. You said it was so I could keep making magic."

"I remember that." I kissed her on the temple.

"I started hearing this song in my head just then. And I felt...I felt the impulse to tell you something important, but I couldn't. I had a knot in my throat."

"Babe." I hugged her tighter.

"All you heard was 'We all live in a yellow submarine,' but for me it will always be the first time I said *I love you* looking into your eyes, even if I used other words to say it."

My heart skipped a beat. And I realized we were a puzzle that had been put together with the passage of years. The difference was that Leah had always had all the pieces, and I had taken years to find them.

85

Leah

I HAD ALWAYS LOVED HIM. But I used to love him from afar, looking at him up on a pedestal, unable to touch him. The things we can't reach or can't have always acquire a certain added value, like those paintings no one pays attention to until they find out they're by a famous artist of the day and cost a fortune. For years, I had idealized Axel, I knew that. That he bewitched me. That I worshipped the ground he walked on. That his approval every time I picked up a brush meant everything to me.

Not anymore. Now I had him in front of me and, in a strange way, only now was he flesh and blood to me. Real. So real. With his defects, his shadows, all his magnitude, a thousand times better and a thousand times more interesting than the perfect Axel who had lived in my head.

And loving him added a new dimension.

More shades. More colors. More everything.

86

Axel

MAYBE IF THE FEELINGS LEAH stirred in me had been lukewarm, I could have avoided them, stopping it before it happened, keeping up a barrier. But no, they were like a hurricane that sweeps through and upturns everything. Like something long dormant that suddenly awakens. Like the apple they say you shouldn't taste, but it's so shiny and tempting and perfect. Like the unexpected.

I could say it was chance. That Leah wound up in my house. That I struggled to strip her bare layer by layer. That I fell in love with her after finding what I found, when all that was left was her skin against my fingers...

I could say that...

But I'd be lying.

87

Leah

I HAD GOTTEN TWO BS and an A on my last three exams, and I was excited when I got home. Axel hugged me and said we had to celebrate. It was a warm spring Friday. I put on a loose dress and sandals. We went to Nimbin, a suburb to the west of Byron Bay, an artists' and ecologists' refuge, the most alternative town in Australia, where all the hippies gathered.

We walked down the streets and looked at the colorful facades covered in drawings. We'd been walking a few minutes when Axel's fingers started rubbing mine, and soon we were holding hands. Seeing his expression, I understood. He had decided to take me to eat somewhere where we wouldn't have to worry about anything. And I liked that feeling of being able to walk hand in hand with him like a regular couple, which was just what I wanted us to be. I opened my mouth to tell him, but he guessed it.

"Not yet, Leah."

"Okay."

The midday sun accompanied us when we sat on a patio to have lunch. We were relaxed, and we spent the trip back in the car talking nonsense. Axel told me it was impossible to touch your nose with the tip of the tongue. I struggled to do it.

"Let it go." He rolled his eyes.

"This from the guy who always tries to find the logic in everything, or some proof to the contrary. I was just checking," I joked.

"I don't do that," he said, defending himself.

"Of course you do. You can't stand not understanding something."

"Like what?"

"Dad's beetles, for example."

"Do they somehow make sense?"

I wasn't used to talking about him, about them, without someone forcing me into it. Without Axel doing so specifically. It saddened me to realize I missed my parents and wasn't even allowing myself to remember them, to keep them close and carry them around with me.

"They do make sense," I said. "He did them for Mom. She loved beetles because she had an amulet of one that my grandfather gave her when she was little. In ancient Egypt they were considered a symbol of protection, wisdom, and resurrection. When she fell in love with my father, before they started going out, she said she used to spend the days picking daisies in the garden of her house and pulling off the petals, saying, 'He loves me, he loves me...'"

"Isn't it supposed to be, *he loves me, he loves me not?*"

"Exactly, but she didn't want to imagine any other possibility, so she changed the rules and that's that." I couldn't help smiling as I thought about Mom. "She told him on their third date. So for him, the beetle was her, good luck, full of those *I love yous.*"

Axel started laughing. "Jesus, fucking Douglas, I still remember the day I asked him and he told me I should keep thinking about it. I could have spent my whole life trying to figure it out and I would never have gotten anywhere. You know what? He loved that, having a laugh at my expense."

We were silent for a few minutes.

"It's beautiful," I said.

"Him portraying things only they could understand. The rest of the world could see those beetles sliced open down the middle and think it was just weirdness. And for him it was love, one of the many ways he had of looking at it."

Axel sighed and his expression darkened, but I didn't ask him what he was thinking, because I knew he wouldn't tell me. Back in Byron Bay, he took a detour.

"Where are we going?"

"I want to show you something."

He stopped in front of a contemporary art gallery. There were several in town, but this one was the smallest, and it was special, maybe because of its rustic facade or its charm. He seemed nervous.

"I never told you this before, because…I didn't want you to get scared or take a step back, but I promised Douglas something once. I told your father that I didn't know how, but I would…get you to show your work in a gallery."

"Why'd you do that?"

"Because I failed to keep another promise."

"Which one? You don't have to lie to me."

"That I would. Show my work here. Because that was my dream, but so long ago that I don't even remember the feeling of wanting such a thing. When I told you I needed to talk to someone about them, with you, I was being serious. Not just because I miss them, Leah, but because your dad…if I take him out of my life story, you'll never know me entirely, understand? I owe a lot of what I am to him."

I held back to keep from crying, and his fingers glided softly down my cheek, but he pulled away when he noticed something outside the car. I turned. All I saw was a short-haired girl whose head turned when she met my eyes.

"What is it, Axel?"

"Nothing. It's nothing."

"You know her?"

"She's a friend."

He started the car, and we went home. I looked at the door of the art gallery we were leaving behind in the rearview mirror, and we didn't talk about it again for the rest of the day. We made dinner together. We put on a record. We made love in his bed and embraced afterward in the silence of the night.

I couldn't fall asleep. The tips of my toes were burning, and I knew that sensation very, very well, but it was three in the morning, I didn't want to wake him. I got up when I couldn't take it anymore. I walked barefoot on tiptoe through the living room, leaving the door to the bedroom cracked. I turned on a lamp on the table, which gave off a faint orange light, and went for my art materials. I unrolled a sheet of paper on the floor and knelt on the warm wood. I took a deep breath, feeling the solitude of the moment, holding on to it before opening the paint box and sliding my fingers over the tubes, caressing them, remembering them…

I grabbed a yellow. Then a carmine red.

Then a petroleum blue, a mauve, a purple, a salmon pink, a chocolate brown, turquoise, dark amber, apricot, mint green...

I mixed them all. Felt them all. Found myself in all of them.

88

Axel

DOUGLAS SHOWED UP AT MY house with a bag of prepared food and two beers in his hands. He didn't say a word before going to the kitchen and taking everything out. I was a little angry as I watched him. Not at him. Maybe at me. I don't know. I put the cigarette I was about to light before he arrived behind my ear.

"Bad day, no? Lots of those lately."

"You don't say?" I hissed. "Why are you here?"

"Some host you are…"

"It's not you, it's just… Don't worry about it."

I opened a beer and took a sip. Douglas looked around at the disorder in the house. I hadn't picked up in days. The floor was full of unfinished paintings, sketches, spots of paint I hadn't bothered to clean.

All I could feel was frustration. "I just can't do it. I can't."

"That's not true, Axel. Come on, look at me."

"You're right, it's worse. I don't want to do it."

He twisted his beer around in his hand while he looked at me. I saw disappointment in his eyes. I had to hold back from crying like a fucking boy in front of him about all I'd ever wanted to be and would never achieve.

"If you tell me, I'll understand."

I got up and ran a hand through my hair. "It's everything. It's...this house, this place. The idea I had about what it would be but isn't. I'm suffocating. It's like having a noose around my neck the whole damn day." I walked back and forth, stepping on my paintings, but I didn't care. "I don't even know why I wanted to do this. Paint. I've forgotten. How can you forget something that was supposedly your dream, Douglas?"

"Tell me just one thing: what is it that comes between you and your canvas?"

"Me, damn it. Me. I don't feel anything. I don't have anything to capture, anything I want to record. I don't want to make just *anything*. If that's how it's going to be, I'd rather never touch a fucking brush again. And the harder I try to find something that's important enough to me to give it my all, the worse it is; the more frustrated I get. I can't. I've tried for months, and...I can't. Supposedly this is what I studied for, and I promised you I would do it and I would show my work in a gallery and..."

I brought a hand to my chest, and Douglas got up and hugged me. I held him tight. I needed it; I needed to know that even if I hadn't done it, even if I hadn't scratched that goal off the list, he would still be there with me, because painting was one of the strongest things that had brought us together since I was a boy, and I was afraid if I let it go he would pull away from me or something would change.

"That's enough, son. That's enough." He patted me on the

back. "You don't have to do it anymore, hear me? No one's forcing you. You've started a war and you're only fighting against yourself, and you're never going to win. Fuck painting. Fuck everything, you hear me? The first thing is to be happy, feel relaxed when you get up every morning."

I wanted to cry from relief.

I took a deep breath. I breathed, I breathed, I breathed...

Douglas squeezed my shoulder and the disappointment on his face turned to pride. I didn't know why, but I didn't ask either, because seeing it was enough. He made the tension disappear, grabbing our dinner and taking the two boxes of noodles out to the porch. We ate our meal in silence, each lost in his own thoughts. I was about to go get some tea when he stopped me with a smile.

"Wait, I've got something better."

"No fucking way." I started laughing when he took out a bag and shook it before my eyes. "Looks good. Give me that."

He laughed uproariously there in the nighttime as I took the weed from him and went for a rolling paper. A half hour later, we were both high and sitting on the porch steps with an open bottle of rum, our feet in the grass growing in the sand.

He took a hit and coughed. "I'm too old for this."

"You'll never be too old for anything, Douglas. Can a thought get old? I don't think so. You can always be what you want to be."

"Don't get all philosophical on me at this hour, boy."

I took the joint from his hands. He looked at me askance as I blew out the smoke and observed the smoke rings disappearing in the darkness.

"So fuck painting."

"Fuck painting!" I repeated, euphoric.

"I always liked that about you, the way you just grab on to life and bend it to your will. You remind me of myself. You know, sometimes there are just two options: go up or go down, move forward or move back, grab on or let go, close or open... Shades of gray are fine, but they're not everything. Sometimes you've got to go big, take risks. Like in love."

"Screw love," I mumbled.

"I don't buy that from you. You're an easy target, you know. Tell me you know that, Axel. You need to be on guard."

I looked at him from the corner of my eye and raised a brow. "You've smoked too much."

"No. I'm talking about you, how you are. Trust me, I know what I'm saying." He brought a hand to his chest, looking happy. "Axel, you paint or don't, and one day you'll love or you won't, because you won't know how to do things any other way."

I lay back and looked up at the stars. "Well, love doesn't seem to be in a rush..."

"There are things it's worth waiting for."

"How did you know Rose was the one?"

"How could I not?" He wrinkled his forehead, disconcerted. "Hell, one look at her and the world stopped right as I heard the notes to 'I Will' in my head. I never had a doubt."

"You're lucky," I whispered, and then two ideas came together all at once. Maybe it was a coincidence that she popped into my head while we were talking about love. Or maybe not. I would never know. "As far as that promise I made you, since I've just been screaming, 'Fuck painting...'"

"You don't owe me explanations, Axel."

"It's not an explanation, it's a revelation." I sat down quickly, a little dizzy. "She'll do it. Leah. Your daughter. It makes sense, no? Now I understand; it was clear from the beginning. Have you seen what she does? She'll fill galleries. And I think...I think that's her destiny, not mine. That's fucking it."

"She's really good, yeah. She's special."

"You know what, I think I will keep my promise. I'll have an exhibition one day; the only thing is, I'll do it with her. I'll be the organizer. Same thing, right?"

Douglas laughed, and I did too.

It was almost dawn when I decided to go inside and look for my cell phone in my desk, because, unless I was wrong, I had left it there a day or two back. I found it and called Rose. I told her not to worry, that her husband was going to sleep at my house. But twenty minutes later, she showed up.

"I can't believe it," she said when I opened the door and she saw Douglas on the couch.

"It's my fault, I swear." I let her in. "Coffee?"

"Yeah, because it's that or drag him out by his ear."

"I've told you before, he loses track of time; he doesn't realize it."

"Axel, we know each other. Make me that coffee."

I suppressed a smile and poured her a cup. She was wearing baggy jeans and a few blond hairs were hanging out of her wild ponytail.

"Sorry for calling you at this hour."

"It doesn't matter, you had to tell me. What were you all doing? Trying to save the world, as always?"

"Trying to save me, if you believe that," I confessed.

"Don't be silly. You're perfect the way you are, Axel Nguyen." She softened up and pinched my cheek. "Someday you'll realize it, and then you'll accept all your defects and let in someone else, and they will too."

"Sounds very nice," I said ironically.

"It will be." She looked at me with bright eyes, then I looked away, uncomfortable, because I had the sense that she knew something about me I couldn't figure out, and that was a strange and irritating sensation.

"We should wake him up."

Rose nodded, and the two of us managed to get Douglas into the passenger seat of the car. She gave me a kiss on the cheek.

Later I started picking up all my paintings, drawings, and art material scattered all over the floor of the living room. When I finished, I took it all to the bedroom and looked for a ladder. I left the things on top of the wooden wardrobe, not worrying about the dust they'd gather. It was relief. Happiness. Peace.

I went back out on the porch feeling lighter, without that weight on my back. I lit a cigarette and took a sip from the bottle of rum. I decided I would start the next day doing the thing I liked most in the world: getting lost in the waves. I knew that I would try and be happy from then on, that I would take all the things I wanted from life, the things that fulfilled me, and discard the rest, and I wouldn't feel guilty for it.

And that was how I started a new stage.

89

Leah

I WAS STILL PAINTING WHEN the first rays of sunlight appeared on the horizon. I was about to fall over from exhaustion, but I couldn't stop. Every time I finished a line, I needed to start the next one; every time I added another tone, I needed to mix more...

I turned around when I heard a noise behind me.

Axel was there, his hair unkempt, so handsome that I went breathless when I saw his eyes had focused on the piece of paper on the floor of his living room. I couldn't have deciphered his expression in a million years. It was full and, at the same time, desolately empty.

"Axel." I stood up slowly.

"Don't say a word," he whispered and walked over to me in two long steps. He grabbed my cheeks and kissed me. A slow, soft, eternal kiss.

He pulled me into his chest while he contemplated the drawing: the explosion of color, the delicate but firm lines, the whole.

It was him. His heart. His heart full of vivid colors,

vibrating in the center of the paper. Stars shot from one of the arteries shining on the upper part. Lower down was the water where it floated. And there were glimmers of light and splatters on each side.

"It's for you." I looked up.

I hugged him tighter when I felt him tremble.

90

Axel

I SAID GOODBYE TO HER for the last week of the month with my heart shrunken, as though I feared she would never return. Because that wasn't an option anymore. There are things you can choose at a certain moment, and then they're no longer in your hands; you've crossed a point of no return. She was one. If I turned back, I would find a wall.

But not turning back was complicated too.

Oliver. Every time I thought of him, I suffocated a little more. Maybe that's why I avoided him. I did it at the end of August and I followed the same formula at the end of September. I didn't want to see him. I didn't want to fuck my life up even more. I rejected every plan he proposed, offering a million excuses, and I spent the week shut up in the house, in the sea, cutting through the webs of sorrow Leah had left in her absence. A person can change your perception of situations no matter how used to them you are. The things I liked before now seemed to be missing something.

I should have known it was a bad idea not going to family

lunch and claiming I was sick, because, obviously, my mom showed up at my house that morning with an arsenal of food and a bag from the drugstore.

"Shit," I grunted when I opened my door.

"What a mouth you have."

"Believe me, some people like it."

My mother gave me a light smack on the back of the neck before going to the kitchen and leaving everything on the counter. She started putting the fresh food in the refrigerator and then placed a hand on my forehead.

She frowned as only she could. "You don't have a fever."

"It's a new special kind of flu."

"Does your belly hurt? Are you tired?"

"Mom, I'm fine. You didn't have to come."

"Someone's got to take care of you if you're sick, honey." She inspected my face, lifting my eyelids and tugging on my cheeks. "You don't look bad."

"I'm handsome, that's why."

"I thought you'd be a wreck."

"Is not showing up to lunch that big a deal? Let me breathe a little."

"Breathe? You live like a hermit here, cut off from the world…"

I rolled my eyes and flopped down on the sofa.

"I don't like you trying to weasel out! You know how many people would give anything to be with their family? Remember Miss Marguerite? Her daughter lives in Dublin and they can only see each other once a year. Can you imagine?"

"Yes, and I'm enjoying it."

355 ALL THAT WE NEVER WERE

She threw a cushion at me. "You need to start reconsidering your life."

"It's funny that you of all people would tell me that."

"What are you insinuating?" Wrinkles appeared in her forehead as she arranged the cuffs of the jersey she was wearing. She sat next to me in an easy chair.

"You know. A time comes when you have to make certain decisions, right? How long has it been since you said you were going to retire and leave the café to Justin? It seems like an eternity."

"That's not your business," she hissed.

"Mom." I sat up, though I was reluctant to, because the last thing I felt like doing was having a heavy conversation, especially when my life was a total chaos, and I had no idea how to deal with it and untangle all the knots that had appeared in the past few months. "Justin is going to end up leaving, and he'll be right to do it. You promised him he could run the business, that he could do with it as he saw fit, and you're not keeping your word. What's the problem? You should be ready to stop working and enjoy your life with Dad."

My mother's lower lip twitched. "It's not that easy, Axel."

"Explain it to me then. Tell me."

She cracked. She looked at me with tears in her eyes and breathed in deep. "Everything was supposed to be different. We were supposed to retire, Leah would go to the university that year, and we and the Joneses were going to travel all over the world, carefree, knowing you all were living your lives, and then...then it happened. And nothing will ever be the same."

People are like that. We make plans; we have dreams, notions, goals; we focus on making them a reality without asking ourselves what will happen if they don't. I had decided years back I wanted to devote myself to painting, and I never envisioned any other form of life until I was deep in the black hole. It's easier to ignore the negatives and go straight for what we want. The problem...the problem is, then it's harder to accept the blow.

I stretched out a hand toward my mother. "I understand. And I know how you feel. But you can't just stay anchored there, Mom. It's hard, but life goes on."

"It's not the same. You're young, Axel; you see things in a different way. What do I have left? Rose and I used to fantasize about spending the afternoons cooking and drinking wine and chatting in the backyard, but now...the café is the only thing I have left. Being at home is unbearable; I need to stay busy to keep myself from thinking."

"I'm going to get dressed," I said, getting up.

"Thank you, honey," Mom said, smiling amid tears.

So an hour later I was at my parents' house, sitting in front of Oliver and beside Leah at the table, surrounded by food, voices, and laughter, though all I could think about was how fucking good she smelled, how I wanted to bend down and give her a kiss, like Emily and Justin did, about how the only thing that kept me from grabbing her, dragging her off to the bathroom, and stripping her naked was my last shred of common sense.

Who could have told me things would end up like this?

I felt a jab of desire when I felt her leg brush mine under the table. She looked at me when she noticed I tensed up, and I got lost in those turquoise eyes for a second, sinking, finding myself in them.

"I'll be right back. I'm going to grab a smoke." I got up suddenly.

"Wait, I'll come with you," Oliver said, following behind.

I leaned on the concrete barrier with a few plants climbing it and lit my cigarette before passing him one. The street was calm. The midday sun was reflected in the windshields of the cars parked out front. I took a long drag.

"Everything good in Sydney?" Every word was a struggle to pronounce.

"Better than here, I'd say. What's up lately?"

I shrugged. I wanted to run away. "Weird times," I managed to say. "It'll pass."

"I hope so, because it sucks to come here for a week and not see you, damn it. You're not all fucked up about painting again, are you? Hey, Axel, look at me."

I shook my head and expelled smoke. I felt so guilty... "Remember what you said to me a few months ago? About that chick of yours, Bega. How sometimes you aren't looking for something but it just appears." I rubbed my chin and stubbed out my cigarette. "Forget it, it's nothing."

"Fuck that. Tell me. I'm listening."

I looked at the hand he had just rested on my shoulder and felt the ground give way beneath my feet. I could have just out and said it. Get it over with. I knew Oliver; I knew how he reacted during conflicts, but none that we'd experienced had ever been *Hey, I'm fucking your little sister, cool?* And uncertainty and cowardice mingled in my stomach. But I did take one step forward, or backward, I don't know.

"I've met someone special."

In theory I'd known her for nineteen years, since she was born, but I didn't specify that. I analyzed Oliver's incredulous expression.

"You? Shit...I mean, cool. I don't know what to tell you. The only advice I can give is take it slowly and don't push too hard the first few months, because that's something you'd do. Shit, don't look at me like that..."

For the first time in ages, I wanted to punch my best friend.

"You know exactly what I'm talking about. You get excited and then you get bored. You get bored of your own dreams, Axel."

"That's not completely true."

I sounded cold, strange. Oliver looked at me and shook his head. He threw his cigarette on the ground, stepped forward, and hugged me. Fucking Oliver. A part of me wanted to be angry with him because it would be easier.

"I was trying to make things better, not worse. I'm sorry I've been gone these months, man, but I don't know, call me if you need something or want to talk." He pulled away and looked at me not like a friend, but like a brother. "Come on, let's go inside before your mom comes out and pokes us with the first thing she gets her hands on."

I smiled and followed him inside.

October

—

(SPRING)

91

———

Leah

"I WAS GOING TO DIE if I spent another minute without seeing you."

Axel started laughing and picked me up in his arms as he kissed me. When we got to his room, he dropped me on the bed and lifted my shirt to kiss my stomach next to my belly button. I trembled.

"You're exaggerating." He laughed.

"You aren't dying to be with me?"

"To kiss you. To touch you. To fuck you."

"Same thing," I said, defending myself with a grimace.

"It's not, but you know that, right, babe?"

I nodded, but actually I didn't know. I didn't understand. Not yet.

92

Leah

I HAD SPENT MONTHS WITH a five-hundred-piece puzzle in front of my nose, not knowing how to solve it, where all the pieces went. But little by little, it all started to come together. I guess there wasn't just one moment; instead it was all my talks with Axel, looking at myself in the mirror, making decisions. With the passage of time, I saw myself more clearly, I took off my raincoat, and though the wounds still ached, I let them air out and heal. He came, love pulling on that invisible thread that had stirred up feelings I thought no longer existed. Routine, classes, listening to what people said around me. Painting, color, emotions to get out. And finally I found myself talking to Axel about my parents on the porch, remembering them and rescuing them from that place full of dust where I had kept them hidden for a year.

Everything went back to…normal. Life went on.

93

—

Axel

IT WAS THE FIRST SATURDAY in October and Leah hadn't gone to school; she'd had a break for the past few days. So we had killed time kissing each other all over, talking, staying up late at night, or trying new recipes in my little kitchen. In the afternoon, she would study for a while or draw, and I loved the feeling of watching her from my desk as she worked, so focused, so lost in thought.

That day I went by myself to surf for a while, and when I came back, she was crouched down on the porch painting with some watercolors she had bought with Blair on Wednesday. I liked that, her going out with her friend, hanging out with people, going back to being the girl she had been before, but with more layers.

I lay down beside her, still wet. The afternoon colored the sky orange.

"What you doing?"

"Just colors, mixing them."

She took the heart-shaped sucker out of her mouth and bent over to give me a kiss. I held her there, bringing back her strawberry flavor on my tongue. She went on painting. I sighed and stayed there, relaxed. I closed my eyes, and at some point, sleep overtook me. When I awoke, she was sitting next to me with her legs crossed and dragging a fine brush over my hands.

"What are you doing?" I asked, groggy.

"Painting. You like?"

"Sure, what guy doesn't like having daisies all over his hand?"

Leah laughed. She was light. She was happiness.

"I like it if it makes you laugh that way."

The curve of her lips turned more pronounced. Leah slid the brush over the skin of my wrists, tracing out a small heart right where my pulse was beating faster and faster. I swallowed and stared at her.

"Remember the day I asked you if you realized I was going to die?"

Leah nodded and went on painting in silence.

"I couldn't really explain to you what I wanted to say. The thing is, we're all going to do it. Die, I mean. But do you know that? Have you thought about it; are you convinced of it? I think if we did think about it more, if right now we stopped and repeated to ourselves the absolute truth that we're going to croak, maybe it would change things in our lives, maybe we'd get rid of the stuff that doesn't make us happy, be more aware that every day might be our last. And I'll bet you can't guess what it is I can't stop thinking about."

She looked at me. The brush trembled in her hand.

"That I wouldn't change a single thing. If anyone asked me where I'd want to be right now, I would say right here, looking at you, lying on this porch." I watched her eyes grow moist before she embraced me.

"What would you say if I told you I feel the same? I can't stop thinking about it. About being with you. About how I don't want to go to college and be apart from you."

I sat up quickly. The moment was ruined. "What are you saying? Are you kidding?"

She wrinkled her forehead and breathed deeply. "I don't want to be away from you."

"God damn it, Leah, don't think anything like that again. And never...never give up something of yours for anyone. You're nineteen. You're going to go to college and you're going to live that stage the way I did too. I'm not going anywhere; are you listening to me?" I grabbed her chin and she nodded her head. I gave her a soft kiss. "It'll be fun, you'll see. You'll go partying, you'll meet people, you'll make new friends. In fact, you know what? You and I are going out today. We should do it more." I extended a hand and helped her up.

She didn't say anything, but I could see through her gaze. I saw the doubts, the questions, the fears. At the time I didn't want to face them, just cover them up and keep moving. We didn't talk more before getting dressed and going out to dinner. We went to the Italian place where I had eaten with my father weeks back. Leah relaxed and started to joke around when they served the appetizers. I loved seeing her smile. It filled my chest with a unique warm feeling. So I devoted myself to that the whole night, making her smile and laugh, saying stupid stuff just to experience those moments with her.

Then we took a walk on the beach and wound up at Cavvanbah without realizing it. I greeted my friends a little nervously. They soon realized Leah was Oliver's sister and included her in the conversation. I stopped being so tense around the third drink.

"Don't leave without telling us how you manage to live with him without throwing yourself into the river with your pockets full of stones," Tom said, already drunk by then.

"He's got his good side too." She looked at me from the corner of her eye.

"Bullshit. We've never seen it," Gavin said and laughed.

"Well, he's not a bad cook," she responded with a smile.

"Does he put on an apron and everything?" Jake joked, nudging her hard.

"Yeah, a pink Hello Kitty one." Leah started laughing.

She'd had two beers and seemed as drunk as me. I finished my drink in one sip while Madison came over to the table. She stared daggers at Leah, and I shifted uncomfortably when I remembered the day she had seen us at the art gallery in the car. It had been nothing, right? Just touching the edge of her mouth, an affection-ate gesture...

"You all want anything else?"

"Another beer," Leah said.

"Better not," I said. "Bring us the check."

Madison licked her lower lip and looked at me. "Should I wait for you when my shift's over?"

Maybe it was just my perception, but the silence that fell over the table was dense, and I could read understanding in Leah's expression. I prayed it wasn't that clear to everyone else.

"Nah, we're going," I said.

Madison looked back at Leah when she brought the check, then wandered off among the tables. I paid for the last round, we said goodbye to my friends, and we took the road to my house hugging the coast and passing through tropical vegetation. I grabbed Leah's hand when we were a ways off. She was distant, quiet, pensive.

"What's up with you?"

"Nothing. It's just…" She shook her head. "Forget it."

I stopped on the side of the road when my house became visible. I held her hips softly. It was silent apart from the singing of the crickets. "Tell me things. Don't ever hold back with me."

"It's just… That was uncomfortable. Seeing you with her."

"She's just a friend," I replied.

"One you fucked," she guessed.

"Exactly. We just fucked. That's all."

"What we have is different," she ventured.

"Totally different." I bent down and kissed her.

I ran my lips slowly over her tongue until she started panting, then slid my hands under her skirt and played with the seam of her panties until I pushed the fabric aside and felt the dampness on my fingertips, on my skin. I didn't care if we were outside; there was no one around. Just darkness. Just us. I sank a finger into her softly, and she arched, leaning against my chest. I held her around the waist.

"Look at me, babe. With you, it's always more, so much more. Different. Another way of living. I thought I knew before but everything's different. Don't you feel that?" I whispered, and when she nodded and a sigh escaped her, I felt pushed to move my fingers faster, deeper. I wanted to mark her with my hands. Draw her, her pleasure; the two concepts together. "Let's go home."

We stumbled down the road until we reached the door. I slammed it closed as Leah unbuttoned my shirt and pushed it over my shoulders. I took off her T-shirt and dropped it in the middle of the living room before lowering her skirt. We kissed as we walked to the bedroom, tripping, hugging, panting, her hanging around my neck and pressed into my chest.

"What the fuck have you done to me?" I whispered.

Because that was the question that consumed me at all hours of the day. At what exact moment had I lost my mind over her, what was the phrase or gesture that made it happen, when did I start belonging to her—because I did, even if my pride would never let me say it aloud.

"I want to give you everything." She looked at me and shivered.

"You have."

When our lips collided fiercely, she knelt in front of me. I held my breath. She took me into her mouth and I thought I would die. I breathed deeply, slowly, almost in time to her movements, which were slow and soft at first, but then turned more intense. God damn it, were they intense. I sank my fingers into her hair. Fuck. Her lips. Her tongue. Her mouth felt incredible. I tried to control myself, to hold back a little longer, but a shiver of pleasure ran though me when her eyes looked into mine as she caressed me with her mouth.

"Babe...I'm going to come..."

I tried to pull away, but she kept going. I put my hands on the wall in front of me and let out a hoarse cry when I emptied myself between her lips. It was devastating. From another planet. I closed my eyes and sucked in a breath of air, shaking like a little boy. I wanted for her to come back from the bathroom a minute later to grab her cheeks and kiss her over and over. Leah laughed as she hugged me.

"Jeez, I guess you liked it."

"It's not that…" I picked her up and carried her to the bed.

"What is it then?"

"Love," I whispered.

I know what lust was, pleasure, the longing to reach climax. But until she came into my life, I had known nothing of love, the need to satisfy another person, to give them everything, to think about them before you.

"Axel, what do you think of love?" she asked, lying in the white sheets.

"I don't know. Nothing in particular."

"You always have an answer for everything."

"I guess I think of you."

"That doesn't count."

"Well, that's the only truth I have. All I know is that I would happily spend my whole life like this. Talking with you. Fucking you. Dreaming of you. Everything with you. Do you think that's love?"

Leah smiled, cheeks red.

She was so precious I wanted to draw her.

94

Leah

WE ARE ALMOST NEVER AWARE of how happy we are when we are. We usually remember it and value it afterward: that family meal that you thought would be dull and turned out to be a blast, things that happen and you have no idea they'll turn into stories you'll always remember, that afternoon when you end up cracking up with your best friend until your stomach aches, the day you're lying on the sand being kissed by the hot sun and you think you have it all. Those kinds of moments you enjoy so much you don't stop to treasure them because you're there, right there, living them, feeling them, in the present.

But with him, I couldn't stop thinking about it. *Happiness*, the word was on the tip of my tongue every morning, just before I woke and gave him a slow kiss. I think it was because a part of me already knew it wouldn't end well, that I needed to hold on to all those moments we were experiencing together because I would remember them for years and they would be the only thing I could hold on to.

95

—

Axel

I NOTICED SOMETHING. A SOFT crack, but I didn't pay any attention to it until I heard the noise of a couple of steps on the wood of the living room floor. I opened my eyes wide. I don't know how the fuck I managed to get out of bed and put on a bathing suit from the top drawer, my heart suddenly in my throat. Leah murmured something incomprehensible, still half asleep, but I hardly paid attention. I crossed my room in two long steps and grabbed the door frame. Shit. Fuck. Shit.

Justin looked at me, keys in his hands, an incredulous expression on his face. His eyes veered toward the clothes we had left scattered around on our way to the bedroom, and then looked into Leah's empty room before staring back at me.

"What the fuck have you done, Axel? What the fuck…?"

He brought his hands to his head, and I closed the door so Leah wouldn't come out just then, even if the situation couldn't get any worse. Justin's expression said it all. There was nothing to explain, he'd grasped everything.

I swallowed slowly. I could hardly breathe. "I told you that key was for emergencies only."

"Fuck me! That's all you've got to say to me? Are you out of your goddamn mind? Where the fuck is your head? Of all the things you've ever done, I swear, this is... You've crossed the line this time. But you don't get that, do you? You think you're above everyone else; you just stare at your belly button and everyone else can go fuck themselves."

"Lower your goddamn voice. You're going to wake her up."

Justin looked at me in shock. I was too, because that was far from the best thing I could have said at that moment, but I was angry and scared and more bewildered than I'd ever been. I bit my tongue to keep from saying anything else stupid and walked out the back door. My brother followed me. The morning sun was burning high in the sky. I walked down the trail until the grass gave way to sand. Then I stopped and took a few deep breaths, keeping my eyes focused on the sea.

"It's not what you think, it's not some fling..."

The wind rustled my brother's brown hair. "Explain it, then. Make me understand, because right now I don't know what to do with this, Axel. This never even passed through my mind..."

"Mine either. What can I tell you, Justin? It just happened. What do you want me to say? I fell in love with her. I didn't want to, but I also don't know what's wrong with it. It doesn't feel wrong."

"Fuck, Axel." He walked away a bit.

I gave him time and a little space. I waited in the middle of the beach while he walked back and forth with his brow furrowed, muttering the occasional curse word. I would have laughed in any other situation, but that day I was about to have a heart attack. I walked over to him when my impatience got the best of me.

"Justin, say something. Say whatever."

"You're in love with her?" He looked at me cruelly.

"Don't make me repeat it."

"Today's not the best day for you to joke around, Axel. Fine, it happened, let's accept that. Things like this do, but that doesn't change the thing that really matters. You need to talk to Oliver. Now."

"I can't. Not yet."

"Why?" He crossed his arms.

Because I'll fucking lose him. Because I hate the word conse-quences. *Because I'm scared of what will happen.* "I need to find the perfect way to tell him. When I do, I need him to understand. It's not that easy, okay? At first, I just wanted to see where it went, but now...it's even more fucked up."

"You've really screwed up this time."

"God damn it, Justin, I know!" I shouted.

But then, instead of replying with one of his usual stiff replies, he walked over and hugged me. I stayed there feeling dull and cold because I couldn't remember the last time I'd hugged my brother. I clapped him on the back, still surprised, and drew the hug out as I recalled my father talking about Justin's jealousy when we went out to dinner. My brother looked at me and shoved me on the shoulder.

"Everything will be okay, you'll see. Who else knows?"

"No one."

He raised an eyebrow.

"What did you expect?"

"It's fine... I mean...well...I don't know."

"You don't have to do anything," I said.

"Yeah. But if you need to talk or something..."

"I'll call you. Thanks, Justin." We went back to my house. "By the way, what brought you over here? Oh, and give me back my key. You broke the rules."

"I'm keeping the key. I had some free time, I just assumed you were out surfing, and I thought I could come by and join you; you could give me some quick lessons. I called you, but you didn't pick up, obviously."

"Why would you want surfing lessons?"

"Why not?" He looked me in the eye.

"Because you haven't done it in two decades."

"It's never too late. The other day I heard Emily say she thought these surfer tourists were hot. I think she was on the phone with a friend. And now I can't get it out of my head. Lately we've been doing it less because with the kids, it's just impossible, and look at me, I've got a gut now, and if I'm optimistic, I've got five more years before my hair falls out."

I laughed, and he punched me in the shoulder.

"You're an unlucky bastard. Don't be an idiot though. What does her thinking tourists are attractive have to do with what you guys have? They're two different things, Justin. And you somehow got lucky enough to have a wife who adores you, who's fun and smart and very fuckable."

"Stop talking about Emily that way."

"Take the stick out of your ass."

Justin stood still for a moment when he saw Leah in the kitchen making coffee. She smiled at him. "Want one?"

"Thanks, I'm on my way out though." He looked at the two of us as though trying to put us together for the first time, then huffed, said goodbye, and left. I exhaled the breath I'd been holding as I walked over to Leah. I hugged her from behind and kissed the nape of her neck.

"We've got to talk, babe."

96

Leah

WE AGREED THAT WE WOULD tell Oliver on November first. I would have liked to do it myself, because I felt ready, strong, self-assured. I felt full of color and part of me wanted to share this with my brother. Axel smiled when he heard me and shook his head. He kissed me on the edge of my lips. He said he had to do it himself, Oliver was his friend, he loved him...and I respected that. Then he asked me for a favor, something he'd been putting off for months and that we needed to do first. He told me slowly, speaking softly, tentatively. I know he was frightened of what I'd say. I know he was worried I'd burst into tears and close up inside myself, but when I heard him, all I felt was an uncomfortable tingle in my stomach followed by curiosity. And...need.

97

—

Leah

I OBSERVED THE BLURRY COLORS we were leaving behind as we drove down the road. It was sunny, with no clouds. I turned my head to look at Axel's profile, and I tried to memorize the image: him driving, relaxed, with an arm hanging out the window, the little scar on his left eyebrow from when he had hit himself on his surfboard when he was sixteen, his jaw, just shaved that morning, when I insisted on passing the razor back over the places where he'd left stubble; he was neglectful like that with everything...

He stretched out a hand and rested it on my knee. I was nervous.

"Remember, Leah, you don't have to do this; it's only if you want to. If you get cold feet, just tell me, and I'll turn around right away and we'll do something else, just spend the day out or have lunch on the beach. I just wanted to give you all the options."

"I know. But I'd rather stick to it."

I don't know how long we were in the car because my thoughts were elsewhere, in a place full of memories I was slowly blowing the dust off of. It might have been an hour. Or maybe two. When we stopped in the middle of a development of white houses, the knot in my throat was so big I could hardly breathe.

He gave me his hand. I took it.

"You ready?" he asked, unnerved.

"I don't think I ever will be," I admitted, "so we might as well get it over with."

I opened the door and got out. Humidity impregnated the air, and nothing was audible but the singing of birds and the hissing of the tree branches shaking in the wind. The place was filled with a sense of ease. I looked at the mailbox with the number 13 and the two-story home with the white fence around the small yard with its carpet of grass and a few toys lying around.

I walked toward the entrance. Axel followed me.

I rang the doorbell. My stomach clenched when she opened the door. She was a young woman, around forty, with a sweet gaze, pale skin, slightly sunken cheeks. Tension encircled us.

"I was waiting for you. Come on in."

I could see her hand was trembling as she leaned on the door frame. It was hard for me to say the words, but I knew I needed to do it on my own, for me, because he had been beside me from the beginning, supporting me and lifting me up, helping me to keep going, to get stronger. I tried to control my angst.

"It's okay... Don't come in..." I whispered.

Axel seemed surprised, but stepped back and put his hands in his pants pockets. "No worries, I'll be here waiting for you. Don't rush."

I followed the woman inside, and my heart started pounding

when she closed the door. I looked at her living room, the framed photos of two smiling children with gap teeth, the comfy, familiar-looking sofa where I ended up sitting down.

She asked me if I wanted something to drink, and when I shook my head, she sat down in a chair in front of me and started rubbing her hands together. "I'm a little nervous," she began.

"Me too," I admitted in a hoarse whisper.

I looked at her. I looked at the woman who had changed my life, who one day, after a twelve-hour shift at a hospital, closed her eyes for a few moments behind the wheel and crossed over her lane into the opposing one, where we were driving while the first notes of "Here Comes the Sun" played. I thought I should feel hatred and rage and more pain, but when I felt around inside myself and looked, all that was there was compassion and a bit of fear of how unpredictable life can be. Because that day I had been on the other side, but on any other day, I could find myself in her shoes, because there are things you can't foresee and almost can't forget. And when she told me in tears how sorry she was, I realized that my work in that house was done.

98

Leah

IT'S FUNNY HOW THINGS CHANGE. Some changes take years, a whole life, others happen in minutes. When I walked into that house, I was a different person from the one who came out just half an hour later. All it took was a couple of words. Often we see everything through filters, and then one day we start stripping them away and what's left is reality.

When I came out and saw Axel leaning on the side of his car with his arms crossed, my knees trembled. Because I saw him more clearly. More mine. More him. More perfect. More everything. And I ran to him with my heart in my throat as if he were the one solid thing in the world, my world, the point everything else revolved around.

I hugged him. I grabbed his body, trembling but conscious of every detail: the softness of his skin, how good he smelled, how much I loved him, how important he would always be to me. I hid my head in the hollow of his neck and we stayed there, holding each other and swaying in the middle of the street, closing a trunk together that was full of pain before but where there were now only beautiful memories I never wanted to hide again.

"Months ago you said I thought you were an insensitive bastard because you kept pouring salt in the wound. And you were right. I thought about it." I took a deep breath, getting lost in his blue eyes. "But you also said...that one day I would thank you, that I should remember that conversation..."

"Babe..." His voice was hoarse.

"Thank you, Axel. For everything. Thank you thank you thank you." I hugged him again, this time harder, almost knocking him down against the car, and we stayed there a few minutes in silence, clutching each other.

99

Axel

I TURNED UP THE RADIO when "A 1000 Times" started playing and put on my sunglasses as we drove away from that development and headed toward the coast. I looked at Leah out of the corner of my eye for a second, keeping that image for myself, her with her eyes closed, singing softly, the midday sun caressing her eyelashes, the tip of her nose, and her smile. And I remembered one of the first things Douglas taught me when I was young, that light was color, that without it there was nothing.

We stopped to buy some sandwiches and ended up on the beach. There was no one there, just some surfers far off. I took a big towel out of the trunk and stretched it out over the sand. Leah lay down, stretching her arms, and I had to suppress the urge to cover her with my body and caress her all over. I sat down beside her and waited until she sat up to give her some food. When she finished the last bite, she stood up, walked to the shore, and let the water splash her legs. I contemplated it, absorbed in how it seemed to fit in with the landscape, in the beauty of that picture, the peace that warmed my chest as I saw her there, so whole, so happy, so herself.

She ran over to me smiling and flopped down on the towel, her eyes squinting from the sun. Leah kissed me on the neck, the jawline, the eyelids, the lips. I let out a soft moan and got hard. I squeezed her against my body.

"You're my favorite person in the world."

I laughed. "And you'll be the end of me," I whispered.

Leah drew spirals with her fingertips on my shoulder and moved slowly down my arm. She asked me to close my eyes and try to guess what she was tracing out on my skin. I took a deep breath when I made out *I love you. Love, Submarine.* I liked how it made sense for us and no one else.

"Axel, do you think...do you think you could draw me?"

I opened my eyes and my pulse started racing. "I don't know. No, I couldn't."

Her face was inches away from mine. "Why? Tell me, please."

"Because I would be scared of trying it and not succeeding." I laid her out next to me. With one hand, I pushed her knotted hair out of her face before stroking her cheek with my thumb. "I'm going to tell you about the night I decided never to paint again."

And I told her everything, holding nothing back, and I didn't have to tiptoe anymore around any mention of the Joneses. I let her see how important her father was to me, how fucked up I was, how unhappy I'd been in those days.

"You never tried to go back to it?"

"No, everything's still there on top of the dresser."

"But Axel, how's it possible..."

"Because I don't feel it the way you do. And if I don't feel it, if I'm just doing *something*, then it's better not to bother getting my hands dirty. I told you, the day you understand me, you'll see yourself better. Because you've got magic, babe. You've got it all."

"But it's so, so sad, Axel."

"It doesn't matter." I bent over her and kissed her slowly.

"So I'm going to have to spend my whole life wondering what I look like through your eyes, how your hands would draw me..." she sighed as she embraced me.

I couldn't answer because I had a knot in my throat and her words awakened a charge I thought I'd forgotten. One I'd buried. Not very deeply. I'd just abandoned it. That was all.

"Wait. I know. I've got an idea!" She smiled at me.

A half hour later, we were in the car debating the details. When Leah knew for certain, we got out and walked to the tattoo shop on the corner at the end of the street. I explained the particulars to the guy behind the counter reading a newspaper. He gave us a thumbs-up and we walked into the studio.

The guy handed me a marker. I walked over to Leah slowly while she lifted her shirt, leaving the edge of her breast and her entire flank exposed. I took a deep breath. I sat in front of her and slid my fingers over the skin covering her ribs and the right side of her torso.

"Don't overthink it, Axel."

"It's forever..."

"I don't care, it's your handwriting."

I held my breath as I ran the marker tip over her skin, which rose up in a patch of gooseflesh. I slid it softly up and down and up again, tracing out every syllable, every vowel, just for her.

I pulled back when I was done. I read it: "Let it be."

The song we danced to on the porch the first night I kissed her. The night when everything started to change for us.

"You like it?" I asked.

"It's perfect."

The guy got his materials ready and walked over. I watched meditatively as my letters were engraved in her skin, how every trace, every drop of ink seemed to unite us forever in a memory that was ours alone.

100

Axel

IT WAS THE SECOND-TO-LAST SATURDAY in October when I walked into my parents' house with an anniversary gift in hand. They weren't going to celebrate until the following Friday, when Oliver was back and we would all go to dinner at Justin and Emily's house. They had planned things so Mom wouldn't have to cook that day. At six in the evening, I rang the door.

My father opened and hugged me. "How's it going, dude? You look good."

"You too. I like that pendant."

"It's a tree of life from the Kabbalah," he said proudly.

I accompanied him inside. Mom came out to greet me and asked me if I wanted anything. When I said no, she furrowed her brow.

"Nothing? Not even a little tea?"

"No, I'm good."

"Orange juice?"

I rolled my eyes and sighed. "Fine, an orange juice."

"I knew you wanted one." She winked.

My father sat in his easy chair and asked me about my recent work.

Mom passed me the juice a few minutes later and sat down with her hands crossed over her legs and a curious expression. "I don't want to be rude, honey, but why are you here? You're worrying me."

"Why does everything make you think of something bad?"

"Believe me, every time they used to call me from your school, I would pray it was for a good reason, a trophy or an unexpected A, but it never happened. I realized I was only ever right when I thought it was something bad. You know I adore you, dear, but…"

"For fuck's sake, that was forever ago!"

"That mouth!"

"I just wanted to bring you two your anniversary present." I got up to take the slightly bent envelope out of my pants pocket. My mother's lower lip twitched when I handed it to her. I waited nervously while she opened it, trying to decipher her expression, but it was almost impossible because she was excited, surprised, but also scared, with a tense face.

"A trip to Rome…" She looked up at me. "You're giving us a trip to Rome?"

"Yeah." I shrugged.

"But that's…so much money…"

"It's your dream, isn't it?"

My father looked at me with gratitude.

"I don't know…I don't know if we can do it…" Mom put the plane tickets in her lap and brought her hand to her lips. "There's the café and…other things. I have the cake competition…"

Dad took a deep breath, and I saw determination in his eyes when he turned to her and grabbed her by the cheeks. I wanted to get up and leave, let them have that intimate moment to themselves, but I couldn't move.

"Honey, look at me. We're going. And it's going to be the first trip of many. We'll dip into our savings account, we'll get on that plane, and we'll start a new phase. Are you listening to me? It's time to move on, Georgia."

She nodded slowly, almost like a little girl. Sometimes emotions and the way we assimilate them don't have much to do with age. I thought about that and the different ways we all have of accepting the same thing, loss. I guess in a way life consists of trying to jump over the pits that show up along the way and spend as little time as possible lying on the ground uncertain how to get up.

I stood. My parents insisted I stay a while longer, but instead, I kissed each of them and said we would see each other on Friday night. I knew they needed to be alone, and I...wanted to be back with her.

Maybe because I missed her. Maybe because I'd gotten used to spending every second by her side. Maybe because I knew in a few days, everything would change.

101

Axel

I WALKED IN THROUGH THE back door and saw Leah's surfboard on the porch. I smiled at the thought of her feeling the need to get lost in the waves in my absence. I saw her through the door. Her back was turned, and she was kneeling on the floor in front of a big canvas with a palette full of fresh gobs of paint. All she had on was her bikini from earlier, and I caught a spectacular view of her ass.

I took off my shirt and walked over to her. She looked at me over her shoulder and smiled.

"Don't move," I said before I knelt down beside her. I hugged her, slid my hands under the fabric covering her breasts, and brushed my thumb against her nipple until she panted and dropped her brush. "I missed you."

I closed my eyes and touched her all over, kissed her tattoo, sank a finger inside her, and her back tensed against my chest. I kissed her neck. I grabbed her by the hair. I smelled the sea on her skin and all I wanted was to lick it. I ran my tongue down her spine and felt every twitch in her body. I stopped thinking about anything. Except for her. Me. Us. How precious she was, how full of color...

I wasn't thinking when I stretched my hand out to the palette next to us and buried my fingers in her paints. Then I ran them over her body: her back, her buttocks, her legs. I colored her with my hands on top of that canvas.

She sighed. "Axel..."

There was so much longing in her voice that I almost came when I heard her say my name that way. I held my breath and pulled her bikini bottoms down in one go. I unbuttoned my pants and took them off as I lay beside her and held her over the canvas in my arms stained with paint.

I pushed inside her. I closed my eyes.

I couldn't see her face, but I could hear her rapid breaths. I rammed her again, holding her hips tight. Harder. Deeper. Leah moaned, shouted. I clenched my teeth and grabbed more paint and my hands covered her with it while I pushed inside her over and over, and it was never enough, nothing filled the hole in my chest at the uncertainty of whether or not this was forever. When her skin was covered in paint and sweat, I pulled away and turned her around, because I wanted to fuck her with my eyes, too, with my hands, with every gesture.

Leah's breathing was agitated and her bare breasts rose and fell rhythmically. Her eyes were shining and pinned on me. Full of everything. Love. Desire. Need. Our gazes intertwined while I traced a blue line from her cheek to her belly button, slowly, so slow that every touch between her skin and mine was pleasure and torture at the same time. Her soft lips opened as she squeezed me against her, smearing me with the paint that covered her while I contemplated her, enchanted.

"I'm so fucking in love with you…"

"Kiss me." She sank her fingers in my hair and pulled me close until our lips met.

She tasted like strawberry. She tasted like strawberry again.

She moved her hips in a circle. I exhaled and clenched my teeth.

"I could spend my whole life like this, fucking you and looking at you and kissing you." I moaned and grabbed her ass to ram her deeper.

Leah bit my lip when I held her wrists down on the canvas and moved my hips against hers, making her mine, getting lost in her, giving her everything.

"Fuck, babe…fuck…"

She came. Her back arched, she moaned into my mouth.

Her eyes were glassy when she opened them again.

I kept ramming her. More and more and more…

"Tell me you love me," she said.

I pressed my forehead into hers. My heart sped up, pounding hard, and I ran my lips softly over her, tasting her, tasting her tension, about to explode. I took a deep breath when she kissed me on the heart, in the middle of my chest, then I lost control and exploded with a groan that I silenced against her warm flesh.

I hugged her. Silence. I brought my mouth to her ear. "We all live in a yellow submarine."

I didn't move for what seemed like an eternity. Because I couldn't. I was still inside her, over her body, and all I could think was that it was perfect, that there are things we seem destined for and that just have to happen. I breathed against her neck until she moved her arms to wrap them around me, and the touch of her skin made me open my eyes. I wrinkled my forehead and pulled away from her. I stood up. I looked at her lying there over that surface that was once white and that was now full of color, of us making love, of the image her body had made next to mine.

I held my breath. Something jerked in my chest.

"What is it? What are you looking at?"

"The greatest work of my life." I grabbed her wrists and pulled her up.

There it was. A painting. Mine. Hers. Ours.

Leah hugged me. I was incapable of looking away from that whirlpool of colors, of random lines, of our story made art. That day I understood that you didn't have to think to represent, that what would be scribbles and blotches to everyone else could be, for us, the most beautiful painting in the world.

I crouched down, grabbed it, and went to the bedroom.

"Axel, what are you doing?" Leah followed me.

I grabbed my toolbox and took out a hammer and anchor screws. Ten minutes later, the painting was there, taking up the entire wall over my bed. And I knew that it would stay there forever. I turned back to Leah, my breathing still far from calm.

"It's not dry yet," she whispered.

"It will dry. Come here, babe."

She got into the bed. She was still naked. I squeezed her against me, skin to skin, heart to heart, and kissed her softly, slowly, putting everything into it...everything that filled my chest in that instant.

102

Axel

LIFE IS THAT: UNPREDICTABLE.

One day you think you know yourself well, and the next you find yourself looking in the mirror surprised. One day you think nothing can happen to you...and then it does. One day you're convinced you'll never fall in love with that girl you watched grow up in the backyard of your house, and then you lose your head over her as if you've been waiting your whole life to find out the full meaning of the word *love*. One day you realize you've left aside that brother who was always there in the shadows, afraid of coming close to you and being rejected. One day you're sure you know how your best friend will react to any situation and... you're wrong.

103

Leah

I HADN'T SLEPT FOR SEVERAL nights since Oliver came back on Sunday and I went home knowing that at the end of the week, Axel would talk to him and tell him everything. A part of me wanted to get it over with, the way you tear a bandage off in one go. Another was scared, and the uncertainty was suffocating me.

I looked at the dress I had left on my desk chair and was planning to wear that night to the dinner at Emily and Justin's place. It was black, discreet, but it made me look sexy, I thought, but maybe that had more to do with how I felt when Axel's hands touched me than with the garment itself.

I got out of bed just as Oliver entered my room.

"I'm going to Cavvanbah to have a drink with some friends." He tucked his printed shirt into his pants. "Should I come pick you up, or do you want to meet at the Nguyens'?"

"I'll see you there."

"Cool. Give me a kiss, pixie."

I wouldn't have let him go if I had known what would happen just a few hours later...

104

Axel

IT WAS A WARM SPRING night as I arrived at the house Justin and Emily had bought in the suburbs a few years back. I walked down the driveway, and my nephews ran out from behind some bushes where they had been crouching. I laughed when they attacked me with a couple of water guns. I managed to get one away from Max and shoot him in the face until he ran off.

I greeted Emily and then went to the backyard where the table was set in the middle of the grass. Justin was standing further off at the barbecue grill. I came up behind him and clapped him on the back while he watched the meat roasting.

"Were you a good brother? Did you keep me in mind?"

"You've got a vegetable lasagna inside."

"I fucking love you," I laughed.

Justin shook his head before flipping the hamburgers while his children ran back and forth. "How's everything?" he asked.

"It is what it is."

I looked back when I heard the door open and I saw Leah emerge. My heart stopped. She was precious with that smile...

with that dress that I wanted to tear off immediately. I walked over and kissed her on the cheek. Justin was tense when he greeted her and asked her if she liked her meat well done.

We spent a while fooling around with Max and Connor, who didn't stop even for a second, and then we took the dishes to the table. My parents appeared just as I was setting down a dish, and I went to say hi to them.

Oliver was a few feet behind them.

His brow was furrowed and his mouth contracted in a thin tense line. I guess when I saw that, I should have known what was going to happen. After he made his way through the people in front of him and reached me, I couldn't avoid the first punch. Or the second one. My family started shouting all around, but all I could think of was the searing pain and what had caused it, because I knew a part of me deserved it, and because at least that way, I could give Oliver some satisfaction.

I stumbled with the third blow, but I managed not to fall. I heard Leah screaming at her brother, but neither of us took his eyes off the other, as if all the threads that had held us together since we were eight were breaking one by one. In my mouth was the metallic taste of blood. I spit on the ground. Oliver stepped toward me again. He didn't seem even close to finished, but Justin grabbed him from behind before he could reach me. I think he must have realized I wasn't going to defend myself.

"How the fuck…? How could you?"

I didn't answer. What the hell was I going to answer? I was about to say, "It just happened," but I knew that wouldn't be enough. I saw it in his eyes. The hatred, the incomprehension, the disappointment.

"What's going on here? Boys..." My mother's voice was trembling and her eyes were open wide.

Connor started to cry, and Emily took him and his twin inside while I rubbed my sore jaw, trying not to look at my parents. "We need to talk..."

"I'm going to kill you, Axel!"

Justin held him tighter.

"Tonight. My house," I continued, and I don't know why the fuck I sounded so cold and calm, because inside, I was dying. I'd always been like that though. It had always been hard for me to show my emotions in tense situations. "In an hour. I'll be waiting for you."

"You're a piece of shit," he hissed.

If I'm honest, he wasn't entirely wrong.

"Axel, just get the fuck out of here," Justin said.

I decided that would be best and left, not looking at Leah, because if I did...if I did, I would know for sure how this was going to end. I could still hear Oliver shouting at his sister to get her things, ignoring my parents' questions and Justin's attempts to calm him down. In the car, I pounded the steering wheel, then turned the key and sped off.

The first thing I did when I got home was grab the bottle of rum. I took a few sips straight from the neck while walking toward the bathroom to look at myself in the mirror. I spit the last gulp into the sink because my mouth was still bleeding. I could put two and two together. I didn't need to think about it long, knowing Oliver had gone to Cavvanbah that afternoon. Madison must have seen enough—much more than I had thought. I tried to calm myself down. I drank a little more, and a few minutes later, I heard the knock on the door. He almost beat it down. I opened up.

"Fucking son of a bitch…" Oliver came through like a hurricane.

He punched me again. I couldn't dodge that one, but afterwards I wrapped my hands around his back and pushed him against the wall. There was so much tension between us, it was hard for me to breathe.

I spoke through clenched teeth. "I haven't defended myself yet, but I promise you, you try to hit me again and I'll hit back. Believe me, Oliver, that's not what I want, but you're backing me into a corner. So I'm begging you; fucking listen to me."

I let him go and walked a few steps back.

His shoulders wriggled and he snorted like an animal, walking from one side of the living room to the other. He punched the wall closest to me, then ran his hands through his hair before finally raising his head and looking up at me for once.

"How could you, Axel? How the fuck….?"

"I don't know. I just…"

"You don't know? What the fuck kind of response is that? Do you realize what you've done?"

"It just happened." I had a stone in my throat, and it kept growing and growing, choking me. "I didn't want to, but…I need her." It came out like that, thoughtless. The least appropriate thing I could say.

"You need her? Sure. What about her needs?"

I didn't answer. I wasn't capable of telling him she needed me; I wasn't sure if it was true.

"That doesn't matter, does it?"

I wanted to knock that sardonic smile off his face. "Yeah, it matters. It's the only thing that matters to me."

Oliver punched the wall again, and I saw the skin peel away from his knuckles. When he scowled at me again, a muscle tensed in his jaw. "Do you not see? She's a girl! She's nineteen!"

"No. I don't see her that way. And she's an adult."

"An adult? Oh, well that makes it all okay, doesn't it? Tell me one thing then, Axel. When did you stop seeing her as a little sister? How long have you been waiting for this to happen?"

I became furious. Now I was the one out of control. I ran over and slammed him against the front door, grabbing him by the neck. "Don't you ever insinuate anything like that again."

"What's the matter? Truth hurts? You've fucking brainwashed her. You know what she said to me when I dragged her into the car? That she doesn't want to go to college. That she wants to stay here with you. Really sweet, right? For her to spend all her life shut up in your goddamn hermit's cabin. Brilliant, a promising future, right? The very reason I've spent an entire goddamn year busting my hump."

"It's not true. That's not true." It couldn't be. I let him go.

"You would never have let this happen if you really loved her. Tell me one thing, Axel. Do you even know what it is to put other people before yourself? No, right? You don't know what that is. You're incapable of repressing your desires, because you always come first, and second, and third. It's always about you." He put a hand on his chest. "Before me. Before anyone."

If I could just breathe... But I couldn't, I couldn't... "It wasn't supposed to be like this. I wanted to tell you, but I didn't know how..."

Oliver's eyes were glassy. *Shit.* I turned around, went to the kitchen, and grabbed the bottle of rum. When I came back, he was on the floor, breathing deep, trying to calm himself down. I sat by the other edge of the wall and drank. Silence embraced us. The strangest silence of my entire life, because really, it was full of noise. My heart was pounding out of my chest. I took another long sip before speaking, because my mouth was dry and the words were crushed together and wouldn't come out.

"I'm sorry, Jesus, I'm sorry," I whispered. "I know I fucked up, I know I didn't do right, but...I love her. I didn't even know I could feel this way about someone. I don't know how it happened or when; there wasn't a precise moment. But it happened, and I would do anything for her."

Oliver hid his head between his knees. It wasn't a good sign. I took another sip even though I was nauseated and waited, waited, waited...

"Then don't chain her to you."

I held my breath and looked at him. "What does that mean?"

"It means this shouldn't have happened, that she's nineteen and she's been through a fucked-up situation. She has to go to college and have fun and go out and live her life, the same as you and I did in our day. Don't take that from her."

I grew tense, hesitated... Hesitated because I had thought that same thing way too many times and it frustrated me that it was true. That she hadn't had the chance to be with more guys before me, that her experience was so limited. I had chosen her after learning, trying, fucking, understanding many things. She had chosen me because I was all she knew. *You're my favorite person in the world*, she had said. I asked myself how many people Leah had even known if she hadn't even left Byron Bay.

I hated the idea that Oliver might be right. "I don't know if I can do that," I confessed.

He reached over, grabbed the bottle, and took a sip. "You can. And you owe it to me." He rubbed his face from exhaustion. "I trusted you, Axel. I told you to take care of her, I told you she was all I had left, the thing that mattered most to me, and you…"

"I'm sorry." The words came from my soul.

Oliver shook his head. His eyes gleamed. He took another sip. "You know what? The problem isn't that you've got feelings for her. The problem is you didn't stop it, that you did things the way you did them. You lied to me, you didn't talk to me, you just threw away a life's worth of friendship because you're a fucking coward."

He leaned against the wall and struggled to get up. I did the same, and we looked at each other in silence.

"How can I fix this?"

"You already know, Axel." His voice sounded firm.

I wanted to vomit, but I nodded slowly. I stood there in the middle of the living room while Oliver turned toward the door. Before turning the knob, he looked at me over his shoulder. I saw a whole life together in that last look.

I held his stare, but I didn't say a word.

And Oliver walked out of my house. Out of my life.

105

Axel

"I CAN'T TAKE ANY MORE, damn it."

Oliver placed his hands on his knees and huffed, drained. We were at Cape Byron, and we had many stairs still to go before we reached the most isolated section. I turned and pulled on him, helping him stand up straight. It was hot and muggy, and Oliver's eyes were still red and swollen three days after his parents' funeral.

Leah was supposed to be there too, but keeping in mind the amount of tranquilizers she was on and her absolute refusal to come, my family had said they would do so instead. But Oliver said no, he didn't want to share that moment with anybody else, it was his thing, and so I was the only one to accompany him. Because there were no secrets between us. We were more than brothers.

We kept climbing under the morning sun and the clear sky. It was a pretty day. Calm. I remember because I thought the Joneses would have liked it, the serenity of every step we took, going higher and higher.

The sea breeze greeted us when we reached the peak. I looked out at the views: the immense ocean, the waves hitting the rocks, the intense green of the grass we were walking on, and in the distance, a group of dolphins bursting through the calm surface of the water.

Oliver squeezed the bridge of his nose. "I don't know if I can do it."

"Of course you can. Let me."

I grabbed the backpack he had just thrown on the ground and opened it slowly while he walked a few feet away, trying to calm down. I took out the two urns and placed them on the damp grass, trying to keep my hands from shaking. Oliver came back, looking at the ground. I stepped forward, hugged him, and clapped him on the back.

"You ready?" I asked.

He handed me Douglas's urn and grabbed Rose's. I had expected he would do it alone, so I stood there a moment before I could react. I walked to the cliff's edge beside him. We looked at each other. Oliver took a deep breath. And we let them go without another word. We stood there, in front of the sea, together. Saying goodbye.

November

—

(SPRING)

106

Leah

I BURIED MY FACE IN my pillow when I heard Oliver, who spoke to me from the door of my room. Hard. Angry. Disappointed. Unwilling to understand.

He talked about college, about how he would move back soon, how he would just go to Sydney to arrange everything and then he would come back for good. Then we would make plans. We'd find a dorm in Brisbane, I'd take my final exams, he'd help me move, and we'd spend a few days together in the city so I could get to know it.

All I wanted to do was shout. But what I offered him was silence. A silence that exasperated him and that helped me keep whole.

When he couldn't take it anymore that day, he came to my bed and made me turn around to look at him. He sat there on the edge of it, furious. I wouldn't meet his eyes.

"Do you realize all I've done for you, Leah?" His voice was quaking. My nose started tingling, and I wanted to cry. "You're going to spend the next few days with Justin and Emily, and you're not going to give them any trouble, all right? Hey, look at me." He pulled my hair out of my face. "You already know this is for your own good. All this was my fault. I should never have left you here, not in the state you were in."

"You're not listening to me. I told you. I've always loved him; this is real..."

"You don't know Axel. You don't know what he's like when he gets into a relationship, how he just shoves away all the things that stop interesting him. Has he ever told you how he stopped painting? Has he ever told you how when something gets complicated, he refuses to fight for it? He's got his black holes too."

A tear—just one—escaped me.

"You're the one who doesn't know him," I whispered.

He looked at me with sorrow and I wanted to erase that expression. It infuriated me to see him judging Axel and not bothering to understand a single word of all I had told him those past few days, how he didn't respect me, how he thought he could come between us, acting like all this was a mistake.

I sent one last message to Blair before getting off of Justin and Emily's sofa and walking on tiptoe to the door. I hadn't heard from Axel in a week. A week of silence, of uncertainty, of going to bed every night in tears because I didn't understand what was happening. I needed to see him and be sure he was okay, that this was just a pothole we would forget, leaving it behind with the passing of time. Oliver would eventually understand.

So I asked my best friend for a favor, and all I had to do was go out the door without making noise and come back a little later, at midnight. But I screwed up and hit my knee against a table in the living room, bringing my hand to my mouth to keep from shouting. The lights turned on.

Justin was looking at me. He was wearing blue pajamas. "Leah. What are you doing?"

"I have to see him. Please."

He rubbed his face and looked at the clock on the shelf. "This is a terrible idea."

"I won't be long, I promise."

"Two hours. If you're not back in two hours, I'm going to look for you."

I thanked him with my eyes, because he was the only person who seemed to understand us. I left, walking past the fence, and saw the red car parked beside it. Kevin was in front behind the wheel, sitting next to Blair. I got into the back seat, hugged her as best I could, and he took off toward the house where I had lived for the past eight months, a place suddenly alien to me, as though I hadn't set foot inside it in years.

"Thank you for this," I whispered.

Blair stretched her hand back to grab mine. I squeezed it between my fingers, as in the old days, as though we were out on one of our wild late-night adventures. I wanted to laugh, more from the nerves that were making a mess of my stomach than from anything else. I took a deep breath when Kevin parked out front.

"No rush. We'll be here waiting for you."

I said goodbye to them and walked around the house to the back porch. I saw him before I made it there. When I saw his eyes,

I grew tense, because that stare wasn't the one I'd known in those last days we spent together. It was different, colder, more distant, vaguer. I walked up the steps. Axel was leaning on the railing with a cigarette in his hand. He put it out before looking me over slowly from head to toe. I shook.

—

107

Axel

LEAH HESITATED, BUT A SECOND later she took off running toward me and hugged me, clutching my body, killing me a little inside. I closed my eyes and took a deep breath, but it was a mistake, because that only made her scent envelop me. I made the biggest effort of my life when I grabbed her shoulders and pushed her away softly.

"What's happening? Why aren't you answering your phone?"

I rubbed my chin. I didn't know what the fuck to say, I didn't know how to deal with that, and all I could do was avoid looking at her, concentrating on anything else on the porch, because the idea that this would be our last memory together was so sad, and it seemed to stain everything else.

"Axel, why won't you look at me?"

Because I can't! I wanted to scream, but I knew I couldn't run away. I had tried it, the way I had with other things that were too much for me, as if some part of me were determined to ignore the advice I gave everyone else. Finally I looked up. And she was so precious...angry, but full of emotions that seemed to overflow in her eyes. Trembling, but standing there before me, not stepping back. Brave.

"I'm sorry," I whispered.

"No, no, no..."

I looked down. She ran her hands across my jaw and lifted it up. If there was ever a moment in my life when my heart broke, that was it, the instant when Leah slipped her fingertips over the bruises on my right cheek and my busted lip. I closed my eyes. And I fucked up again. I let her stand on tiptoe and cover my mouth with hers in a frightened, tremulous kiss. I grunted when she squeezed against me. Her hips pressed into mine. Her arms around my neck. Her tongue with its taste of strawberry and everything she had symbolized in my life: breaking with routine, opening up to another person, intense, vibrant color, nights under the stars, moments we had lived in that house that would be ours alone forever...

"Leah, wait." I pushed her away slowly.

Fuck. I didn't want to hurt her. I didn't...

"Stop looking at me like that. Stop looking at me as if this was a goodbye. Don't you love me? You told me...you told me we all live in a yellow submarine." Her voice broke, and I bit my lip, holding back.

"Of course I love you. But this can't be."

"You're not being serious." She brought a hand to her mouth, and I watched her erase the kiss that we had just given each other, taking it away in her fingers.

I came close to her. Every inch that separated her body from mine was fucking torture. And when I thought of how far apart we would be after that, I wanted to hold her until she begged me to stop.

In another life, at another time, I would have...

"Listen to me, Leah. I don't want to come between you and your brother, because I know you, and I know you'll end up regretting it."

"That won't happen. I'll work it out with him. I just need time, Axel."

I continued because I had no other choice but to continue. "And you're young, you're going to go to college, and you need to enjoy that time without anyone tying you down, without me, without this fucked-up situation." I was suffocating as I watched her eyes grow damp. "Grow, live, like I did in those days. Meet guys, have fun, be happy, babe. I can't give you all that."

"Are you suggesting I go out with other people?" She held my eyes, trembling, crying, with a grimace of incredulity.

And I...I wanted to die, because the very idea of someone else's lips touching hers, other hands holding her...

"Axel, tell me you're not being serious. Tell me this was a mistake and we'll start over from zero. Come on, look at me, please."

I took a step back when she tried to touch me. "It was a mistake, Leah. That's what I want to say."

She brought a hand to her chest. Her cheeks were coated in tears, and this time, I couldn't wipe them away. I had gotten so used to holding her up when she was in pain in those months, helping her to channel it, to face it, to accept it...and now I was the source of her pain.

"Why are you doing this?"

"Because I love you, even if you can't understand."

"Don't love me like this!" she shouted in a rage.

We looked at each other for a few seconds in silence.

"I'll still be here," I whispered.

She laughed amid her tears and wiped her cheeks. "If you break up with me now, you know I'll never come back."

"I'm sorry," I repeated and looked away.

That's how things were. How they needed to be. I'd been tossing it around for days, like staring at a picture from a thousand different angles trying to understand every line and every shadow. And I had reached the conclusion that everything was against us, that our relationship had been pretty, idyllic, but that it wasn't real. She had molded to me. To my routines, my life, my house, my way of understanding the world...and selfishly, I wanted to keep going like that, because it made me happy, but there was something that didn't fit, like a puzzle piece you've wedged in between two others, and even if you aren't sure for a while, you realize it doesn't belong here, that it needs to go somewhere else.

Leah came close to me before I could light another cigarette. Looking at her...it hurt. I needed her to go now, before I ended up doing something I shouldn't again or going back to staring at my own belly button.

"What were we all these months, Axel?"

"Lots of things. That's not the problem, the problem is all we never were. We didn't just bump into each other one day at a bar, it's not like I looked at you and liked you and came over to ask for your number. We didn't go on a date. I didn't say goodbye to you with a kiss in front of the door to your home. We couldn't even walk down the street holding hands without thinking of anything else. We never could have all that."

"But I never cared."

I lit a cigarette. I should have thought about how Leah was, how she wouldn't give up, would hold onto what she felt because she lived for the emotions that shook her, and they determined her world. I closed my eyes when I felt her arms embracing me from behind. *Fuck, why? Why?* I couldn't take it anymore. I turned around and she let me go. She was still crying. She was still trying to understand. I thought I would try to drive the nail in deeper.

"What the fuck do you want? A farewell fuck?"

She blinked. Her eyelashes were gleaming with tears. "Don't do this, Axel. I swear I won't forgive you."

"Believe me, I'm trying to be delicate, but you're making it hard for me."

"Oliver was right." She sobbed, and finally, she took a few steps back, pulling away from me. "You're incapable of fighting for what you love."

I looked at her and clenched my teeth. "I guess that means I don't really love then."

I was able to see the exact instant when her heart shattered before my eyes, and I did nothing to avoid it. I stayed there, imperturbable, wanting it to be over soon, to forget the moment when Leah's eyes met mine for the last time. And I saw hatred. And pain. And disappointment. But I held on. I held on until she turned her back to me and hurried down the porch steps. I watched her walk off up the drive as I had so many other times, but it was different, because there wouldn't be more. She wouldn't come back the next morning pedaling her orange bike. There wouldn't be more mornings together or more nights of words and kisses and music.

There are end points that you can feel in your skin...

I stood there a few minutes without moving, still anchored in that instant that had vanished and was now part of the past. Then I went inside and took a drink from the first bottle I found. I smashed it against the sink, grabbed another, and followed the scent of the sea to the beach. I lay on the sand and drank and remembered and repeated to myself that this was probably the biggest mistake of my life.

I don't know when I finally returned home. But I know my heart was pounding against my rib cage, and I had to light one cigarette after another to keep my hands busy and my fingers still. Because the impulse was there...shouting at me, whispering to me. I grabbed the stepladder and went to my room. I climbed up and looked at everything. I looked at my failures piled up on top of that dresser, full of dust and spiderwebs. And when I realized I was incapable of facing them, I went back down and stayed there, still and silent in the middle of that room that had been ours.

I sat on the floor with my back to the wall and looked up at the painting over the bed. The notes of a song about yellow submarines floated through my head and accompanied me through the night, until I understood I had lost her forever and that those traces of color and skin and afternoons making love were all I had left of her.

—————————

I got up when the doorbell rang. It was already morning, and I think I was still a little drunk, because I stumbled as I walked through the living room. I opened up. Justin was there with a coffee in one hand and a portion of cheesecake in the other.

"I, uh…I just wanted to see how you were."

"Got it."

"Are you okay, then?"

I think it was the first time I ever answered that kind of simple question sincerely. I was too used to just quickly saying yes and it was hard for me to find the words and get them out. "No, I'm not okay."

"Shit, Axel, come here."

He hugged me. I let him. And I felt it, felt that I had support, a friend, my older brother. I'd had to get down in the mud, all the way up to my neck, to see what was in front of me the whole time. I remembered what I told Leah when we went to Cape Byron about that graffiti I hadn't managed to see for months. That feeling of missing a chapter of my own life shook me again.

108

Leah

I'D BE LYING IF I said it didn't hurt. That falling out of love wasn't hard. That I didn't spend nights crying until I fell asleep, exhausted. That when something breaks, it doesn't leave behind a bunch of tiny shards that can't be put together again. That it wasn't like feeling Axel's hand reaching through my skin, grabbing my heart, and tearing it out. Lies. But ironically, the worst thing was losing him. Yeah. The most unbearable thing was knowing that the boy who had been by my side since the day I was born would no longer form part of my life. That I would never again feel that pull in my abdomen when I saw his mischievous smile. That he wouldn't nudge me during family meals. That he would never see all that I wanted to paint. That there wouldn't be any more birthday presents, and I wouldn't hear his hoarse laugh when Oliver told one of those stupid jokes no one else ever got. That he wouldn't be the love of my life, that unreachable boy who made me melt with one look.

Not anymore.

December

—

(SUMMER)

109

Leah

I LOOKED OUT THE WINDOW at the landscape we were leaving behind while Oliver drove in silence, and I swallowed the tears when I realized I no longer had anywhere to return to. Byron Bay was no longer our home because there was little to go back to there. The Nguyens had promised they'd visit me at school, that all I had to do was pick up the phone if I needed anything, that it would all work out...but a part of me knew it wouldn't. There are things that change, and then they'll never be the same. Similar, maybe. Sure. But not the same. If only life was like a ball of modeling clay, moldable, malleable, something sorrow and disappointment left no marks on.

My brother parked in front of a furniture and décor store when we got to Brisbane, and he grabbed my hand. I trembled from his firm self-assurance.

"Come on, pixie, turn that frown upside down."

Almost two months had passed since the beginning of November, when I saw Axel for the last time, but it felt like an eternity. I was still sore with my brother for not understanding me, but worse still, because he had been right about a lot of things. Too many. Things that are so ugly you don't want to see them until somebody forces you to, because for me, Axel had always been perfect. Even with his defects, I had idealized him, put him on a pedestal. I'd looked up at him that way since I was a child, and in the last few days I had not stopped thinking about it, and how maybe not everything about him was clear and pristine, how he also had sharp angles and shadows. I couldn't get out of my head that phrase he had whispered in my ear that night when he came home, lips red from kissing someone else: *"You know what your problem is, Leah? You're stuck on the surface. You look at a present, and all you see is the shiny wrapping paper, and you don't think about how there might be something rotten inside."*

"You could help me a little," Oliver said, peeking into the window of the passenger seat.

"Coming." I got out of the car.

I grabbed my carry-on bag and he took the two big suitcases. The blue midday sky rested above the streets full of strangers. I couldn't help but remember how in that same city, Axel had kissed me, truly kissed me, for the first time, without my asking, while we danced to "The Night We Met" before ending up in the bathroom of that bar discovering each other with our hands. I took a deep breath, looked up at the dorm buildings that would be my new home from now on, noticed the furniture store in front of us, and...I felt a need. Like a bolt of lightning.

"Can you...can you wait for me for a moment?"

"Now, Leah? I'm going up," Oliver replied.

"Okay. I'll be right there."

I went inside and walked straight to the counter. I could have strolled through the aisles, which were full of precious furnishings, but I had just seen it in the window and I didn't have eyes for anything else. I asked the woman who attended to me how much it cost and hesitated when I heard the number, but I followed my impulse, and a minute later, I walked into the building, striking my ribs against the front door. I muffled a groan of pain.

"Are you out of your mind?" My brother appeared.

"No, it's just... I liked it. A lot."

"Jesus, Leah. Give me that."

Oliver grabbed it and carried it to the elevator. We traveled up one floor. A long narrow hallway full of blue doors greeted us. Mine was number 23. Just as I had seen in the photos before we decided to rent it, the room was small, with a bed, a desk, a closet, and a bathroom hardly big enough for two people to squeeze into. But I didn't mind. I opened the little window to air it out and left my belongings on the wooden table.

"Where should I put this?" Oliver asked.

"There, just lean it against the wall."

"Might I know why you've bought a mirror?" He placed it carefully so it wouldn't fall, then shook off his hands.

"I don't know. I just liked it. It's pretty."

And I want to see myself in it every morning.

Oliver knew I was keeping my real thoughts to myself, but he didn't insist; he just helped me open my luggage and hang my clothes in the closet. We spent the afternoon together, and when he had to leave, I felt a hole inside myself that kept getting bigger and bigger. I was afraid to be alone. I was afraid to stumble, fall, and not have anyone there to pick me back up. I was scared of what would happen when I was left alone with my thoughts, everything I would find when they got stirred up and I decided to confront what I felt, because I could feel my emotions pushing and pushing, trying to break out.

A month would go by before I started classes at the university, but Oliver had to go back to work and he thought it would be best for me to get used to the city and the people I would share my residence with.

He looked at me and opened his arms, and I jumped into them.

"Call me whenever you want, no matter the hour," he said, and I nodded, pressing my face into his chest. "Eat right, Leah. Take care of yourself, okay? And remember that if you ever need me, all you have to do is tell me and I'll grab the first flight out. You'll see, this will be fine. It's going to be good for you. Like starting from zero." He pushed me away to be able to look at me and kissed me on the forehead. "I love you, pixie."

"I love you too."

Oliver had always hated goodbyes. Not me. I looked out the window and watched him as he put on his sunglasses and got into the car. He started it up, turned, and got lost on the streets of Brisbane.

I turned around and faced the girl who looked back at me from the tall mirror in its sculpted wooden frame. We were the same. Neither of us had on a raincoat full of holes. I thought it was a good idea to remind myself of that every morning, to start the day smiling at myself. Or at least trying. *You'll be fine*, I repeated. *You will*. Because it can't rain forever in your heart, can it? I grabbed my headphones, lay in bed, and closed my eyes after putting a strawberry sucker in my mouth while a Beatles album surrounded me with familiar notes and voices. I suppressed the urge to cry.

And I thought...I thought of things that used to exist and now didn't...

Everything can change in an instant. I had heard that phrase many times throughout my life, but I had never stopped to consider it, chew on it, savor the meaning those words can leave on your tongue when you've digested them and they've become your own. That bitter feeling that accompanies every *what if* that awakens when something bad happens and you ask yourself if it was avoidable, because the difference between having everything and having nothing is sometimes no more than a second. Just one. Like back then, when that car swerved into the opposite lane. Or now, when he decided that he didn't have anything to fight for and the black and gray lines ended up swallowing all the color that had floated around me months before.

Because, at that second, he turned right.

And I wanted to follow him, but I hit a barrier.

And I knew I could only keep going by turning left.

TO BE CONTINUED...

Can Leah and Axel
reconcile their love?

Read on for a sneak peek as
their story continues.

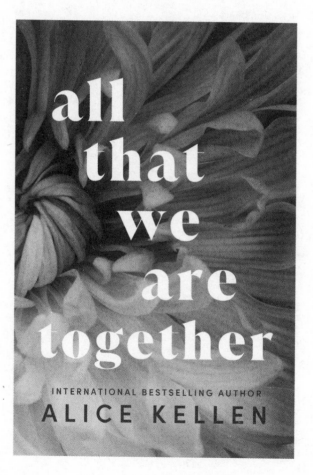

all
that
we
are
together

INTERNATIONAL BESTSELLING AUTHOR
ALICE KELLEN

PROLOGUE

IT SCARED ME THAT THE line between hate and love was so fine, so slender that you could jump straight from one extreme to the other. And I loved him... I loved him in my solar plexus, with my eyes, my heart. My entire body reacted when he was near. But another part of me hated him. I hated him with my memories, with words never uttered, with scorn, and was incapable of opening my arms and offering him forgiveness, however much I wanted to do so. When I looked at him, I saw black, red, throbbing purple: emotions welling over. And feeling something so chaotic for him hurt me, because Axel was a part of me. He always would be. Despite everything.

November

—

(SPRING, AUSTRALIA)

1

Leah

MY EYES WERE STILL CLOSED when I felt his lips sliding down the curve of my shoulder, before they traveled further down and left a trail of kisses next to my bellybutton; sweet kisses, delicate, the kind that make you quiver. I smiled. Then my smile disappeared when I felt his hot breath on my ribs. Close to him. Close to the words Axel had once traced out with his fingers on my skin, that *Let it be* that I got tattooed there afterward.

I shifted, ill at ease, then opened my eyes. I put a hand on his cheek and tugged until his mouth met mine and a feeling of calm swept over me. We took off our clothes in the silence of that still and sunny morning, a Saturday just like any other. I held him as he slid inside me. Slow. Deep. Easy. I arched my back when I needed more, one last hard intense thrust. But that didn't give me what I needed. I wedged a hand between us and stroked myself with my fingers. We came at the same time. I was panting. He was moaning my name.

He flopped to one side, and I stayed there looking at the smooth white ceiling of his room. It wasn't long before I sat up in his bed and he grabbed my wrist.

"You're going already?" His voice was soft.

"Yeah. I've got stuff to do."

I got up and walked barefoot to the chair where I'd thrown my clothes the night before. From between the sheets, hands folded behind his head, Landon watched me getting dressed. I adjusted the thin belt of my skirt, then threw my tank top over my head. I slung the bag my brother had given me for Christmas over my shoulder and pulled my hair back in a ponytail on my way out the door.

"Hey, wait. Don't I get a kiss before you leave?"

I walked back to the bed smiling and bent over to kiss him. He tenderly stroked my cheek then sighed with satisfaction.

"Will I see you tonight?" he asked.

"I can't, I'll be in the studio until late."

"But it's Saturday. Come on, Leah."

"Sorry. How about dinner tomorrow?"

"OK."

"I'll call you," I said.

I walked down the stairs beneath the warm gray morning sky. I took my headphones out of my backpack, grabbed a lollipop, and stuck it in my mouth. I ran through the crosswalk just before the light turned red and cut through a park full of flowers on the way to my studio.

Well, not really my studio. Not exactly. Not totally.

I had worked hard all through college to get a scholarship that would allow me to have a little space for myself. And this was it.

When I stepped in, the scent of paint permeated everything. I dropped my junk in a plush armchair and grabbed the smock hanging on the back of the door. I was knotting it as I walked over to the painting overlooking that old attic space.

I shook as I observed the delicate outlines of the waves, the splatter of foam, and the iridescent sunlight that seemed to radiate from the canvas. I grabbed the wood handle of my palette knife and mixed colors as I went on glancing from the corner of my eye at that canvas that seemed in some eerie way to be challenging me. I picked up a brush and felt my hand shaking as my memories crashed down. There was a trembling in my stomach as I remembered the night I had to come running because I needed right then to paint that stretch of beach I knew so well, even if it had been three years since I'd set foot there...

Three years without that bit of sea, so different from all the others.

Three years in which everything had changed.

Three years without seeing him. Three years without Axel.

ABOUT THE AUTHOR

Alice Kellen is an international bestselling author of romantic fiction. She writes stories with universal crossover themes such as love, friendship, insecurities, loss, and longing for a brighter future, connecting with younger and older readers alike. She lives in Valencia, Spain, with her family.